The Days of Elijah

Book One:
Apocalypse

Mark Goodwin

For information on preparing for natural or man-made disasters, visit the author's website, PrepperRecon.com.

Technical information in the book is included to convey realism. The author shall not have liability or responsibility to any person or entity with respect to any loss or damage caused, or allegedly caused, directly or indirectly by the information contained in this book.

All of the characters, places, and incidents are products of the author's imagination or are used fictitiously. Any resemblance to actual people, places, or events is entirely coincidental.

ISBN: 153362626X
ISBN-13: 978-1533626264

DEDICATION

May He grant you according to your heart's desire, and fulfill all your purpose.

Psalm 20:4 NKJV

This book is dedicated to the hundreds of readers who read *The Days of Noah* series and emailed me, requesting that I continue the story. Thank you for reading, for your support and your wonderful words of encouragement.

ACKNOWLEDGMENTS

A most heartfelt note of appreciation to my beautiful bride and constant companion. Thank you for your patience, encouragement, and support.

I would like to thank my fantastic editing team, Catherine Goodwin, Ken and Jen Elswick, Jeff Markland, Frank Shackleford, and Claudine Allison.

FOREWORD

The Days of Elijah was written in response to a massive show of support and requests from readers of my previous series, *The Days of Noah*, asking that I continue the story of the characters in that series who were left behind by the rapture.

Having not originally intended to continue *The Days of Noah* series, and having the main character, Noah Parker, whose name graced the title of that series, caught up and translated into eternity, left me unable to continue the saga as *The Days of Noah*.

Since I therefore needed to continue the story of Everett Carroll, Courtney Hayes, and Elijah Goldberg by creating a new series under a new title, it is inevitable that I will get additional readers to *The Days of Elijah* who are unfamiliar with my previous work. For the sake of those new readers, and as a refresher for those who have been with the story since the first book of *The Days of Noah*, I have attempted to provide an adequate synopsis in the prologue to cover how Everett, Courtney, and

Elijah have come to be in such a position, at such a time, and in such a relationship to each other as to make *The Days of Elijah* a stand-alone series of books.

However, to cover the minutia and details of the events that have transpired and the personal interactions that have taken place through the course of three books, would be unfair to the readers of *The Days of Noah* series, forcing them to sit through a rehashing of literature that they are already familiar with. It is my hope that the prologue will contain enough information to bring the new readers up to speed without exasperating those who are already aware of Everett's plight, all while providing a sufficient backstory.

If you are a new reader and you find yourself wanting to know more about how the America of *The Days of Elijah* came to be, or if you desire a more intimate understanding of who Everett, Courtney, and Elijah are as people, I invite you to read *The Days of Noah* trilogy. I'm sure you'll enjoy it.

I realize that the timing of the rapture in this book and the previous *Days of Noah* series doesn't fit perfectly into any of the major eschatological views. I have written it in that manner on purpose, so as to not grant preference to any of the predominant schools of thought. The chronology of the rapture in *The Days of Elijah* would probably be best described as a hybrid pre-wrath viewpoint. The important thing to remember is that this is a fiction book. As Derek Gilbert of SkyWatch TV says, "Eschatology is too important of a subject to get your doctrine from the fiction aisle."

Trust me when I tell you that I've heard exceptionally compelling arguments for the pre-trib, pre-wrath, and mid-trib schools of thought.

Just as I have afforded myself some poetic license with the timing of the events in the last days, so I have blended some conjecture into my interpretation of how these events might play out and in what manner they are related to historical facts, other biblical events and characters, and conspiracies. Please keep in mind that while I incorporate elements of truth in all of my writing, this is a fiction book. And while it is fascinating to study the events of the last days and fun to speculate how these mysteries will be revealed, many of these prophecies will not be fully understood until they have come to pass. As Paul said in I Corinthians 13:12 "For now we see through a glass, darkly; but then face to face: now I know in part; but then shall I know even as also I am known." So, as you find yourself coming across parts of the book that don't line up with your understanding of prophecy, and you most certainly will, remember, it's just a novel.

The purpose of *The Days of Noah* and The *Days of Elijah* are not to promote any particular eschatological view, but rather to demonstrate just how bad conditions could deteriorate for the American Church before the return of the King. And within that purpose was the secondary mission to encourage the American Christian to balance his or her spiritual and physical preparedness efforts to be ready for the dark days ahead.

A tertiary set of goals has developed with the

writing of *The Days of Elijah*, and that is to describe the terrible events of the final days on earth, so as to encourage the unbeliever to accept Christ while the chance still remains, motivate the believer to reach friends, family, and neighbors with the gospel, and to be an extra-biblical guide for those who may have been left behind by massive disappearances of Christians, to tell them what happened and what to expect in the coming years as the wrath of God is "apokalypse" or revealed.

PROLOGUE

But as the days of Noe were, so shall also the coming of the Son of man be. For as in the days that were before the flood they were eating and drinking, marrying and giving in marriage, until the day that Noe entered into the ark, And knew not until the flood came, and took them all away; so shall also the coming of the Son of man be. Then shall two be in the field; the one shall be taken, and the other left. Two women shall be grinding at the mill; the one shall be taken, and the other left. Watch therefore: for ye know not what hour your Lord doth come. But know this, that if the goodman of the house had known in what watch the thief would come, he would have watched, and would not have suffered his house to be broken up. Therefore be ye also ready: for in such an hour as ye think not the Son of man cometh.

Matthew 24:37-44

Twenty-six-year-old Everett Carroll was recruited straight out of grad school, from George Washington University into the CIA. His position as a Directorate of Intelligence Officer was a fancy way of saying *analyst*, but he knew it was an opportunity he couldn't turn down.

The job, located in an office park a few miles west of the main CIA campus, started at $88,000. It was understood that part of the pay was considered compensation for keeping your mouth shut, not asking questions, and doing exactly as you were told.

His sense of moral duty and curiosity got the better of him when he discovered that the agency was involved in less than savory activities which were funneling money through massive credit card fraud to keep black box projects funded, and possibly pad the pockets of rogue agents. His direct superior, John Jones, circumvented Everett's curiosities before he made a mistake which could have cost him his job, his freedom, or his life.

John Jones had been a field agent prior to a gunshot wound which landed him a desk job just outside of Langley, at the CIA outpost where

Everett worked. During his time in the field, Jones had learned things about the CIA and the government, pieces of a puzzle that were creating a complete, horrifying picture.

Jones confided in Everett that he was not long for this world. He was, in fact, dying of lung cancer. Jones told the youthful analyst that he saw things in Everett which reminded him of himself, in another time. Perhaps as a means of catharsis, or perhaps as a way to pass the torch to a younger generation, Jones, through a series of clandestine meetings with Everett, revealed to him the CIA's involvement in a conspiracy to bring down the current economic and political system to make way for a new global order.

In anticipation of the coming economic collapse, Jones had prepared a cabin in the mountains of Virginia, stocked with food, ammo, and weapons. He encouraged Everett to make a contingency plan, to be ready to survive the tumultuous times that were heading his way. As their friendship grew, Jones eventually invited Everett and his girlfriend, Courtney, to come to his cabin when the chaos began. Unfortunately, Agent John Jones, would not live to see the fulfillment of his own warnings. Lung cancer claimed his life just as the dominos of conspiracy began to fall.

Everett's girlfriend, Courtney Hayes, also worked in the intelligence community. Her job at H and M, a contractor for the NSA, gave her just enough insight into the events going on behind the scenes of the collapsing global financial system that convincing her to take action wasn't a difficult sell.

Everett's best friend from work, Ken, and his girlfriend, Lisa, required much more persuasion. Despite the fact that Ken had access to the same information as Everett, his ability to suppress his curiosities, and his desire to be a loyal employee allowed him to deny the facts until he could no longer contest Everett's claims of the need to prepare for the collapse.

Finally, the malaise did arrive, just as Jones had predicted. Global markets melted down, toppling the faith in all fiat currencies around the world. Next, a false flag attack against America's energy infrastructure created a massive fuel shortfall and a collapse of commerce in the country. The event was blamed on Christians and patriots who were hunted down like criminals, rounded up, and detained in massive prison camps around the US.

Everett, Courtney, Ken and Lisa abandoned the city for John Jones' well-stocked cabin in the Appalachian Mountains near Woodstock, Virginia, just hours outside of the DC metropolitan area.

A vast segment of US law enforcement officers and military personnel refused to cooperate in the witch hunt for the so-called domestic terrorists blamed for the attacks. Many of them joined the patriots in a retaliatory strike against the US government. Without the support of law enforcement and the military, the ginned up assault on Christian patriots soon failed.

When the smoke cleared, America was not the country it had been. The chains of tyranny had been loosed, but the decay of anarchy and famine would consume what little remained.

The United Nations seized the opportunity to ride in on a white horse, providing a solution which promised a better world. UN Secretary General, Angelo Luz was granted sweeping new powers to institute a new global monetary system, using an electronic currency. His plan for peace involved the ban of weapons and all individual religions. He only allowed participation in the new singular world religion which promised equality and acceptance for all.

Everett lay back on the couch and sighed. "I feel like being bad."

Courtney smiled. "What do you mean?"

"I'm going to break the ration protocol and make another pot of coffee. Besides, maybe the smell will wake Ken and Lisa up. They never sleep this late."

Courtney furrowed her brow. "I know. I'm getting a little worried. Do you think I should check on them?"

"Let them sleep."

"They've been sleeping. It's bad enough that they stay up all night keeping watch. If they sleep all day, they'll get seasonal depression disorder. They need to at least see the sun for a couple of hours a day." Courtney jumped up from the couch.

"People in Alaska don't see the sun for weeks sometimes. Spring is right around the corner. They made it this long; they'll be okay. Leave them alone."

Courtney turned and winked. "What if they're dead? Are you just going to leave them in there until they start stinking?"

Everett couldn't help but laugh at her macabre humor. "They're not dead!"

Courtney knocked on the door. "Lisa, Ken, can I come in?"

Everett listened for an answer. None came.

Courtney knocked a little harder and spoke a tad louder. "Lisa, Ken, are you awake?"

A silly thought crossed Everett's mind. *What if they are dead*? He got up from the couch and walked to the bedroom door. "Ken, bro, wake up."

Still no answer. Everett turned the knob and opened the door. "They're not here."

Courtney looked in to confirm. "Do you think they went up to Elijah's?"

Everett walked into the room and pulled up the blinds to let some light in. "Why is the bed messed up? Lisa always makes the bed. Look, Ken's boots are here, and his coat is still hanging on the back of the chair. You think he hiked up the mountain in a pair of sneakers and a windbreaker? Not in this weather."

Courtney put her hands on her hips and looked around. "Well, they couldn't have just disappeared."

Everett's heart began pounding the second he heard the word, *disappeared*. "Turn on the radio."

"Why?"

Everett ignored the question and went to grab the small AM/FM radio sitting on the kitchen table. He switched it on and quickly tuned in to the local Global Republic Broadcasting Network affiliate.

The reporter had a thick British accent.

"Secretary Luz and Pope Peter will be issuing a joint statement in a press conference at five o'clock Eastern. After their statement, the new Global Republic press secretary, Athaliah Jennings, will take questions from reporters.

"The Vatican has issued a formal statement about the mass disappearances, saying that it was an expected event, and as difficult as it may be to believe, it was caused by alien life forms. The statement goes on to say that the beings who caused the disappearances are not hostile to the humans who remain on earth. Some analysts expect the pope to say that the Vatican has been in contact with the aliens for quite some time and that the disappearances may turn out to be for the good of the planet."

Everett turned the radio off. "They're gone."

"Why did you turn it off? The radio was telling us what happened!"

"No, it's not. It's a cover story." Everett put his back against the wall and slid down to the floor.

"For what?"

"For the rapture. Jesus came to get the Christians. All that stuff Ken and Lisa tried to tell us about. It's all true."

Courtney sat on the floor next to Everett and took the radio out of his shaking hands. "Let's not jump to conclusions. We don't know anything for certain. Let's put our coats on and go see Elijah. Ken and Lisa might be up there."

"They won't be. And Elijah won't be there either. They're all gone. All the Christians."

Everett stood and went back into the bedroom. He sat down at the small desk and turned on the ham radio.

"Who are you calling? I thought Spindle was captured?"

Everett found the frequency. "Ken was staying in contact with the rest of his cell. I want to see if any of them are still here."

Everett pushed the talk button. "This is Undertow. I'm looking for Minecart."

A despondent voice came back. "Hello."

"This is Undertow; is Minecart there? Have you heard anything about Spindle?"

A woman sobbing in the background could be heard when the voice came back over the radio. "No. They're gone. All of them. It's just me and my girlfriend, Sarah."

Everett keyed the mic. "You shouldn't use your real names. Come up with a pseudonym, anything. How about I call you Mr. Black?"

"It doesn't matter. They told us this would happen. We didn't believe them. You have no idea what is coming next. Earthquakes, famines, plagues . . . judgment. Judgment is coming upon the earth. Sarah was training the women when it happened. They were in the woods performing a tactical drill one second, and the next, they were all gone. She turned around, and the rifles and clothing were lying on the forest floor. She thought it was a joke at first."

Everett's hand began to shake. "I know you're distraught now, but you really shouldn't use your real names, not even the names of the people who disappeared. Let's call your girlfriend Ms. White."

"Whatever. Like I said, it doesn't matter now. And don't believe the news. It wasn't aliens."

"I know; it was the rapture. We missed it too. Just hang in there. We'll be in touch."

"Maybe. I gotta go." Mr. Black cut the feed.

Courtney took Everett's hand. "It just doesn't make sense. There's a logical explanation for all of this. Come on; get up."

Everett was just shy of being in a state of shock. He had no will to fight Courtney, who was insisting that they drive up to Elijah's house. He stood up and let his arms hang limp as she put his coat on him. "We're too late. They were right. Jones was right; Ken was right; Lisa was right; Elijah was right. Now I believe them, but it's too late."

Courtney grabbed his hand and pulled him out the door. "Everyone is going to be at Elijah's house. Everything is going to be fine." She opened the car door for Everett, gave him a nudge to sit down, and then closed the door on the passenger's side of the BMW. Backing out of the driveway in a hurry, she slammed into a tree trunk. "Sorry about that, but it will be worth it to find our friends."

Everett said nothing about hitting the tree.

Courtney drove up the mountain and pulled into Elijah's drive. She blew the horn twice. Elijah came to the door.

"Look, what did I tell you? Elijah is still here. I bet you anything that Ken and Lisa are inside drinking tea."

Elijah walked out onto his porch as Everett and Courtney got out of the car. "Are you okay? You gave me quite a scare with the horn blowing."

Courtney chuckled. "Sorry about that. Everett was convinced that you, Ken, and Lisa had all disappeared. He had me sort of shaken up with the whole thing. I guess I was a little panicky."

Elijah furrowed his brow. "Yes, well, come inside. Come inside."

Everett walked in and looked around. "Are Ken and Lisa here?"

"No." The old man closed the door behind them.

Courtney looked confused. "Oh, do you know where they are?"

Elijah's eyes were compassionate. "Why don't you two come sit down in the kitchen; I'll put on a pot of tea."

Everett followed him into the kitchen. His voice was frantic. "It was the rapture, right? Jesus came to get the Christians, right? Why are you still here?"

Elijah put the tea bags in the kettle and filled it with water. "Yes, Messiah came for his saints. It was what you call the rapture." Elijah turned on the gas stove and put the kettle on the burner. "Why am I still here? Now that's a long story."

Courtney's eyes were worried. She seemed to be grasping the weight of the situation. "Tell us, please."

Elijah sat down and folded his hands. "I was sent for such a time as this. Let's think of our present predicament in the terms of international warfare. Just before a nation or, in this case, a kingdom declares war on another kingdom, the first thing that kingdom will do is close all of its embassies. And, of course, it will call all of its ambassadors home.

That is what has happened. The ambassadors of heaven have been called home. The only ones left are those who act in an intelligence or warfare capacity, like secret agents."

Everett looked at Elijah. "So there are others besides you?"

Elijah nodded. "One other. We were sent to bear witness to the coming times and pronounce judgment against the nations on behalf of Messiah."

"Are you an angel?" Courtney looked very confused.

"No. I'm a man. God has seen fit to grant me a rather . . . unique existence. I was whisked away and then sent back. I can tell you, I didn't miss it. But I won't be around that long anyway."

Everett had no idea what the old man was talking about. "Now I believe. I believe Jesus is real, but it's too late."

Courtney looked at Everett and nodded. "Lisa tried to tell me over and over. It just didn't make sense. But how else can it be explained? The disappearances; it's exactly the way she said it would happen. She said they would all just be gone someday. And she said the world would go through the most terrible time in history, even worse than what's happening now. And we're too late."

Elijah smiled. "You're too late to be caught up. It's true; that ship has sailed. But, as long as you have breath in your lungs, it's not too late to repent, call upon the name of the Messiah, and be saved. He is merciful and patient, not wanting that any should perish but that all should come to repentance and be saved."

Everett looked deeply into Elijah's eyes. "I repent; I'm sorry that I didn't believe. I believe in Jesus. I believe he is God. What do I do? What do I say?"

"Me, too." Courtney held Everett's hand as she looked at the old man.

Elijah held his hand up. "Don't tell me; tell him."

Everett fell to his knees. "Jesus, forgive me. I've heard you knocking. I've found an excuse not to listen every time. But now I know. You are God."

Courtney cried out, "Forgive me, Jesus. I'm sorry I didn't believe. Lisa told me what terrible days are coming. I pray that you will help us get through them."

Elijah stood and poured the tea. "Welcome to the family. Now for our next order of business; repentance means turning away from your sin. If Jesus really is Lord, as you have said then you will allow him to be Lord of your life. The two of you are living in sin."

Everett had no idea what Elijah was talking about. "What do you mean?"

"You're not married."

"Oh." Everett paused for a second. "Courtney, will you marry me?"

Courtney smiled, and tears of joy streamed down her face. She wrapped her arms around Everett's neck. "Yes, I'll marry you. Elijah, will you perform the ceremony?"

"Yes, but it should be soon. When I get my marching orders, I have to go, right away."

Everett looked at Courtney. "Tonight?"

She nodded with a grin from ear to ear. "Tonight!"

Everett felt peace like he'd never felt before in his life. That uneasiness he had felt, ever since Jones started confronting him about believing in God, was gone. He was in love with Courtney, more than ever before. They were about to go through the worst period of time since the creation of the earth. They had missed the rapture, but they hadn't missed heaven.

CHAPTER 1

This know also, that in the last days perilous times shall come.

2 Timothy 3:1

Everett held the door open for Courtney when they got back to the small cabin, which was just a few minutes' drive down the mountain from Elijah's place. He closed the door behind her and locked the latch out of habit. He leaned up against the wall and stared blankly trying to process everything that was happening. Everett ran his hand through his hair and tossed the car keys on the table near the door.

Courtney walked over and took his hand. "Are you okay?"

"Yeah." His voice was despondent as he

continued to stare at nothing. "I just don't know what to think. I don't know where to start. There're so many things to figure out. So much stuff to do. And Ken . . . I'll miss him . . . and Lisa. They were our best friends. I'm really going to miss them."

"Can we just focus on getting married for now? We can figure out how we're going to survive the Great Tribulation tomorrow. Unless . . ." Courtney's voice cracked as she dropped her head.

"What?" Everett turned his focus on her. "No! Courtney, that's the one thing I'm sure about. You're the only person I have left in the world. Of course I want to marry you. Yes, we'll focus on getting married today, and worry about everything else tomorrow." He pulled her close and held her tightly.

She sobbed. "I know they are in a much better place, and I know we're about to go through hell, but I miss Lisa so bad. It's like she just died."

"I feel the same way." Everett stroked her hair as she leaned on him and cried.

After a few minutes of standing by the door with Everett and weeping, Courtney took a deep breath, dried her eyes, and walked toward the back bedroom that had been Ken and Lisa's room. She walked in and sat down on the bed.

Everett followed and sat next to her.

She picked up Lisa's Bible that Elijah had given her. Courtney flipped through the pages. "I wonder where we should start."

"Revelation. That's where Jones found most of the information about the last days."

Courtney paged through from front to back. "Do

you think Ken and Lisa are sitting up there with John Jones right now?"

Everett chuckled at the thought. "Yeah, probably laughing at how hard-headed we were."

"I don't see it. I'm almost to the end." She kept thumbing through, a few pages at a time.

"Does it have a table of contents?"

Courtney shrugged as she kept flipping. "Ah, here it is. All the way in the back."

"I guess that makes sense, if it's about the end times. I thought we were going to focus on getting married. Unless . . ." Everett bit his lower lip.

"Stop it, Everett. You know I love you." She shot him a playful look with a slight grin, and then went back to looking over the pages of the Bible. "I would have married you the night we met."

"Really? I was so sure I'd blown my chances that night with my smart-alecky comment. I thought you'd never go out with me."

"That's what you were supposed to think." Courtney continued scanning the pages.

Everett reclined on the bed. "Ouch." He turned over to find out what had scratched his arm. "Oh, it's Lisa's ring."

Courtney turned to look. "Can I see it?"

Everett handed it to her.

"It fits." She slipped the small diamond ring on her finger, and then pulled it back off. "Do you want to give it to me again?"

Everett took the ring as Courtney handed it to him. "Are you sure you don't mind having a hand-me-down engagement ring? You won't feel weird about it?"

"It's not like we can go to the mall and pick one out. Besides, Ken didn't have anything to trade for the ring at the flea market. You gave him the coins, so technically, you paid for it. And it will always remind me of Lisa. It won't creep me out."

Everett knelt beside the bed and took her hand as he slid the ring back on her finger. "Courtney Hayes, will you marry me?"

"Yes, Everett Carroll, I will." She pulled him up from the floor and kissed him, lying back on the bed.

Seconds later, Everett pulled away. "Let's go get married and come right back."

"Okay, good idea." She gave him one more kiss. "I'll go get ready. I'm going to need about an hour. I want to be really pretty for you."

Everett smiled. "Okay, that's reasonable. I can wait."

"Great, get your clothes out of the loft and get dressed down here. You can't see me until I'm ready."

"Sure thing." Everett climbed up the ladder to the loft and retrieved the best clothes he'd brought out to the cabin. He took his slacks, shirt, belt, and shoes downstairs. Everett hadn't brought a tie or suit jacket out to the cabin, so he looked through Ken's closet. He tried on Ken's jacket. It was too big, but he figured he could get away with wearing it. Everett had been devoted to going to the gym each morning before work prior to the collapse, so he'd been in good shape. But like everyone in the post-crash world, he'd lost weight. Even if he had brought a jacket, it would likely fit him almost as

Mark Goodwin

loosely as Ken's. He found a nice tie from Ken's closet as well. Everett wouldn't look perfect in the oversized coat, but he wanted to look as nice as possible.

Everett was ready in less than fifteen minutes. He had some time to kill. He retrieved Lisa's Bible and brought it to the kitchen table. Everett had no idea where to start. Suddenly, a thought hit him. *Obviously this stuff is all true after all. Maybe God would show me where to start.* Everett looked up. "God, I'm new at this. If I'm going to get it all figured out, I'll need a little help. I'd appreciate it if you would show me where to start." Everett looked back down at the book in his hands. "Oh yeah, thanks. I mean, amen." Everett closed the book and opened it to a random spot. He looked down. "The Gospel of John. Hmm, well, it is the beginning of a book. I suppose that could be a sign."

As Everett began reading, the words came to life and he started to understand everything Lisa, Ken, John Jones, and even Elijah had been trying to tell him.

An hour later, Courtney called out as she descended the ladder. "I'm ready."

Everett looked up from the Bible to see his bride-to-be standing by the ladder. She was stunning. Her white dress was shorter than anything you'd typically see even the attendants wearing at a wedding, much less the bride. But Everett didn't care; she was gorgeous. And with her toned athletic form, she wore it well. His heartbeat quickened. "You're beautiful."

Courtney had her long blonde hair up in a

braided bun and had spent more time than usual applying eye makeup, lipstick, and blush. Courtney looked down at her short dress then back up at him. "Thanks. I didn't have much to choose from in the way of white dresses. I hope this isn't offensive to Elijah."

"I think he's glad to see us doing the right thing. And you certainly won't hear any complaints from me." Everett stood and walked over to kiss her.

"No, no. You'll have to wait. Besides, you'll smudge my makeup." She winked and slipped her heels on.

Everett tucked his holster in his pants and grabbed his Sig. "Then let's get going. I'm not sure how long I can wait."

Courtney grabbed her coat. "Would you mind getting my Mini 14 from upstairs? There's a good chance we'll see a deer on the way up the mountain."

"And you're going to gut a deer on your wedding day?"

She looked at him like he was mad. "No. Of course not."

Everett needed no explanation. Obviously it wasn't out of the question for him to gut a deer on his wedding day. She was right, times were tough and they couldn't afford to miss the opportunity to take some game. Those occasions were becoming less and less frequent. Since the collapse, deer was the primary source of meat in the Appalachians, and they would soon be hunted to near extinction. Everett climbed the ladder, opened the safe, grabbed the Ruger and an extra magazine, locked the safe, and then hurried back down. He opened the front door. "After you."

Courtney walked out onto the porch. "Kind of chilly for heels and a short dress."

Everett locked the door. "But it's sunny. March is just a few days off. Spring will be here before you know it."

Courtney held his arm as she walked down the stairs to the car. "Look at us, running off to get married like we don't have a care in the world. And on the day of the rapture. Right when the whole world is getting ready to come unglued." She paused by the car and began to cry again.

Everett put the rifle in the back seat and held her close. "It's going to be okay. Whatever comes, we'll get through it. We managed to survive this long; now that we've got God's help, I know we'll make it."

"And I miss Lisa so much right now. I wish she could be here, to be my maid of honor." She looked up and dried her eyes. "Now look, I've ruined my makeup."

Everett handed her a tissue from his pocket. "You're still beautiful."

She blotted around her eyes with the Kleenex. "You really believe God will get us through? What were you reading?"

"Um, John. And yes, I really believe." He opened the car door for her.

She sat in the BMW. "Is it about the last days?"

"No." Everett closed the door, walked around to the driver's side and got in. "I actually prayed and asked God what to read."

"And he told you to read John?"

"Not exactly. I just opened to that page. But it felt divinely inspired. It's about Jesus. It gives me an idea of who he was . . . or is, rather. He's nothing like the hippy I had pictured him to be in my mind. You'll have to read it when we get home."

"Okay, I'll do that. I suppose getting to know him is probably more important than finding out which catastrophe is next, but I'm pretty curious. We need to get an idea of what's coming so we can prepare for it. Which reminds me, I hate to spoil the mood by rushing through our wedding, but I would like to be home by five so we can hear what kind of garbage Luz and the pope have to tell us about the disappearances."

"That makes sense. And I'd like to squeeze in something akin to a honeymoon. You look awfully cute in that little dress."

She winked. "Oh, we'll definitely make time for that."

Minutes later, they pulled up to Elijah's cabin, got out of the car, and walked up to his porch. Everett knocked on the door. He turned to Courtney as he waited. "Are you excited?"

She smiled and nodded. "Yes. Do I look like a raccoon with my runny mascara?"

He chuckled. "No, you look like the woman of my dreams."

The weathered hinges of the door creaked as it opened. Elijah said, "I didn't expect you back so soon."

Courtney tugged at the hem of her dress. "Sorry, are we interrupting? We can come back later."

Elijah opened the door all the way and held out his hand. "No, no, don't be silly. What could you possibly be interrupting? Come in, come inside. Let's get the two of you hitched before someone gets cold feet. I'm always happy to accommodate the work of the Lord."

Everett laughed. "Thank you, we appreciate it." Elijah's quirky mannerisms and lighthearted attitude quickly swept away any anxiety that might have been stirring in Everett's stomach.

Elijah looked Courtney over. "And you look absolutely splendid. Is that Lisa's ring?"

Courtney twirled the ring on her finger. "Yes, do you think she would mind?"

Elijah put a hand on each of Courtney's shoulders. "I think she'd be glad you were putting it to good use. And I can assure you that she would be ecstatic that the two of you came to faith in our Messiah. Never once did she leave my home without asking that I pray for the two of you, for your eyes to be opened and your hearts to be filled with Yeshua's love."

Everett nodded as he rolled his eyes in contemplation. "I probably don't know who that is."

"It's just the Hebrew name for Jesus. Most languages have variations on how a name is pronounced. John in English is Juan in Spanish, you know. Which reminds me, how did your reading go today?"

"It went well; it was very informative. The words on the page, they seemed to jump out at me and . . . wait, when did I tell you I was reading the Book of John?" Everett recollected everything they'd talked about since they arrived at Elijah's.

"Ah, no matter." Elijah led the way into the living room. "Let's get this show on the road. I'm sure you two lovebirds have more important plans for your wedding night than sitting around here, gabbing with some old man. Did you want a long ceremony or a short one?"

Courtney blushed at Elijah's comment. "We enjoy your company very much, Elijah. We're probably going to have a lot of questions -- about the Bible and about what's coming on the earth, you know, the tribulation and all that."

Elijah found three candles and lined them up on his fireplace mantle. "Yes, well, I'll teach you what I can. And the Spirit, he'll guide you and show you everything you need to know. He's the best teacher of all." Elijah lit the center candle. "But for now, let us rejoice, both for your wedding to each other, and more importantly, for becoming part of the family of God." He stuck his finger in the air for emphasis.

Elijah slid the coffee table out of the way to make room for them to stand near the mantle. "Now, short or long?"

"We don't want to put you out," Courtney replied.

Everett winked at her. "And like you said, we do have other plans."

She slapped his arm playfully. "That depends on whether Everett wants to embarrass me anymore this evening."

Elijah snickered as he retrieved his Bible. He turned to Ecclesiastes 4 and began reading. "Two are better than one; because they have a good reward for their labour. For if they fall, the one will lift up his fellow: but woe to him that is alone when he falleth; for he hath not another to help him up. Again, if two lie together, then they have heat: but how can one be warm alone? And if one prevail against him, two shall withstand him; and a threefold cord is not quickly broken."

Elijah closed the book and set it on the coffee table nearby. He handed Courtney and Everett the two unlit candles. "It is good that the two of you have each other to help you through the terrible times that are about to fall upon the earth. You're going to need all of the help you can get. But don't be deceived. The enemy has long perfected the art of planting seeds of division in the hearts and homes of even God's most devoted. To keep your marriage strong, you need that threefold cord which is not quickly broken. If the two of you will weave your lives around your relationship with God, dedicating time each day to prayer and reading his Holy Word, you will have a three-strand cord that can withstand all trials. Everett and Courtney, place the wicks of your candles to the lit candle which represents the Spirit of God and your willingness to be bound to each other through him and this covenant you are committing to, here before God today."

The two of them lit their candles.

"Everett, do you take Courtney as your wife, forsaking all others?"

"I do."

"And Courtney, do you take Everett as your husband, forsaking all others?"

She looked at Everett. "I do."

"Then I pronounce you man and wife. The LORD bless thee, and keep thee: The LORD make his face shine upon thee, and be gracious unto thee: The LORD lift up his countenance upon thee, and give thee peace. Kiss your bride, Everett."

Everett placed his candle on the mantle as did Courtney, and the two of them embraced in a long, passionate kiss.

Elijah cleared his throat as a sign that the kiss had lasted long enough. "I'll make a special meal tomorrow, and we can have a little reception if you want to come around about noon tomorrow. I would have prepared something today, but it was short notice."

"Thank you. You really don't have to. We should make lunch tomorrow and invite you down," Courtney said.

"I insist. You two enjoy each other. Make a little time to read your Bible. Write down any questions that come up and I'll do my best to answer them." Elijah led the way to the door.

Everett shook Elijah's hand as they walked out the door. "Thank you so much, for everything."

Everett and Courtney got in the car and headed down the mountain. Everett let the BMW idle slowly down the hill, with his foot gently tapping the brakes. He looked from side to side out the windows for game.

"Are you doing this to torture me?" Courtney bent over the seat and put her hand on his leg.

Everett chuckled. "What am I doing?"

"Going so slow. You know I want to get you

home."

"You're the one who said we couldn't afford to miss the opportunity to get a deer."

"That was before we were married. I don't know what I was thinking. Let's just get home."

"If you say so." Everett smiled and took his foot off the brakes. Just then he looked down the hill at their cabin. There was a truck in the driveway. "Now who could that be?"

Courtney looked down the hill. "I don't think it's well-wishers, wanting to congratulate us on tying the knot."

Everett pulled to the side of the road and stopped the car. "Somebody just came out the front door and put something in the bed of the truck. We're getting robbed!"

Courtney took her heels off and tossed them in the back seat.

"What are you doing?" Everett asked.

"We have to slip around through the woods and hit them from the back."

"You can't run through the forest barefoot. You'll get frostbite or cut yourself on a branch. And you sure can't run an ambush in a white dress. I'd see you on the other side of a crowded nightclub dressed like that, forget about going through the woods and not being spotted."

"We have to do what we have to do. We need our supplies if we're going to get through this."

Everett put the car in reverse and started driving back up the hill slowly. "I'll find a spot up on the hill where I can get a good shot from cover. You take the car back up to Elijah's. See if he has some shoes and clothes you can borrow. Send him to back me up if he can."

"I don't want to leave you."

Everett got out of the car, retrieved the rifle from the back seat, and handed Courtney his pistol. "It's the only way. I'll be all right. Go. Drive slow until you're out of earshot so you don't alert them."

"Okay, I love you." Courtney moved over to the driver's seat.

"You, too." Everett blew her a kiss as she steered the car backwards, up the mountain, and out of sight.

Everett checked the chamber of the Mini 14 to make sure it was loaded. He stuck the spare 20-round magazine in his back pocket and stepped off the road into the tree line. Immediately, his foot slipped on a wet patch of decomposing leaves. He grimaced as he looked at the bottom of his shoes. "Horrible shoes for the woods. But I don't really have any options here. I'll just have to move slow," he whispered.

Everett carefully moved between the trees and down the hill to a position where he could see the cabin. He took small steps and tried to keep one hand on low tree limbs to help balance himself and prevent another slip. Soon, he found a large rock formation jutting up from the forest floor. It was almost too far away, but if he could hold the rifle steady enough, he was sure he'd be able to hit a man-sized target down by the cabin. Everett lay prone on the ground at the side of the rock and took aim. He could see the pickup truck and the cabin, but none of the burglars. He waited, taking careful aim at the path between the vehicle and the porch. Seconds later, a man appeared carrying a cardboard box. Everett waited for him to reach the truck to load the box in the back. When the man paused, Everett pulled the trigger.

Pow! The shot rang out through the forest, and the man fell, spilling the contents of the box. "Ahhh! I'm shot! Greg! Help me!"

Another man ran to his assistance -- Greg, Everett assumed. When he bent down to help the injured man, Everett took another shot. Pow! The shot echoed off the side of the granite mountain and Greg fell motionless. Everett had a clear shot of the injured man. He could have easily put him out of his misery, but the man was proving to be an effective lure for the other hostiles.

"Johnny! I need help man! I'm bleeding real bad!" the injured man called out.

Everett couldn't see the next man, but he heard his voice call out, "Just be still. I'll help you in a minute. Where did the shot come from?"

The injured man replied, "I don't know. But I need to stop this bleeding. I'm going to die!"

"I have to find the shooter, or he's going to kill us both. Just stay calm." The voice was insistent.

Finally, a third figure emerged from the side of the porch. Everett could see the man clearly. He wore a camouflage ball cap, jeans, and a brown jacket. The man had a sandy-colored beard and was looking straight in Everett's direction. Everett lay still with his head down and the rifle flat on the ground. He peered up and waited to see what the man would do. The man racked a shell into his shotgun and continued to scan the woods where Everett was positioned.

Everett's mind raced and he whispered to himself, "I've got range on this guy. There's no way he could hit me from that distance with a shotgun… unless. Unless he has a deer slug and gets off a real lucky shot." Everett watched as the man began walking up the hill in his direction. Evidently, the man had figured out the angle and direction of the shots that had killed Greg and injured the other man.

"I'm hurting over here, Johnny! I need help." The injured man's voice was filled with pain and fear.

Everett quickly calculated his odds. "His chances of hitting me are getting better and better with every step." Everett pictured the shot in his head before he popped up to take aim. Then he mustered up the courage and made his move. Everett raised his rifle, still in the prone position, and took aim.

Immediately, the man saw the glint of light from the moving rifle barrel and prepared to return fire. Everett pulled the trigger. He heard the sound of the shot from the Mini 14 ring out and the blast from the shotgun in quick succession. Everett quickly rolled behind the cover of the rock and examined himself. "No blood." He took a deep breath and exhaled his relief. Everett peeked around the side of the rock. The man -- Johnny, he assumed, lay face down on the forest floor.

"Johnny! Where are you? Johnny?" The injured man continued to call out to what seemed to be his last hope for rescue.

"If there was anybody else in the cabin, I'm sure he'd be calling to them, since Johnny isn't responding." Everett talked through his reasoning to keep his racing mind in focus.

Everett heard the BMW coming down the road. "I've got to make sure the guy doesn't have a gun before Courtney gets down there." He circled around the fallen body of Johnny, keeping his sights trained on him, in case he still had some fight left in him. "God, forgive me, but I have to keep my wife safe." Pop! Everett put another shot in the back of Johnny's head for good measure.

He continued working his way down the hill, being careful not to slip. In addition to the sleek-bottomed shoes, Everett now had shaking legs to increase his risk of falling. He made it to the truck and slowly worked his way to the corner where he could see the injured man.

The man was lying in a growing puddle of blood. "Johnny?"

"Johnny's gone. Let's see your hands." Everett called to the man.

"Where's Johnny?" The man rolled over, placing his hand near his stomach.

Everett had a split second to decide if he was trying to hold his wound or if he was going for a weapon. "Rats!" He couldn't take the chance. Everett gritted his teeth as he fired the rifle once more. POW! The man fell limp.

"Everett! Are you okay?" Courtney's voice called out from the road.

"I'm okay. Stay where you are. I'll come to you." Everett surveyed his surroundings before moving slowly in the direction of Courtney's voice. He reached the car where Courtney and Elijah stood with guns drawn. Elijah held an aged-double barrel shotgun with what looked like an old Civil War-era haversack, filled with shotgun shells, slung over his shoulder. Courtney stood behind the car with the Sig grasped in both hands, wearing her short white dress and knee-high green rubber boots.

"You're going duck hunting?" Everett couldn't resist laughing.

Courtney voiced her annoyance. "Shut up, Everett! The boots were right by the door and easy to put on. I had to get back here as fast as possible. Are there any more intruders down there?"

Everett looked back toward the cabin. "I don't think so, but I haven't cleared the house."

"Then let's get it cleared." Elijah stepped forward.

"Okay, we'll stack up to enter. I'll go straight. Courtney is behind me. She'll go right and Elijah, you'll be behind her and you'll go left when we get in the door. Just give her shoulder a squeeze to let her know you're ready to go. Once the living room is cleared, we'll stack back up and clear the kitchen. Courtney, you'll watch the ladder coming down from the loft, and Elijah and I will clear the back bedroom. Once the lower level is clear, we'll clear the loft.

Elijah chortled. "What are you? A CIA secret agent?"

Everett looked at Courtney. She looked like she was thinking the same thing Everett was. Could Ken have told Elijah more than he was supposed to?

There was no way to know. Everett gave Elijah a silly grin as if it were intended as a joke. "No." After all, he was a low-level analyst, far from an active field agent like John Jones had been. Nevertheless, Everett had seen his share of classified footage of forced entries and knew a thing or two about what to watch out for. "I just watched too many movies."

Elijah smiled, like he knew better.

Everett said, "Elijah, I know you're a man of God, so I don't want you to have to take a human life, but if it comes down to it, you have to be prepared to kill. Otherwise we're all at risk. If you can't do it, tell me now. Courtney and I can clear the house on our own."

"It won't be the first time." Elijah showed no emotion in his response.

Courtney looked shocked by his answer. "Oh?"

"Not even close." Elijah motioned forward. "Come on, let's get going."

Everett was glad Elijah was willing to do what was necessary to clear the house, but the old man was becoming more mysterious by the moment. Everett led the way down the road to the front door. Everett stood by the entrance, Courtney stood behind him, and Elijah was last in the line. Everett gave a nod to signal that he was ready to enter. He felt Courtney's hand squeeze his shoulder, and he quickly moved in the open door. No one was in the living room. Everett moved to the doorway leading into the kitchen and waited for Courtney and Elijah to stack up behind him. They cleared the kitchen, and Courtney covered the ladder from the loft while

Everett and Elijah cleared the back bedroom, checking under the bed and in the closet. Everett exchanged weapons with Courtney before climbing the ladder into the loft. This was certainly the most dangerous room to enter because of the slow access and total exposure while entering. Again, Everett found no one in the loft. "All clear," he said after checking every possible hiding place.

Courtney sat down on the bed and pulled her rubber boots off.

"I wanted some wedding pictures of you in those boots. Why did you take them off so fast?" Everett chided.

She smirked. "I'm done being the laughing stock of the mountain. And I don't want any reminders that we had to take out hostiles on my wedding day. It's not the best sign."

Elijah smiled. "But you must be grateful that God has delivered you from the hands of your enemies. I'd say that's a pretty good sign."

"Here's your boots." Courtney handed the green rubber boots to Elijah. "Thanks for letting me use them."

Everett sat down on the mattress and hugged his wife. She'd been through a lot for one day. Her best friend had disappeared; she'd repented of her unbelief in Jesus; they'd gotten married, and been robbed. Any one of those things would be enough to qualify for a very emotional day, but all together, it took a strong woman. He admired her strength, but it was obvious that it was taking its toll on her and she needed comforting.

"Well, you're safe now. I'll be going back to my

home." Elijah laid his shotgun near the entrance to the ladder and began descending.

Courtney dried the single tear that was running down her cheek. "Can you stay for a little while? The joint statement by the pope and Luz is coming on the radio at five. Why don't you hang out and we'll drive you back up the mountain after it's finished."

Elijah looked at Everett. "I don't want to be a bother."

Everett shook his head. "None at all. We'd appreciate your commentary on what the two of them have to say. Lisa told us something about them -- Luz being the antichrist and the pope being his false prophet, but I didn't take her seriously until now."

Courtney brushed the leaves and dirt off the front of Everett. "Your jacket is ruined. And there's not a cleaner around for miles. Why don't you change and we'll try to clean up that mess outside before the speech. I'll put on some work clothes if you guys want to wait for me downstairs."

"I'll be in the kitchen." Elijah continued down the ladder grabbing his shotgun when he'd reached a point where he could bring it down.

Everett pursed his lips as he found some jeans and a t-shirt.

Courtney must have seen the disappointment in his eyes. She whispered, "I'll put my little white dress back on later if you want."

His pulse quickened as he grinned. "Okay." He kissed her, swiftly changed into his jeans and t-shirt, and climbed down the ladder.

"I really appreciate you coming over. You didn't have to help us," Everett said to Elijah.

"You would have done the same for me," Elijah replied politely.

Everett nodded. It was true, now that he'd come around to the truth, there was nothing in the world Everett wouldn't do for the old hermit, but prior to the disappearances, Everett had been very skeptical and standoffish to the man. He regretted that he'd not been more kind. And now that he was about to go through the Great Tribulation, he was even more remorseful that he'd not listened to the old prophet's exhortations to be reconciled to God earlier. Everett sighed. There was no use beating himself up over the matter. That was water under the bridge.

Everett made his way out to the front and surveyed the carnage as he waited for Courtney. Elijah followed him out and over to the bed of the truck.

Everett looked in the back of the pickup. "Oh great. Look at this. They cut the wires to steal the ham radio."

"Wires can be spliced much easier than a radio can be replaced." Elijah looked at the cans, boxes, and buckets of storable food in the back of the truck. "I believe it was a divine act that you were able to prevent them from stealing your means of communication."

Everett picked up the contents of the box that the man was carrying when he shot him. "This guy was stealing my coffee. Now that's divine intervention!"

Courtney soon joined them. "What are we going

to do with the bodies?"

"I don't know, bury them I guess." Everett continued to pick up the food items that had rolled away when the box was spilt.

"You'll have a hard time digging graves by hand." Elijah stomped his foot twice. "The ground is still frozen for one thing. Another thing, this high up in the mountains, about half the time you dig, you'll hit rock before you get to six feet deep."

"Do you have any suggestions?" Courtney asked.

"Birds have to eat," Elijah said.

She protested, "Oh, gross! I'm not leaving these guys lying around here to rot and get eaten by the animals!"

Everett thought about digging three graves, in frozen ground, high in the mountains. "We could drag them down in the forest where we wouldn't smell them or see them. We never go hunting down the mountain anyway. We always stay as far away from town as possible."

"Better yet, string them up a tree on the road coming up from Woodstock. Hang a sign around their necks saying, 'Looters will be shot on sight.' It will deter similar incidents. Perhaps it will save the life of someone else contemplating coming up here to make a bad decision." Elijah stood with his arms crossed.

Courtney made a face of disgust. "I don't know. It sounds so nasty."

Everett was certain that he did not want to dig those graves. "I agree with Elijah. It's practically a public service."

"You guys take care of the corpses and I'll get

the groceries put back on the shelves. What do you say?" Courtney took several food items from the back of the truck.

"I'm not leaving you here by yourself," Everett said firmly. "Ride with us and stand guard. Elijah and I will string up the bodies."

"Maybe you should ask him, before volunteering him." Courtney nodded toward Elijah.

"I'll assist you. It helps to make my home safer as well." Elijah helped Courtney bring in more things from the truck.

"Okay, that's the plan. You guys get the truck bed cleaned out and I'll find some rope. Then I'll figure out which one of these geniuses has the keys and we'll load them in the truck bed." Everett started walking around to the shed in the rear of the cabin. "But we'll have to hurry if we're going to be done in time to listen to the address at five."

Everett retrieved the rope and tossed it in the back of the truck. He dropped the tailgate and tried to figure a way to load the first corpse without getting blood all over his clothes. He resigned to the fact that he was probably not going to be able to accomplish such a lofty goal. "At least I don't have to dig a hole."

"Let me help you load him in the back." Elijah assisted Everett getting the first body up into the bed, then the second.

"The other one is up in the woods. We'll have to drag him down to the drive." Everett looked at the blood all over his hands and jeans. The two men found the third body and each took a hand to pull him down the hill. Once he was loaded into the back, Everett, Courtney, and Elijah got into the cab of the truck.

"What do you think of my sign?" Courtney held up a cardboard sign which read, "Looters will be shot on sight."

Everett glanced over. "The font looks like something you'd use for a birthday party sign."

Courtney huffed. "It's going to be hanging around the neck of a dead guy with birds eating his eyeballs out. I doubt anyone is going to mistake it for a birthday party." She looked back down at the sign. "Unless I put some balloons in the corner."

"No balloons!" Everett tried to stay focused on the road.

A half mile down the road, Everett pulled to the side. "How's this?"

"Are we going to string them all up in the same place?" Courtney asked.

Everett shrugged. "Yeah, I guess. Why?"

"You know when you're on the interstate and you'll see a billboard, then a quarter mile later you see another one by the same company, then another one in another quarter mile? I think it's effective messaging."

Everett shook his head. "Courtney, it's not a marketing campaign."

Elijah interrupted. "I'll agree the balloons would have been in poor taste, but in a way, this is a marketing campaign. We're trying to let people know how we deal with thieves on this mountain. I'll have to say, spreading them out would be, what did you call it, effective messaging?"

Everett grunted his displeasure as he stood in the

back of the truck and made several attempts to throw the rope over the lowest tree limb. Finally, it fell over the limb and hung just low enough overhead for him to grab it and pull it down.

"Do you know how to tie a noose?" Elijah asked.

Everett didn't even answer, just handed the end of the rope to Elijah. In a few minutes, they had the first man strung up with Courtney's well-crafted sign hanging around his neck. Everett proceeded down the mountain, this time watching for a lower limb. The second man was up in less time than the first. By the time they found the third low-hanging limb, they had a system worked out. Courtney hung the sign, Elijah tied the noose, and Everett hoisted the man up, tying the rope off around the trunk of the tree.

"Four-thirty, I've got just enough time to get cleaned up before the radio address." Everett spun the truck around and raced back up the mountain.

The morbid task was finished and Everett was relieved to be done with it, but he dared not ask himself what more could happen before the day was over.

CHAPTER 2

I am come in my Father's name, and ye receive me not: if another shall come in his own name, him ye will receive.

John 5:43

Before Everett could even get cleaned up from moving the dead bodies, he had to bring water from the stream that ran alongside of the house. As he packed the two buckets, five gallons in each hand, he said to himself, "I'm going to dig a branch off of the stream tomorrow to bring water closer to the house. Hauling water four of five times a day is getting old fast."

Once he was cleaned up, he used the same water he'd washed in to soak the blood out of his clothing. The days of washing hands and letting water run down the drain were long gone.

When he got back in the house, he asked Elijah, "Can I lend you a clean shirt? I can put your shirt in the laundry bucket with mine so it doesn't stain."

Elijah waved his hand. "I'm fine."

Everett looked at the man's shirt. He knew he'd seen blood on the front of it. Maybe not much, but some. However, as he stared at Elijah's clothing, he couldn't see one drop. *How is that possible?*

Courtney peeked into the kitchen from the living room and said, "I'm warming up some venison stew in the fireplace and making some cornbread pancakes. Anybody want some?"

"Yes, please," Elijah said. "You're blessed to have a wife that cooks."

Everett shook his head trying to signal to Elijah not to make an issue out of her cooking. Everett had made a wise crack about wanting a woman to cook for him when they'd first met and she'd never let him live it down.

Elijah didn't seem to understand Everett's frantic attempt to reach him through code and signals, but dropped the subject, nonetheless.

Everett tuned into the Global Republic news affiliate on the small battery operated radio.

An announcer stated that the station was broadcasting from the new press room in the recently-constructed Global Republic General Assembly Building, erected in the National Mall of Washington, DC. Global Republic Press Secretary, Athaliah Jennings, introduced Pope Peter. "Ladies and Gentlemen of the press, please offer your most reverent attention for the Supreme Pontiff of the Universal Church, His Holiness, Pope Peter of Rome."

After a few moments of pious silence, the pope began to speak in English. "Dear Children of the Earth, today has been a trying day. Most everyone knows someone who has been affected by the disappearances. All of you are looking for answers. It is important that you not allow yourselves to be carried away by myths and superstitions, yet just as necessary, you will need to keep an open mind to understand what is happening. First, let me ask that you focus and bring your consciousness to a place of peace, from which we can rebuild, grow, and mature as a planet and as a global culture. The apostle Paul often spoke of the birth pains a new mother must endure to see her child. This present experience is not unlike those pains. But to see the miracle that is to come, we must persevere.

"To the mothers and fathers whose children have disappeared, it was for the good of your offspring. And I promise you, by my throne in Vatican City, you will see them again. They have been taken to a place where they can learn to be the leaders of tomorrow and the citizens that will guide a new illuminated society to a place of harmony with the universe. They are also being preserved from a disruptive period that our planet is having to encounter, due to the poor stewardship of our species. Global warming, combined with seismic instabilities created by massive drilling and mining projects by the world's carnivorous corporations, are going to cause massive challenges over the coming years and this will not be a welcoming planet, especially for the young.

"I understand your hurt and your sorrow, and what must be all-but-unbearable grief at the perceived loss of your children, but trust that they are in good hands.

"Which brings us to the next topic. Where did they go and who is caring for them? The Vatican has sponsored and financed a massive cooperative enterprise between the SETI Institute, the Vatican Research Observatory Group, and the Mount Graham International Observatory. The Search for Extraterrestrial Intelligence or SETI Institute has long been a pioneer in the scientific community to prove that we are not alone. I am pleased to be able to announce to you that, as your hearts will confirm, we are indeed, not alone in the universe. It has been many thousands of years since the beings from beyond our skies have been able to walk and live among us, but they have never been far away. Many have witnessed their comings and goings throughout the night skies across the globe and a fortunate few have even been in contact with them. But, for the most part, they have stayed back, watching from a distance. These Watchers, if you will, have often been referred to as angels, or visitors, even gods by some. We have seen their images inscribed on the walls of the pyramids, heard of their exploits in Greek mythology, discovered their places of visitation among the ziggurats of Central America and read of their contributions to the human race in the Book of Enoch. The Watchers have been instrumental to giant leaps in technology throughout the ages. And they have long desired to once again hold us by the hand, like younger siblings, and guide us into a glorious new age, a utopian existence like that of the fabled Atlantis.

"This leads me to the next explanation. What happened to the adults that disappeared? Unlike the children, who have disappeared from every city, town, and country side around the world, the adults all had distinct commonalities. They clung to a rigid belief structure that would have prevented our species from being able to progress in a positive direction. Some who were influenced by their dogmatic rantings will tell you that it was Christ who came to gather his Church."

The pope paused to allow time for snickering in the press room. He let out a condescending chuckle himself before continuing. "Well, I'm still here."

More laughing could be heard from the members of the press. Then the pope continued. "For those in the Americas, this address will be followed by a short message from the new Global Republic's Minister of the Americas, Richard Clay and world renowned megachurch Pastor Jacob Ralston. They will further assure you that the disappearances were not caused by the mythical rapture. For it was not Christians that the Watchers had to remove for us to move forward, but rather a cult-like subset of people who claimed to be followers of Christ, yet never practiced his compassion, tolerance, and acceptance of those around them. In the world we want to build, under the guidance of the Watchers, we have no room for hate, intolerance, and bigotry disguised as religion. We welcome followers of Jesus, Mohammad, Buddha, Baal, and Ahura Mazda. We invite the worshipers of Shiva, Ra, and Chango; many of these are the names assigned by earth dwellers to the very Watchers who have revealed themselves to us at our center on Mount Graham. We invite pagans, agnostics, and atheists to come together, recognize that we must all share this planet and coexist, and pledge ourselves to the universal good. There is room for everyone and every belief, but we must understand that we all seek the same force of good. The Watchers have done their part to cleanse our planet of those who could not turn from their hate and bigotry, now it is up to us to maintain this environment of peace and love.

"Now I will unveil to you the most important of all the revelations today. Once, the Watchers walked among us, lived in our midst and even procreated with our species, creating the most beautiful, enlightened, and gifted offsprings. There is one such child among us now. Being of man, and of the gods, he is the perfect intercessor between man and gods. Through signs and miracles, he will prove to you that he is indeed this spectacle of grace of which I speak. Most all religions have prophesied of his coming. To the Jew, he is Messiah, to the Muslim he is the Mahdi, for the Buddhist, he is Maitreya, to the Hindu, he is Kalki, and to the Zoroastrian, Saoshyant. Whatever you call him, or even if you have never heard of such prophecies, he is come; come that we might have peace and have it more abundantly.

"Ladies and Gentlemen, I present to you this day, the being of whom I speak, the chosen one, His High and Most Prepotent Majesty, Angelo Luz. Please stand and bow your heads."

Everett looked over at Courtney and Elijah and shook his head in disapproval of all that he was hearing. He had so many things he wanted to ask Elijah, so much that he wanted to say in protest of what was happening and being said over the radio, but he dared not speak, fearing that he might miss some vital piece of information. His brief career in the intelligence industrial complex had taught him to listen if it had taught him nothing else. There would always be time for analysis, and distilling information once the data had been received.

Luz began speaking. "Well, that was quite an introduction. Thank you very much, Your Holiness. Please, lift your heads.

"To the citizens of the Global Republic, I ask for your understanding in having this information veiled from your eyes. While a great many of those in power have been aware of these mysteries, it could not be disclosed to the general public until the proper time.

"As His Holiness explained, much of our secrecy was needed because of the immaturity of those who have been taken out of the way. Inevitably, some will blame me for the disappearance of their children because I am of the Watchers. But please understand, I am also of man and as such, these types of decisions belong to my father and are not mine.

"Like you, I am simply here to do the will of my father. I mourn with you and feel your sorrow, but I ask that you trust me when I echo what the Holy Father has told you; it is for the good of the children and you will see them again. I can't explain how proud you will be of your sons and daughters when they return with an understanding of how to treat one another as well as our mother earth. They will come home with a sense of spirituality and an education that they could have never received from this dimension. That level of consciousness and realization cannot exist while this planet is in its present state, which is why I need a commitment from you to lay aside your grief, roll up your sleeves and get to work so we can prepare the world for their return. The harder we work to repair our society and our broken planet, the sooner the earth will be ready for the return of the children.

"We must heal our mother, cleansing her from pollution, abuse and the exploitation of her resources. We must learn to love each other in peace, acceptance, tolerance, and unity. Only then will my father and the other Watchers trust that the investment they have made in the children is secure and that we are ready to receive the gift of their return.

"Do not despair in the loss of those who have been taken, but rejoice in hope for the soon return of the children."

The broadcast cut and a GR commentator began going over everything Luz and the pope had said.

Courtney was first to break the silence. "I don't understand. I'll admit, I kind of tuned Lisa out when she'd start talking about all of this end-times stuff, which is why I'm still here, but the little I learned from her doesn't fit into what these guys are saying. All of a sudden, they've shifted the entire focus of the rapture to people waiting for the return of the children."

Elijah sighed, "False hope and a false sense of security, that's been the enemy's strategy from the beginning. He told Eve that she would be like God, all knowing, giving her a false hope. Then he assured her that she wouldn't die if she ate of the forbidden fruit, instilling in her a false sense of security. If you are jumping out of an airplane with a backpack that you think is a parachute, you might feel quite secure. The goal of every major religion in the world is to convince people that their backpack is a parachute. But, the Messiah said, I am the truth, the way, and the life, no man comes to the Father except by me."

"Every religion except Christianity, you mean." Everett was sure the old man had misspoken.

Elijah rocked back in the chair. "Like the pope said, he's still here. And the next speaker, Jacob Ralston is the poster child for protestant Christianity as a religion, at least in America. You tell me, Everett; is being devoted to the Christian religion enough to make you a child of God?"

Everett sat with his mouth hanging open. He was confused and had no idea how to answer. "What about me? What about Courtney, and the prayer we prayed to God? Are we in or not? How can I know?"

Elijah held up his hand and closed his eyes. "John says, 'These things have I written unto you that believe on the name of the Son of God; that ye may *know* that ye have eternal life.' There's no guess work. You did not place your faith in religion. You put no false trust in your own deeds or a set of instructions. You and Courtney professed that you believed on the name of the Son of God. Furthermore, you showed that your repentance was sincere by your obedience. You forsook your former ways, refusing to live in sin any longer. That's not religion my friend. That's a relationship of trust and walking in the light as he is in the light."

Everett took Courtney's hand and held it. He smiled as he looked at her. Turning his attention back to Elijah, he asked, "Everything he said about the rapture is a lie. How are people falling for that? It seems so obvious to me. Just listening to the pope speak made me feel sick to my stomach. Then when Luz started in, I wanted to come out of my skin."

Elijah put his index finger in the air. "Remember, only hours ago, the scales were still on your eyes. But now you see, the Holy Spirit makes all things known to you. It is not so for those who will not come to him. They will continue to be deceived."

Courtney shook her head. "So God took the children? All of them? And they're not coming back like Luz said they would?"

"The time of Jacob's trouble is here. It is a time of human suffering that is unparalleled in human history. And it is a direct manifestation of God's wrath. Messiah said of this time, 'For then shall be great tribulation, such as was not since the beginning of the world to this time, no, nor ever shall be.' The children who had not yet reached the age of accountability, like those who had been washed in the blood of the Lamb, are innocent in the eyes of God. He has spared them from the full onslaught of his wrath.

"And no, they are not coming back. That is simply a lie, a distraction to lead people further from the truth. Luz is doing just what his father has always done; dangling a false promise before the eyes of the deceived."

Everett was beginning to trust Elijah and decided to open up to him, just a little. "The man who gave me this cabin, John Jones, he told me the narrative for the rapture had been crafted long ago. He said the power elite and the secret societies have had this story in place for years, in anticipation for the disappearances."

Elijah nodded. "That is true. All governmental powers try to control information to steer the minds of the populous toward their own agendas. This final world empire should be no different."

Courtney asked, "And everything he said about the Watchers, that's all lies too, right?'

Elijah furrowed his brow. "Hmm, not everything. This idea that they are alien life forms, which has been so widely sold to the public, is a lie. Even the sightings of their activity don't mesh with what we know about the physical universe. The way the lights appear in the sky, move at great speeds, then make sudden 90 or even 180 degree turns. And the way they come and go suddenly without being detected despite our most advanced telescopes, they defy the most rudimentary laws of physics. These . . . beings, are not of this realm."

"So they're what?" Everett wanted clarification.

"Demons, fallen angels."

Courtney stared at the ceiling. "And what about Luz being the offspring of a human mother and a Watcher for a father? Is that a lie?"

Elijah crossed his hands as he sat patiently in the chair. "I'm afraid not. In the Book of Genesis, we read that the sons of God went into the daughters of men and procreated with them."

"And do you think Luz is in contact with his father, this Watcher or fallen angel, or whoever?" Everett was trying desperately to get his head wrapped around what he was hearing. Even with what Jones had told him before, this was all new information.

"He is in contact with his father. And he's not just some arbitrary fallen angel."

Courtney crossed her arms. "Then who is he?"

Elijah paused, looking them both in the eyes, one at a time, before he spoke. "His father . . . is Satan."

Chills ran up Everett's spine. Courtney quivered and turned away as if she'd heard enough.

The radio commentator announced that the broadcast to the Americas was being turned over to Pastor Jacob Ralston and Minister of the Americas, Richard Clay.

Everett shook his head. "I can't wait to hear what President Clay has to say."

Courtney corrected him. "Minister Clay. You have to have a country to be a president. The United States doesn't exist, remember?"

Pastor Ralston began speaking. "Minister Clay, before we start, I want to congratulate you on your appointment as Minister to the Americas. It's a much bigger territory than what you were responsible for before the Global Republic charter was signed. But, with the experience you gained as President of the United States, we all have the utmost confidence in your ability to lead these two great continents."

"Thank you, Jacob. And I can't go without congratulating you. The pope has granted you the position of Global Republic Minister of Religion. Next to his position, it's the highest spiritual title in the new republic. You really have your work cut out for you."

"Yes, Minister Clay, I am going to give it my all. But I can't take more credit than is due. The infrastructure for the new Ministry of Religion already existed through the World Council of Churches. The council has long been a friend of the UN, co-laboring with them on so many initiatives. And as you know, Lakeview Church has been a member of the World Council of Churches for many, many years. We'll still be seeing most of the same faces."

Clay quipped, "So what are you telling us Jacob? Other than a new office and some fancier stationary,

I'm so glad that they'll be coming home to a better world."

Clay jumped in. "I don't mean to interrupt, but I just got a tweet from my oldest daughter, Megan. It says 'We miss you Josh but will see you soon.' Hashtag hope4thechildren. Our youngest, Josh was taken and my 19-year-old daughter was shaken up by it. But here she is, focusing on a better tomorrow and the hope of seeing her little brother again."

Ralston replied, "Richard, that is so wonderful. I believe that's what we all have to do. Let's follow Megan's lead and get to work so we can provide a better home when the children return."

Clay said, "I agree, Jacob. But like you said, it is going to take some work. The first thing we'll need our citizens in the Americas to do is get registered. Unfortunately, the disappearances have negated the progress of all the census workers, so even if you've already registered, we need you to go back to the closest census station and re-register. And now for some more good news, production of the Mark implants has been ramped up since they were announced on New Year's Day and all the census stations are fully stocked, so citizens will be able to take their pledge to the republic and have their implant placed on the same day. Commissaries are set up at the largest census station, so they'll be able to purchase staples like rice, beans or powdered milk all at the same time. Your Mark will come with 500 GR credits upon your pledge being administered.

"The generous republic gun buyback program will also add another 150 GR credits to your account for each gun you turn in. The amnesty period for weapons has been extended to match the amnesty period for your pledge and census registration. You'll have until March 15th, but why wait? Get registered, get your Mark so you can start spending your GR credits on much needed items today. This is all going to help jump start economic activity and get the ball rolling."

Ralston added, "And I want to put everyone's mind at ease about the pledge, Richard. You are not pledging against anyone. You are pledging for the good of us all. People are lying if they tell you that you'll go to hell if you take the pledge, which asks you to deny Jesus Christ as God's only Messiah. That is simply not true. Jesus is still the same person and he loves you just as much. This clause is in the pledge because it's part of the dogma of the people who have incited violence against the republic. You can still believe that Jesus is a messiah, but a messiah is simply someone who shows up when you need a little help. It would be unfair to the Most Prepotent Majesty, Angelo Luz to say Jesus is the only messiah. After all, it is totally undeniable that His Highest and Most Prepotent has come along at just the right time when the world needed him most."

"I couldn't have said it better myself. To quickly review the technology in the Mark, it is totally safe and very comfortable. In fact, I just had my implant put in a few weeks back and I didn't feel a thing. Even now, the only time I notice that it's there is when I need to use the phone app, or the commerce app, or the internet search app."

Ralston snickered, "Or the camera, or text, or the map, or email, or games, or listening to music, watching videos on YouTube."

Clay cut him off. "Did you have the speaker upgrade implanted in your ear?"

Ralston laughed. "Don't tell my wife, she thinks I'm listening to her."

Clay chuckled. "I've got to tell you, Jacob, I don't know how I ever lived without my Mark. I start my car with it, turn on the lights, turn off the lights, it sends the security code to let me in my house, my office. I never have to worry about losing my phone, my keys, or my wallet ever again. It's always with me."

Ralston said, "I never remembered to charge my phone, so I was always missing calls and texts. The Mark is powered by an internal bio-charge system. A micro thermoelectric generator utilizes your body heat to power the device and keep the batteries topped off for high-power-usage applications."

Clay added, "And the technology is so efficient. The small pico projector projects your Mark's interface on your arm and allows you to manipulate the Mark like a phone or tablet computer via optic sensors. They call it embeddable tech. The screen on my arm is coming from micro projectors under my skin. The tiny processor, battery, speaker, sensors, and projectors are all just under my skin. The mark on your skin is roughly the size of a freckle."

"Which is where it gets its name, the Mark!" Ralston said.

"I've heard this scripted sales pitch before." Everett turned the radio off. "I can't listen to another second of this. It's like QVC. They're glorified sales men."

"Thank you!" Courtney said as she began serving the stew. "I was thinking glorified entertainers. It was like a really bad cross between daytime talk and late night comedy."

Elijah smirked. "President Clay and Pastor Ralston were never more than salesmen and entertainers. It's somewhat refreshing to see them in a more fitting role."

Everett stood to help Courtney bring the cornbread and utensils to the table. "They sure rolled over quick and acted out their performance as directed."

The three of them ate their simple meal together and Elijah returned home. Courtney and Everett turned in early, and . . . well, it *was* their honeymoon night.

CHAPTER 3

For then shall be great tribulation, such as was not since the beginning of the world to this time, no, nor ever shall be.

Matthew 24:21

Everett took the last pancake from the pan and cracked four eggs. "Good morning, princess." He winked at Courtney as she reached the bottom of the ladder.

"What did you do to me last night?" She wrapped her arms around him and kissed his neck from behind. "And how do you have energy to be up cooking breakfast so early?"

"It's almost noon. I've been up since nine." He poured the eggs in the pan and walked back over to the fireplace, bent down and set the pan on the makeshift grill he'd built from rocks and the old oven rack to cook over the coals.

She followed him into the living room and stretched her arms. "Nine? What have you been doing since then?"

"Reading the Bible. I finished John and read Romans."

"Any good stuff about the Great Tribulation?"

"None, but I feel like I'm getting a better handle on what it means to be a Christian." Everett took a seat on the hearth to stir the eggs.

Courtney walked back into the kitchen to retrieve a coffee cup, returned and sat on the hearth next to Everett. "John and Romans; okay, I'll read that after breakfast."

Everett poured some coffee into her cup. "I'm thinking of trying to contact Mr. Black to invite him and Ms. White to come up here."

"To live with us?"

"Yeah, what do you think?"

Courtney sipped her coffee pensively. "I'm not sure. What do we know about them?"

Everett paid close attention to the eggs, making sure they wouldn't burn or stick. "We know they were part of the resistance. We know they don't believe in Luz or the pope. We know they do believe that the rapture is what caused the disappearances. We need more people than you, me, and Elijah to survive. We have to set up a security watch. Food and resources are scarce, people are desperate and yesterday probably won't be the last time we get robbed or attacked."

She stood with the coffee pot and her cup to take

to the kitchen table. "I get all of that. But do we know if they've committed their lives to Christ?"

Everett followed her with the eggs. "We don't know, but is that fair to judge them? Ken and Lisa accepted us when we weren't saved."

"Ken and Lisa weren't saved either when we came up here. Besides, Jones left this place to you. From Lisa and Ken's perspective, it was come up here with you or take their chances riding out the chaos in DC. What if they get up here and decide the tribulation is too tough? What if they decide to take the Mark and turn us in?"

"These two were on Thinthread's team. They've been risking their lives to fight against the New World Order ever since the false flag attacks were blamed on the patriots and the Christians. I'm relatively certain that they won't flip quite that easily." Everett put the two plates on the table, sat down and began eating.

Courtney looked at him. "Are we going to pray before we eat?"

"Oh, yeah. We should." He laid his fork on the table and bowed his head. "God, I'm still not too good at this, but thank you for providing us food and a safe place to live. We pray that you'll continue to protect us and give us wisdom to make the right decisions." He looked up.

"Amen?" Courtney looked up and smiled at him.

He closed his eyes again. "Oh yeah, amen."

"Okay, so if you think it's the right thing to do, invite them to come up. Do you think they'll trust us? And do you think they'll leave their compound to come here?" Courtney cut her pancake and took a bite.

"I'm sure they trust us. We've been feeding them information, and they've been acting on it. As far as why they would leave their compound, they can't be sure that their position wasn't compromised when Thinthread was captured."

Courtney finished chewing. "I thought Thinthread was taken in the rapture."

"They're pretty sure that he was, but who knows how much information could have been extracted from him in the time between him being captured by the Global Republic and when he disappeared."

Courtney nodded as she sipped her coffee. "I hope it works out. And I hope we can get along with them. But you're right, we'll have a hard time surviving on our own. Should you run the idea by Elijah, maybe get his input before calling them?"

Everett nodded. "That's a good idea. I have to borrow some electrical tape from Elijah so I can get the cut wires repaired before I can use the ham radio anyway. How are your pancakes?"

"Great, thanks. We had roughly a years' worth of food when it was Ken and Lisa. Theoretically, we'd be in the same position if Mr. Black and Ms. White come up here. But they should have some supplies also, right?

Everett sipped his coffee. "They should, but fuel is tight. We'll have to see. Anyway, we shouldn't count our chickens before they hatch. We'll have to wait to hear what they have to say. And Ms. White's name is Sarah."

"Sarah, that's a nice name. She's probably a sweet person."

Everett tilted his head to one side. "Black said she was training the women to fight when the disappearances happened. I'm guessing she is ex-military. She might be a tough cookie."

"A person can be tough and sweet. I'm living proof of that."

Everett laughed. "Yes, you are."

"We can make our stockpile last. Elijah is teaching us to farm in the mountains, we've been blessed with a lot of wild game. Even though it's thinning out, we can kill as much as possible, and make jerky, while it's still available."

Everett nodded. "Spring is right around the corner. We should be able to find wild blackberries, ramps, mushrooms, and dandelion."

"Did you say ramps?" Courtney looked curious.

"Yeah, they're wild greens that grow in the mountains. They kind of look like tulip leaves with reddish colored stems; sort of a garlic smell and flavor. You can cut them up and sauté them or eat them with eggs."

"Sounds good." Courtney stood to clear the table.

Everett got up to help. "Why don't you let me clean up and you spend a little time reading the Bible. I can't tell you how much I got out of it."

She kissed him. "I'm glad I married you, Everett Carroll."

Everett cleaned up the dishes from breakfast then walked out back and mapped out his trench to bring water from the stream closer to the house. He sighed. "I just don't have the energy for this." The previous day had been one of the most draining of his life. The mental and emotional toll of dealing with Ken and Lisa's disappearance, realizing he'd been wrong about God, getting married, and then being in a firefight was more than he'd ever had to deal with at once. Everett sat down on the wood pile and took a deep breath. "I think I'll deal with the trench tomorrow."

"Hey, sleepy head." Courtney gave Everett a gentle nudge.

Everett yawned and stretched out on the living room couch. "How long was I out?"

"Maybe an hour. I told Elijah we'd be at his house by two."

"And what time is it now?"

"Two-thirty, we're late. Sorry, I lost track of time."

Everett sat up. "Okay, I'll be ready in a few minutes. We should carry a backpack with some extra magazines and ammo in case we get hit again. And we should both have a rifle and a pistol."

"I agree. And, I won't be wearing heels and a dress, so I'll be much better backup." Courtney winked and headed toward the ladder to the loft.

"You'll never be in a James Bond movie with that attitude." Everett followed her up the ladder. He opened the safe and retrieved four magazines for the folding stock HK G36C that John Jones had left at the cabin. He placed the mags in his pack, placed two spare magazines for his pistol in his back pocket then grabbed the HK rifle.

Courtney topped off the magazine in her Ruger Mini 14. "If you ever think of a Bond girl that you want to trade me in for, just let me know."

Everett smiled as he watched her replace the magazine and rack the chamber. "There's no one in the world I'd rather be with."

She grinned as she closed the safe and spun the combination dial.

They locked up the house then the two of them headed up to Elijah's on foot, because it increased their odds of seeing a deer, it conserved fuel, and it was a beautiful sunny day for a walk.

Everett knocked on the door when they arrived.

"Come in!" Elijah held the door for them.

"Sorry we're a little late." A heavenly smell wafted Everett in the face as he entered. "Wow! What do I smell?"

"Pizza!"

"You're kidding!" Courtney exclaimed.

"Yes, yes, I know. It doesn't sound like the proper thing to serve for a wedding reception, but wait til you try it. It's no ordinary pizza." Elijah led the way to the kitchen.

"That's not what I meant. I'm astounded that you've managed to make pizza. You never cease to amaze me." Courtney followed the old man.

"What's going on in the sink" Everett took a close look at the array of pans and ingredients.

"I used the last of my goat cheese on the pesto pizza, so I was making another batch."

"How do you make goat cheese?" Courtney was excited.

"Simple. Bring your milk to a gentle boil, pour in a half cup of apple cider vinegar and stir until the curds come together. Strain it through a cheese cloth and colander if you have it, otherwise a clean towel will work just fine. Squeeze out the water, and you have cheese. And you can flavor it if you like. This one is going to be rosemary goat cheese. My rosemary is doing very well in the greenhouse."

Everett watched as the old hermit mixed the rosemary into the strained curds. He pressed the cheese into a clean empty can using a slightly smaller can to pack it. "That's amazing."

Courtney looked at the pizza on the table. "Did you make your own pesto? Don't tell me you shelled out all those little pine nuts from the pine cones in the forest."

Elijah put plates and a pitcher of his sweet herb tea on the table next to the pizza. "I'm afraid you've overestimated my patience. I actually used walnuts instead of pine nuts for the pesto. Most people won't know if you don't tell them. Come now, let's eat."

They all took a seat at the table and Elijah asked God to bless the meal as well as the conversation.

Courtney took a slice of pizza. "Wild mushrooms?"

"Semi-wild. I actually cultivate them in the crawl space beneath the house."

Everett finished chewing, and then explained their reasoning and plan to invite Mr. Black and Sarah to come live with them.

"It's a fantastic idea," Elijah said. "The two of you would certainly be welcome to come stay here for mutual security, but as I said before, when it's time for me to go, I have to leave right away."

Courtney wiped the corner of her mouth. "Where exactly do you have to go?"

Elijah shrugged. "Jerusalem, eventually, but who knows what I'll be sent to do before that."

"Pardon my curiosity and you don't have to answer if you don't want to or can't, but what will you be doing?" she asked.

"Pronouncing judgement, standing witness to the wickedness of this present age, and delivering God's final plea for the inhabitants of the earth to repent."

Everett looked at Courtney, and then at Elijah. He was having trouble comprehending Elijah's job description. "So, sort of like an evangelist? A preacher or something?"

Elijah chuckled as he took a sip of his tea. "Prophet would be more accurate."

Courtney said, "We started reading the Bible, but we've been reading John and Romans, and haven't gotten to the part about the tribulation. That's all in Revelation, right?"

"Much of the tribulation is in Revelation. But to fully understand the time of the end, you would need to study Daniel, Matthew 24, and Luke 21, primarily, but clues are sprinkled throughout all the Scriptures; particularly the Books of Prophecy and Paul's writings."

Everett nodded. "Yeah, you lost both of us there."

"Could you just give us a brief synopsis of what we're looking at, and maybe some kind of a timeline?"

Elijah sighed. "I can try. Let me know if I'm moving too fast or if you need some clarification on something. Believe it or not, all has not been fully revealed even to me. I would always have such a good laugh listening to the various Bible teachers over the radio who thought they had it all figured out.

"In chapter 9, Daniel writes of seventy weeks, or 70 seven-year periods. We know they arc literal seven-year periods, because the first sixty-nine *weeks* predicted the precise amount of time from the order to rebuild Jerusalem until Messiah rode into the city before Passover to be sacrificed as our Passover lamb.

"The final week, or seven-year period was never completed, but Daniel tells us that it will be marked by a final prince that shall confirm a covenant with many for one week, or for seven years. I believe the final seven-year period began when Luz made the agreement for the Global Republic Charter.

"The trouble of this seven-year period is explained in Revelation. Beginning in chapter 6, we read of the first of seven seals being broken by the Lamb of God. The first seal unleashes a white horse, which represents the Antichrist, Angelo Luz. The second horse is red, representing war, which takes peace from the earth. We've already seen much fighting and violence, but I expect we will see even more as the Global Republic pushes to dominate the globe; particularly if China and Russia continue to resist being signatories on the GR charter. The third horse is black, representing famine and want. John says that when the third seal is broken and the black horse is revealed he hears a voice saying, 'A measure of wheat for a penny, and three measures of barley for a penny.' The famine is due both to scarcity of food and a hyperinflationary collapse of global currencies. A measure of wheat for a penny may sound like a good deal, but the Greek word which has been translated as *penny* in that verse is *denarius*, which was a silver coin representing a day's wages for a common labor. Let's say its modern pre-crash equivalent was around $100. You would be purchasing a measure, or just under a quart of wheat for around $100."

Courtney pursed her lips. "Suddenly, it's not such a bargain."

Elijah lifted his eyebrows. "We've already seen the collapse of the monetary system, but I believe the black horse will become a darker omen as the famine intensifies; secondary effects of the other judgments coming upon the earth will greatly inhibit food production and distribution."

"Like which other judgements?" Courtney asked.

"Massive earthquakes; they will disrupt infrastructure and the ability to move goods. The great darkness coming upon the earth. A reduction in sunlight from the volcanic ash after the quakes and the atmospheric steam and debris from the comet Wormwood will hamper farmers' abilities to produce food, which by the way is why you must do all that you can to acquire as much food as possible while you still have the chance."

"A comet? The earth is getting hit by a comet? The Global Republic isn't saying anything about a comet." Everett put his pizza down as he listened.

"Why would they? To create mass hysteria that will ruin their message of peace and love?" Elijah laughed. "They won't tell of it. But you can be sure they know. Mount Graham, the observatory where they supposedly made contact with the Watchers has a binocular telescope named LUCIFER. They know exactly when Wormwood is due to hit."

Courtney ran her hands through her hair. "Elijah, be honest, do we have any chance at all of surviving the next seven years?'

Elijah smiled and reached across the table to put his hand on hers. "Child, with God, all things are possible."

Everett saw that Courtney was getting very upset. He was feeling anxious and his heart was beating fast as well. "So maybe we should just focus on the next major event that we have to survive. I don't think I can handle it all at once."

Elijah nodded. "Yes, of course. The fourth seal unleashes the pale horse. I believe he represents the massive plagues we've seen across Africa, Asia and the US. We may see more typhoid outbreaks, more Ebola, possibly other strains.

"Next is the fifth seal. Rather than some terrible plague, the fifth seal is distinguished by the voices of the martyrs, crying out from beneath the altar. They are calling out for justice and asking how much longer until God will avenge their deaths. They are told that it will be just a little while longer and they must rest until the remainder of their brethren who are to die, have been slain."

"So, what does that mean for us?" Everett asked apprehensively.

Elijah sipped his tea, pausing as if to collect his thoughts. "I suspect the fifth seal will be broken as the great persecution breaks out against your brothers and sisters in the faith. Luz has declared an amnesty until March 15th. After that, he has vowed to not tolerate anyone who will not take the pledge to the Global Republic. Those who refuse to take the Mark will not only be excluded from the world's singular means of payment, but they will also be in violation of Global law."

"March 15th? You think the fifth seal will be broken on that exact day?" Courtney inquired.

Elijah stroked his grey beard as he answered. "It's hard to say for sure, but I don't believe that would be too much of a stretch."

Courtney was quick to launch her next question. "If we can say, with some minor degree of certainty that the fifth seal will be opened on, or around March 15th, could we then estimate the timing of subsequent events or judgements?"

Elijah sighed. "If you were keeping a checklist to mark off the progression of the Great Tribulation and the events that must be endured to reach the Kingdom Age, perhaps it would serve that purpose. But you can't say that because the fifth seal was broken on the 15th that the sixth seal would be opened on the 20th. There's no set time periods, other than Luz's appointment to end the daily sacrifice and exalt himself as God."

"And we've got three and a half years on that one. From the agreement of the GR Charter," Elijah explained.

"Is there a sixth seal?" Courtney asked.

Elijah answered, "Yes. There are seven. Seven seals, seven trumpets and seven vials of God's wrath."

Everett felt the uneasiness arising inside again. "Vials of wrath, that doesn't sound good. Maybe you can just tell us what the sixth seal is. I don't want to get too far into the future, fretting vials of wrath that I probably won't live to see anyway."

Courtney took a deep breath and held Everett's hand as the she listened for Elijah's reply.

The old prophet pushed his plate to the side and leaned his forearms on the table. "Okay, the sixth seal. We'll talk about that and leave the rest for another day.

"When the Lamb opens the sixth seal, the earth will have the greatest earthquake in history, moving every island and mountain from its place. I expect every tectonic plate to shift in this massive seismic event. The sudden and substantial movement of the earth's crust will also trigger unprecedented volcanic activity which will send up an ash cloud covering the entire earth. This is the event you need to focus on the most for the time being. And avoiding the Global Republic, of course."

"But the Appalachian chain isn't on any major faults or seismic zones. We won't feel a quake here," Courtney said.

"This section of the Appalachians is not on a fault, which is why I'm on this mountain, but the whole world will feel it. Where we are now, is in the blue zone, the second lowest color code on the USGS hazard map. That is not true for all of the Appalachians. In fact, the East Tennessee Seismic Zone is a red zone, the second highest rating on the USGS hazard map, and is right in the heart of the Appalachians. While not nearly so bad as the New

Madrid Seismic Zone in Western Tennessee, Kentucky, Missouri, and Arkansas, it won't be a good place to ride out the sixth seal."

"That's where Mr. Black and his girlfriend, Sarah, live," Courtney said.

Elijah sipped his tea. "Then, you'll have an additional selling point when trying to convince them to move up here.

"This will be an unprecedented geological event. No recorded data exists on the effects of a global quake."

Everett took another deep breath in an attempt to calm his nerves. "What can we do to prepare for such an event?"

Elijah sat back in his chair. "Fortunately, we are in a relatively safe zone. Another thing that we have going for us is that we live in log homes. Wood tends to give more in a quake than some other types of construction. Brick for instance, is terrible in a quake. The mortar in between the bricks just turns to powder in a quake. Still, when the quake comes, you want to get outside as fast as possible. And know where you are going to go ahead of time. Those rocks Everett used yesterday for cover in his attack are great for a gun fight, but bad for an earthquake. You do not want to go in that direction when the quake hits. Wherever you choose to go, make sure there are no large rocks above that can come rolling down on you. Probably the direction of the road is your best bet. It is cleared on both sides for the pavement, so there isn't much that can come tumbling down. If you do see something falling in your direction, you have a clear path to move out of the way."

"Yeah, as long as it's not in the middle of the night with no moon." Courtney crossed her arms.

"Sleep with your flashlight nearby and some shoes that you can slip on in a hurry," Elijah said.

"What if the cabin collapses? Then what?" Everett asked.

Elijah stood. "Come, follow me. I've thought about that. I'll show you my solutions.

"Do you have any tents?"

"Yes, we have tents." Everett responded.

Elijah led the way out the back door. "Keep them in your out building. It has that flimsy roof. Even if it collapses, you'll be able to quickly clear away the debris and get to your tents. Keep just enough supplies out there to live on for a few days. You'll eventually be able to excavate the beams and rubble from the cabin and find most of your equipment."

Courtney looked at Everett. "We've got that massive safe upstairs."

"I wouldn't worry about the safe, but don't keep anything you care about directly underneath it on the first floor." Elijah chuckled.

He led the way to the goat pen. "I dug up a pit in this area. The goats pull up any vegetation by the roots anyway, so I knew it would never be good for producing anything anyway. I put several heavy duty five-gallon buckets, a dozen or so, side by side to fill the pit. I laid plywood on top of the buckets and smoothed the excavated dirt over the top."

"What's in the buckets?" Courtney looked at the ground in the goat pen.

"Mostly rice and beans. But if you were to make

a similar cache, you could keep a few items that you might need in the event that your cabin was ever overran by looters."

Everett thought about the idea. "Yeah, maybe we'll do that."

"And your glass jars. You should store them in a place that they would not be easily dislodged. Perhaps you can put cardboard, wood, or even cloth in between to keep them from knocking up against each other and breaking. Perhaps you should also keep a bucket of water next to the fireplace so you can douse the fire before you leave your house when the quake occurs. It would be better to deal with a wet fireplace than have the cabin collapse with a fire burning. In that scenario, you might lose all of your supplies."

Everett tried to notice any telltale signs of where the buckets under the ground began and ended, but he couldn't spot any. "Is this the only cache you have?"

"Don't be nosy." Courtney scolded Everett. "You don't have to tell us if you don't want to."

Everett hadn't meant to pry. He thought about how he'd feel if someone were asking him the whereabouts of all his supplies. "She's right. I didn't mean to be rude. I was just wondering if there were any other ideas you might have for keeping a few items safe through the quake."

"Please." Elijah held up a hand. "I'm not that easily offended. Nor am I that secretive. I know you both, trust you, and believe your motives to be of the utmost sincere nature. Part of the reason I'm showing you the goat pen is so you may use the supplies in the event that I'm not here when you need them. When I leave, I don't expect to be coming back. I hope to have the chance to say goodbye, but I never know. It wouldn't be unlike Him to whisk me away in a moment."

Everett couldn't follow some of the things that Elijah said from time to time. On most occasions, he seemed like a very normal person who spoke in rational terms. But once in a while, he went off the rails and the things he'd say made no sense to Everett, whatsoever. Rather than seek an explanation, Everett politely said, "That's very kind of you. And if you ever need something when we're not home, the offer is mutual. Feel free to help yourself."

Courtney smiled and put her arm around Everett to show her approval of the reciprocated offer.

Elijah turned to go back to the house. "Several cave systems run throughout this area. Shenandoah Caverns, Luray Caverns, and the Endless Caverns are tourist caves, all within a few miles of here."

"Do you know of any cave entrances nearby?" Courtney asked.

"Yes." Elijah opened the back door. "Perhaps we can take a drive tomorrow or the next day. It's not far. Caves are typically situated below the layer of earth which is shaken by a quake. The entrance is usually the most volatile part of a cave. You wouldn't want to be inside when a quake struck and get trapped if the entrance collapsed, but it might be a good place to store supplies. A cave might offer a desirable shelter from some of the other judgements coming upon the earth as well."

"Like what?" Courtney asked as they walked back in the house.

"Scorching heat, massive hail storms, large meteors . . ."

"Okay, okay, okay." Everett put his hand up, interrupting Elijah's reply. "Sorry, but I have to process everything so far. We'll cover all of that later."

"Sure." Elijah smiled patiently. "Would you like me to reheat your pizza? I'm afraid it has gotten cold."

Courtney sat back down. "I love cold pizza, actually."

"So do I. Besides, we're the ones who let it get cold." Everett resumed his place at the table.

"And save room, I made you a cake."

Courtney's mouth was full, but she still managed to show her surprise.

"You really went above and beyond. Thank you so much, Elijah," Everett said.

Everyone conspicuously avoided talk of the impending doom throughout the rest of the visit. They'd said enough about it for one day and it was time to celebrate the wedding and enjoy the good things God had provided. Afterwards, Everett asked to borrow some electrical tape to repair the ham radio, and then he and Courtney returned home, cautiously observing their property as they approached, and quietly inspecting the perimeter before entering the cabin. Finding no signs of trouble, they went inside for the night. Everett drew up the ladder and closed the hatch to the loft. No one would be able to get to them without creating a substantial amount of noise, giving Everett and Courtney ample time to react. Their belongings in the cabin below were still at risk of being taken in the night with no one on watch, but at least they'd be safe.

CHAPTER 4

The earth shall reel to and fro like a drunkard, and shall be removed like a cottage; and the transgression thereof shall be heavy upon it; and it shall fall, and not rise again. And it shall come to pass in that day, that the LORD shall punish the host of the high ones that are on high, and the kings of the earth upon the earth.

Isaiah 24:20-21

After breakfast Saturday morning, Everett got right on fixing the wires to repair the ham radio. He stripped the plastic coating back, affixed the cut wires from the radio to the antenna, battery and other components, wrapping the exposed wire tightly with ample amounts of electrical tape to prevent a short through unintended contact of the wiring.

Courtney stepped into the back bedroom where Everett was working on the radio. "Need any help?"

"I've got this, but I'll need your assistance with digging the trench from the creek to bring the water closer to the house."

"I was offering to hold the tape for you or something, not dig a ditch."

He turned to see if she was being serious. He grinned when he saw the playful look on her face. He turned his attention back to the radio. "Okay, I'll do it myself, but you'll have to haul your own water to the cabin. Don't expect to be getting water from my branch of the creek."

"And don't expect to be sleeping in the loft tonight." She tussled his hair. "But seriously, Everett; isn't it a lot of work to dig a trench from the creek when we don't know if the house will still be standing after the quake?"

"Hauling water is a lot of work too. We know the quake probably isn't coming until after March 15th. Even if it came a week later, it would be a worthwhile project."

She leaned against the desk where Everett was working. "Plus, you'll have to line the trench with creek stones or something to keep it from washing out the trench and to keep the water from being muddy."

"I thought of that. Maybe you're right. Maybe it is too big of a job." Everett switched on the power.

Courtney huffed. "Don't listen to me. It's a good

idea. I'll help you collect rocks, gravel or whatever to line the trench. I think Elijah has a wheelbarrow. That will make hauling rocks much easier, especially up and down these hills."

Everett winked at her. "Thanks."

She looked closer at the radio. "Is it working?"

"We don't have much power. I have to take this battery up to Elijah's to charge later, but I think I've got enough juice to call Mr. Black."

Courtney looked around the room. "Should we move down to the bedroom and offer Mr. Black the loft?"

"It would be easier."

"And if we had to get out fast, when the quake hits, we'd be closer to the door," she added.

Everett looked up toward the loft and calculated the position of the safe. "Yeah, I guess this area isn't at risk of being crushed by the safe falling."

She winced. "I forgot about the safe. We'd have to invade their privacy every time we wanted to get in the safe."

Everett turned back toward the radio. "Yep. There's no moving that thing."

"I wonder how Jones got it up there?" she asked.

"I expect he rented a crane and put it up there when he built the house, before he put the roof on. It certainly proved to be an effective deterrent against theft. So what's the verdict? We stay in the loft?"

"Yeah, I kind of like it up there anyway."

He took her hand. "Me, too. Maybe we can practice getting down the ladder quicker."

"Perhaps we can make a fireman pole to slide

down," she said.

"We'll think of something." Everett found the frequency that Ken had used to contact Thinthread. He keyed the mic. "This is Undertow calling Mr. Black." Everett waited a few minutes and repeated the message. Ten minutes later, he called again.

Shortly after his third attempt, the radio sprang to life. "Go for Black."

Everett made a quick and concise offer for Mr. Black and his girlfriend to join them at the cabin.

Mr. Black had come around to the wisdom of not using Sarah's name over the radio. "I appreciate the offer and we do recognize the need for a group to provide mutual security, but Ms. White and I are well positioned and well stocked in our current location. Would you consider relocating?"

Everett began to make his case. "Can you be sure that your location wasn't compromised when Thinthread and the other member of your team were captured?"

Black was silent for a while then finally replied. "I'm 99 percent sure that the GR could not have broken them in the amount of time between their capture and the time of the disappearances."

Courtney gestured to Everett to let her talk for a while.

Everett said to Black, "I'm going to put you on with Mrs..."

"Grey," Courtney said.

"I'm listening," Mr. Black replied.

"Mr. Black, you're aware of the industry in which our team worked prior to the recent events."

"I've got a pretty good idea," Black said.

"Then you'll trust me when I tell you that . . . our industry had certain provisions, chemical in nature, which could be used to acquire information from certain subjects when time was of the essence.

"Also, you said that you were aware of the subsequent events that are prophesied to follow the disappearances. Would you say you have a clear understanding of the chronology of those events?"

Mr. Black replied, "I've been looking through the Bible of the man who led the studies for the group. I have some general idea, but I probably couldn't teach a class on it, if that's what you mean."

Courtney nodded as she listened. "You know about the seal judgements then."

"I read about them, yes. I think there are seven."

"Right. We think the first four seals are opened, we believe the fifth seal will be opened around March 15th, at the end of the amnesty period for people to pledge allegiance to the Global Republic and have their Mark implanted."

"Go ahead, I'm listening."

Courtney looked at Everett and continued speaking. "The sixth seal will bring a cataclysmic worldwide earthquake. The whole earth will feel the effects. Some of the operations we provided information for, were carried out in and around the East Tennessee Seismic Zone. We don't want to know your location, but if it's anywhere near the ETSZ, it would be a horrible place to be when every tectonic plate on the planet begins to shift."

Mr. Black was silent. Seconds later, he asked, "Could we have twenty-four hours to consider your proposal?"

Everett took the mic. "Sure. We'll be standing by at the same time tomorrow." He clicked off the power and looked at Courtney.

"And now we wait," she said.

He winked. "And now we go dig a trench."

"Ugh!" Courtney protested. "Let's get it over with."

Everett got up from the desk and followed her to the kitchen. They each put their boots on, grabbed jackets and gloves, and then proceeded to go outside.

Courtney asked, "Should we go get the wheelbarrow first?"

"Yeah, I'll take the battery up to Elijah to recharge as well."

"So we're going up in the BMW?"

Everett looked at the old pickup left by the intruders. "Let's take the truck. In fact, I'm going to give it to Elijah. We've already got three vehicles and nowhere to go."

"I like that idea." She smiled and opened the door of the truck and got in.

"I'll be right back." Everett went back inside to retrieve the battery, locked the door on his way out, plopped the battery in the bed of the truck, got in and started driving up the mountain.

Courtney looked out the window. "That satellite dish that Ken built, why couldn't we hook that up to the television and get the news channels?"

Everett pursed his lips. "Even if we could unscramble the signal, I wouldn't have any idea how to get the signal into the television. Ken was the hardware guy. I can't do much until I've got a screen and a key board. If you can get me to that point, I'm lethal, but I'm dead in the water without equipment. What about you? Do you think you can rig up something to feed the signal into the television? Jones has the digital-to-analog converter to bring the signal in from the rabbit ears to the television."

Courtney shook her head. "Not a chance. I'm like you; as long as I have a keyboard and a screen, there's not much I can't do." She paused. "Wait a minute. Why do we need a television? Ken has the dish connected to the router which feeds into the computer via USB. We can just hack right into the satellite service with the computer. We'll run tails and go directly through the dark net, no one will ever know we're there."

Everett grimaced. "I don't know. With internet, we have to transmit the request for service, which could give away our location. If we can figure out a way to run the television, it only receives, so no threat of us being detected."

"If I had a satellite television box, I'm pretty sure I could get inside and unscramble the signal."

"That would be awesome. We'll ask Mr. Black to bring one if he comes."

"He'll come, I'm sure of it." Courtney smiled confidently.

The next morning, Everett poked the logs in the fire, stirring the coals so he could place the grate over the hot glowing embers to start breakfast.

Courtney walked into the living room. "Good

morning."

"Good morning." Everett turned to greet her then resumed his endeavor to prepare the morning meal. "How did you sleep?"

"Like a rock, but my shoulder is super stiff from hauling rocks to construct the Carroll Canal."

Everett feigned a look of arrogance. "Hmm, feels kind of nice to have a waterway named after me."

"Tah!" Courtney exclaimed. "The canal is named after me! Carroll is my last name too. Remember?"

Everett placed the coffee pot on the grate and stood up. "You deserve it. You worked hard. And I'll give you a massage to loosen up that shoulder."

She rolled her eyes. "Yeah, right. A massage; we both know where that will end up."

He held three fingers in the air. "Scout's honor, just a massage, no strings attached."

She put her arms around his neck and winked. "Oh, it wasn't a complaint."

Everett smiled and leaned in for a kiss.

Suddenly, Courtney pulled away. "I heard a vehicle. Someone is on the road"

Everett reached for his pistol. It wasn't there. "Rats!"

Courtney gave him a cross look as she pulled her .380 Tomcat out of her front pocket and handed it to him. "Take this, I'll run upstairs and get your HK."

Everett took the small pistol and peered out the window. He watched as the vehicle came around the trees and pulled into the drive. He called out loud enough for her to hear him in the loft. "All clear, it's Elijah."

Everett slipped the small gun in his pocket and

opened the door. "Good morning."

"I hope I'm not interrupting." The old man was careful to wipe his feet before entering.

"Not at all. To what do we owe the pleasure?"

Courtney returned to the room carrying Everett's backpack where he kept the HK G36C and several extra magazines. The short-barreled rifle was just under 20 inches when the stock was folded and fit easily into the pack. She placed the pack on the floor next to the couch and handed Everett his Sig pistol, with its inside-the-pants holster. "Good morning, Elijah."

Elijah smiled. "Good morning, I hope I didn't frighten you by popping around unannounced."

Courtney took her Tomcat back as Everett handed it to her. "There's nothing to be frightened of if everyone is following weapons protocol, is there?"

"Yes, well, I've come bearing gifts." Elijah clapped his hands together.

"You've done too much. We simply can't accept any more generosity." Everett shook his head.

"But you've given me a truck. Such a lavish gift cannot go without an expression of gratitude."

Courtney put her hand in the air. "Elijah, that truck didn't cost us a dime. You're doing us a favor by getting it out of the driveway."

Elijah turned to go out the door. "Stop your squabbling and come. Come see what I've brought before you get out of sorts; it's such a small thing, really. You'll see there's no cause for all of your fuss."

Everett followed and peeked into the bed of the

truck. "Elijah! No! You can't give us your solar panels!"

"Hogwash! I insist! You are scurrying up and down the mountain every other day to charge your battery for your ham radio or the small ones for your flashlights and your little radio. It's a waste of resources, I tell you. Besides, I'm only giving you three panels. I still have three more."

Courtney asked, "What about your charge controller and inverter? You'll need those."

Elijah dropped the tailgate and began unloading the panels. "I bought a spare charge controller and a spare inverter. At less than $100 each, it turned out to be a good investment. Those simple slips of paper money have no value now, but these few pieces of equipment allow me to settle my debt for a fine vehicle."

Everett reluctantly assisted Elijah with unloading the panels. "Like I said, you don't owe us a thing for the truck."

"You shouldn't argue with a man of God. Read First Kings and see what becomes of those who do. Now where shall we install these?"

Courtney said, "The front of the house gets good morning sun most of the year. The shed around back is totally blocked by trees."

Elijah looked at the roof. "So it does. But, if the screws should cause a leak in the roof, it might be more of a curse than a blessing. What if we mount the panels on the overhang of the porch? I've brought screws with the small rubber washers which are intended to prevent leaks, but if it should leak, you'll be less affected on the front porch than in the house."

"I think we can live with that," Everett said. "I'll get the ladder from the shed."

Two hours later, the panels were installed, the inverter and charge controller were working and Everett's batteries were charging.

"Will you join us for lunch?" Courtney offered.

"I must be going, but thank you. Any word from your friends in Tennessee?"

"Acquaintances, which is really stretching it." Everett slid the couch back in place to conceal the small sheet of plywood where the inverter and charge controllers were mounted just inside the living room window. "We're supposed to call them shortly to see what they've decided to do."

"They'll come," Courtney said confidently.

"It would be best for all concerned in the matter." Elijah nodded.

"We might wait to see what provisions they bring before we make a run to the cave. If they have a lot of stuff, we could probably take a few items with us. We don't have much extra space as it is," Everett said.

"That would be fine. I'll see you soon." Elijah waved as he left.

"We'll call Black then get the trench finished up. I want to dig out a pit deep enough to dip a bucket into, and then line it with creek stone so the walls won't erode and collapse."

"You're not worried that it will become a mosquito pit this summer?" Courtney stuck her hands in her pockets.

"No, the channel will be constantly bringing fresh water in from the creek above us where the channel branches out and the overflow will constantly be flowing back into the creek below where it rejoins the creek. We will complete the entire project, leaving only the last few inches at the inflow tie-in. Then when all of the rocks are in place, we'll open it up."

"Smart, maybe I will name the canal after you." She winked as she headed toward the back bedroom.

Everett followed her in and powered on the ham radio. He keyed the mic. "This is Undertow calling Mr. Black."

"Go for Black."

"Have you reached a decision?"

"We have, but there are a couple of things we need to disclose."

"Okay." Everett looked curiously at Courtney.

"Ms. White has a prosthetic leg. She operates very efficiently. Thanks to her strong will, she is less encumbered by her situation than most able bodied people, but there are some obvious limitations."

"That's not even a remote problem for us." Everett replied.

"We also have a dog, who will serve well as an extra set of eyes and ears."

A female voice was heard in the background. "And a cat."

"And a cat." Black cleared his throat. "The value he would bring to the team is difficult to quantify."

Ms. White spoke again from the background.

"The value is simple. It's a package deal."

Courtney took the mic from Everett as she fought to not laugh. "We love animals. Everyone will be welcome here."

Everett also restrained his amusement. He took back the mic. "Do you have a time frame in mind?"

"Given the logistical challenges and, as Mrs. Grey pointed out, the potential that our current location may have been compromised, we intend to make our first sortie tomorrow. Let us know if that's too soon, but we certainly don't want to be up against the wire, trying to beat the amnesty period. We can provide more details when we meet you face to face. Do you have an intermediate point where we could meet? I'm sure you understand the risks associated with broadcasting the exact details of your location."

"Yes, we could meet you at the gas station, off Interstate 81, Virginia Exit 235, east bound. It's a fairly remote place. You probably won't run into many people there."

"We'll see you there, let's say 2:00 PM."

"Okay, we'll see you then. The verification challenge will be as follows. I'll approach you and ask how's the gas mileage of your vehicle. You'll answer with a color rather than mileage information. Also, we could use any electrical extension cords you might have as well as a satellite conversion box. The older, the better."

"Roger that. We look forward to meeting you. Over and out."

"Over and out." Everett turned off the power.

"We're getting a cat!" Courtney exclaimed. "I've

got to get this place cleaned up."

Everett nodded. "Help me with the channel and I'll help you get straightened up."

"Deal!" Courtney jumped up and headed to the kitchen.

Everett put his boots back on and grabbed his jacket.

Courtney zipped her coat. "Poor girl, I wonder how she lost her leg?"

"In the military I suspect. He did say she was in charge of training the other women in their group. At any rate, I'm glad we decided to let them stay downstairs. I couldn't have made her climb the ladder."

Everett and Courtney spent the rest of the afternoon completing the two-foot-deep narrow channel to bring water to the house as well as the small reservoir to capture the water for easy collection. Once it was tied into the creek, the water flowed steadily. With a few minor adjustments and a small partial dam, Everett was able to significantly increase the water flow toward the house.

CHAPTER 5

For nation shall rise against nation, and kingdom against kingdom: and there shall be famines, and pestilences, and earthquakes, in divers places. All these are the beginning of sorrows.

Matthew 24:7-8

Everett and Courtney pulled into the gas station off of Interstate 81. They saw a green Tennessee Wildlife Resource Agency pickup truck filled to capacity.

Everett pulled up near the truck and got out. He looked at the young single man standing beside the truck. He had on jeans, a plaid shirt, work boots, and a ball cap which was pulled low over very short brown hair. The man had a medium build and a well-kept beard. "How's the gas mileage on your truck?"

The man seemed to ignore Everett as he surveyed the skies and roads in the vicinity. "Purple."

Everett slowly approached the man. "Mr. Black." Everett extended his hand as he walked closer.

Black held out his hand. "Undertow, nice to put a face to the name."

Everett shook his hand. "You can call me Everett. Was . . . Ms. White not able to come?"

Black waved at Courtney. "Call me Kevin. Is that Mrs. Grey?"

Everett motioned for her to join them. "It's Courtney, and we just got married."

"Congratulations."

Courtney shook his hand when she arrived. "Hi! I'm Courtney. Where's Sarah?"

Kevin took one more long look around the area, and then raised his hand, depressing a small mic button on the sleeve of his shirt. "All clear." He looked up at Courtney. "I'm Kevin. She'll be along."

Everett saw movement out of the corner of his eye. He looked over at the bushes along the edge of the parking lot. One of the bushes was standing up. "Is that her?"

"You can't be too careful these days." Kevin lowered his sunglasses to look over toward the bushes.

Courtney looked at Everett with her arms crossed and smiled.

Everett smiled back. He knew she was thinking the same thing he was. These two would be a great addition. No one could ever replace Ken and Lisa, but they'd be reunited soon enough. And Everett was in no particular hurry for the reunion. In the meantime, he'd make the most of life here with Courtney, Elijah and their new *acquaintances*.

Sarah approached and took the hat and face net off of her ghillie suit. She held her rifle, which was also heavily camouflaged, low with one hand. She extended the other to Courtney first. "Hi, I'm Sarah."

"It's a pleasure. I'm Courtney."

"I'm Everett. Nice to meet you." Even through the olive drab face paint smeared across her face, he could see that she was an attractive young woman. He made a conscious effort to remember when she'd walked up. He hadn't noticed that her stride seemed affected by the prosthetic leg. Given, he'd been trying to process the bush standing up and walking, so it wasn't the first thing on his mind, but he was sure he'd have noticed.

Sarah whistled and a less-than-well-manicured dog came running up. The creature looked like it had lived a rough life.

Courtney stepped back behind Everett. "Aww, what a . . . good dog."

Sarah bent down to pet him. "He's beautiful on the inside. You couldn't ask for a more loyal companion."

Everett forced himself to pet the homely animal. "What's his name?"

"Danger." Kevin said quickly.

Sarah continued to pet the dog as she shot Kevin a coarse look. "Cupcake, his name is Cupcake."

"And where's the cat?" Courtney looked toward the truck.

"Sox. He's in the cat carrier in the back seat. He's a little mad right now," Kevin said.

Sarah rolled her eyes. "He's mad because it's a raccoon trap, not a cat carrier."

"If you put water in a milk jug, it's a water jug." Kevin walked back to the driver's side of the truck. "We can follow you when you're ready."

"Let's roll out." Everett walked to the truck, started the engine and led the quick forty-five-minute drive back to the cabin.

When they arrived, Everett unlocked the door to the cabin then helped Kevin carry in some of their personal belongings. "Nice truck."

Kevin followed Everett up the steps. "Thanks. The government agency insignia helps deter would be highway bandits."

"Yeah, there's a lot of that going on," Everett replied. "Did you work for Tennessee Wildlife?"

"No, the sheriff's department. Sarah had some friends she used to shoot and go fishing with who worked at Wildlife."

"Seems like a sheriff's vehicle would be an even better deterrent."

"I'm sure it would be, but everyone who worked with the Sevier County Sheriff's Department is wanted for questioning about an incident where a Global Republic census station was assaulted, and a subsequent insurrection. The former sheriff, Jim Taylor, was one of the people in our group who was captured during the insurrection."

"And let me guess, you weren't far from an ammo dump explosion in Nashville when the insurrection was happening in Sevierville." Everett had been involved in passing the intelligence for most of the activities carried out by Kevin and his former team members, but he had never known any of their names. It felt good to be able to get a little more of the backstory on the resistance members involved.

"I don't kiss and tell." Kevin didn't look offended by the question, but he didn't seem quite ready to lay all of his cards on the table.

Once inside, Courtney gave an abbreviated tour of the house as they walked through. "Your room is in the back."

Everett placed the bags he'd been carrying in the floor of the back bedroom. "Unfortunately, your bedroom is also the comms room. We're a little tight on space."

Kevin looked around. "Where do you guys sleep?"

"In the loft. There's a ladder over by the kitchen." Courtney looked back toward the kitchen.

Sarah ran her hand across the top of the bed. "It's a nice place. You guys keep it really clean."

"Thanks, we try." Courtney smiled.

Kevin looked in the closet. "Do you have any additional storage?"

Everett led the way out of the bedroom. "There's a small shed in the back, but that's it."

"Hmm." Kevin paused. "We have a ton of supplies that we'd like to bring out. How would you feel about building a storeroom on the back of the cabin?"

Everett tried not to show his annoyance. This guy had been in the house less than five minutes, and already he was making changes. As he mulled it over in his head, he understood that some changes would have to be made. After all, he'd asked Kevin and Sarah to uproot their entire life to move up here. "Let's take a walk outside and see what we have to work with."

The girls followed. Courtney looked at Sarah. "Was the place where you were staying, a big house?"

"Too big," Sarah replied. "It was fine when it was full of people, but after they disappeared, the giant empty house was a constant reminder of that day."

Everett walked the length of the backyard. "We were planning to put a garden in this section over here. It gets the most sunlight. I suppose we could run a storeroom back this way, toward the woods. But, I don't know where we'd get construction supplies."

Kevin examined the proposed building site. "I can salvage materials from the house where we're at now. It has a metal roof, which I can tear off. Then I'd just need enough wood to frame out the storeroom. I can use the metal sheets from the roof for the walls of the storeroom, as well as the roof. Since it would be in the shade, it would never get too hot."

"Do you mind if we let Sox out? He's had a long ride in the raccoon trap," Sarah said.

"It's a cat trap, I mean . . . cat carrier." Kevin tried to recover from his misspoken words, but it was too late.

"See!" Sarah pointed at him. "You just admitted it. It's a trap, not a carrier."

Courtney led the way back toward the truck. "Well, let's set him free."

"Can we let him run around in the house a while to get used to it? I'm afraid if we let him loose outside that he'll run off into the woods." Sarah took the trap out of the back seat.

"Sure. I'll get him something to eat." Courtney walked by Sarah.

Everett and Ken took another load of their personal belongings into the cabin. As they walked, Everett said, "There's an old hermit a little further up the mountain that we're friends with. He knows of a cave entrance not too far from here. It might be an alternative to building a storehouse. I don't know how we'd secure any supplies stored there, but it's climate controlled, around 55 degrees all year round."

"Have you been there?" Kevin asked.

"No, but all the caves in this region run about the same constant temperature."

"We might need to do both."

Everett was curious. "Oh? How much stuff do you have?"

"Some members of our group saw everything falling apart as early as last September. They started stocking up for a prolonged period of resource scarcity. One of the members owned a restaurant and they literally ordered pallets of food through her supplier before everything fell apart. The group had well over a year's worth of food for everyone. Not a lot of fancy stuff, but enough to keep them alive until they could start producing their own food." Kevin set his luggage on the floor of the bedroom when they arrived.

"And how many people were in your group?" Everett asked.

Kevin looked at the ceiling, as if he were running a calculation in his head. "We lost a guy in the raid then another family came in. But there were about fifteen of us when the supplies were bought. And like I said, it was well over a year's worth of food each."

"And that was six months ago, so your group had roughly six months of supplies left?"

Kevin shook his head. "No, we still had a year's worth when they disappeared."

Everett did the math, but didn't want to look greedy.

"So a year's worth for fifteen would be three years' worth for five, including the old man up the road." Kevin said it for him.

Everett ran his hand over his head. "We have a year's worth of supplies for four people. We were very well stocked for ourselves and the couple that disappeared, not including the game we've been able to kill and preserve. The old man has been self-sufficient for a long time. He produces more than he can eat and gives us food regularly. Between what he gives us and the game we've shot, our stockpile is lasting a lot longer than originally planned. And the old man thinks he'll be leaving soon; some mission he thinks God is going to give him."

"Last week, I would have thought that sounded like something a crazy person would say, but now, I don't know." Kevin snickered. "Do you think he's nuts or do you believe him?"

Everett gave a subtle nod. "I believe him. I can't explain it, but there's something about him. This is all new to me. Up until last fall, I was a dyed-in-the-wool atheist. I rejected reason and logic and held fast to my beliefs. Nevertheless, the constant barrage of facts and indisputable proof that there was a higher power converted me into a soft-pedaling agnostic. Still, I didn't become a believer until the day of the disappearances."

"And now you buy the whole story? The rapture, Jesus, everything?" Kevin asked.

"Yeah. Ken and Lisa, our friends that disappeared, they said this was going to happen. The man I used to work with and who gave me this cabin, John Jones, he saw it all coming down from inside the intelligence community; the alien cover story for the disappearances, the one-world government, cashless global currency, everything. At this point, the evidence is undeniable."

Kevin pursed his lips. "The people in our group all saw it coming too. You're right. There's no other explanation."

"So, are you and Sarah believers now?"

"We believe the disappearances were caused by the rapture. So, yes, we believe God exists and that he's causing all of this."

"But?" Everett waited for the rest of the explanation.

Kevin exhaled deeply. "But that doesn't necessarily mean we agree with it all. I hope that's not going to be a problem."

Everett chuckled and put his arm around Kevin's shoulder. "No problem at all. As I look back and see how patient Jones, Ken, Lisa and even God himself have been with me, how can I do anything else but accept you right where you're at. But I'll warn you. If he's called you, God will not stop until he's made his case."

Kevin looked a little unsure about Everett's answer, but eventually offered his hand. "Fair enough."

The two men walked back out to the truck for another load. Kevin stopped and leaned over the side rail of the truck bed. "I saw the trees on the side of the road when we were coming up the mountain. Were you on the decorating committee?"

"I helped. They're more functional than aesthetic," Everett replied. "And they didn't look nearly so bad when we first strung them up there."

Kevin snorted. "Yeah, well, whatever works. I suppose the birds are responsible for making such a mess out of them. But you're right, it is an effective deterrent. It sent chills up my spine and I've seen a lot of action, both with the resistance and in the desert. At any rate, it's good to know you can do what you have to do when trouble comes a knockin'."

Everett nodded. "I thought it would have bothered me more, but I'd already had such a lousy day, with Ken and Lisa disappearing. Courtney and I had just tied the knot and I wanted to come home and be quiet. When I saw those guys in my house at that time, I snapped. I felt absolutely nothing about what I did, zero remorse. I hope that doesn't make me a bad person."

"Not at all. You did what you had to do. But don't be surprised if it's not as easy next time. And don't be surprised if regret rears its ugly head when you've had a chance to slow down and catch your breath. Emotions are a fickle thing. But always keep in mind that you were just doing your job, to keep your wife safe and protect your home."

"Thanks." Everett knew Kevin was speaking from a position of experience.

Kevin was quiet for a moment. "So, between the four of us, we have close to five years' worth of food, provided we can get it all here without any trouble."

"That's a good start."

"A good start?" Kevin furrowed his brow.

Everett nodded. "According to Elijah's calculation, we've got seven years to survive."

Kevin shrugged. "We can produce enough food to make up the difference."

"I hope you're right. Are you aware of the specific judgements that are coming down the pike?"

"Sword, famine and plague, generally. We always half listened when the others would get into all of that stuff." Kevin paused. "What, specifically would keep us from being able to produce food?"

Everett gave a brief synopsis of what Elijah had told him about the effects on crops from the ash cloud caused by the volcanic activity which would accompany the first big quake, the hail and meteor showers.

Kevin looked concerned. "Maybe we should try to put together another couple years' worth of food before the amnesty period ends."

"We can worry about that later. First let's focus on getting what you have, up to the cabin. That's going to take a few trips," Everett said. "Fuel is kind of hard to come by. How far is your drive?"

"Just under 400 miles each way," Kevin replied.

"That's a lot of gas." Everett put his foot on the bumper of the truck.

"We've got a lot of gas, for now. It's well hidden, but the stash will be discovered sooner or later; either by looters or by the Global Republic. I used about a tank to get here. I brought gas cans for the return trip. We've got more trucks back at the house, but no more gas cans."

Everett turned toward the cabin. "Jones had 2 five-gallon cans here, and I bought 2 more. Elijah might have a couple we could borrow. Would that be enough?"

"Yeah, and we'll fill your car with whatever is left over in the cans before we leave. A vehicle is the best storage tank around."

"Great, let's get the rest of your stuff in the house, and we'll work out the details after dinner. We've got a big pot of venison stew simmering. You guys had a long trip. I'm sure you're hungry." Everett helped Kevin get the remainder of his things from the truck. Everett was happy to see the ammo boxes beneath the rifle cases in the back seat.

Kevin took out two of the cases. "Do you have a

gun safe?"

"It's stuffed full, but I could move some of the ammo out to make some room for a few long guns."

"Yeah, I've got a couple high-end pieces, some nice stuff a couple of the guys left behind; an HK 416, and an Armalite AR-10. Armalite makes a decent gun, but this one is tricked out. PVS-14 flip-to-side night vision scope and an EOTech reflex site."

Everett said, "I've got a HK G36C. It's got all high-end optics as well."

"Wow, that's a nice gun. For some reason, Benny, the guy you called Thinthread, always made you guys sound like DIA or CIA analysts."

Everett snickered. "That's a fairly accurate assumption. The man who left me the weapon, Jones, he spent several years in the field."

"National Clandestine Services?"

"Something like that." The whole secret-agent spy thing was over for Everett, but it would take a while to erase all of the programing that the Company had indoctrinated him with. And even then it would likely take more than a few hours to open up.

Kevin arranged the rifle cases and ammo boxes along the wall. "We've got a ton of hardware. Everybody on our team had multiple weapons and being with the sheriff's department, we had plenty of ammo as well."

Everett nodded. "Bring whatever you want up, but there's a limit to how much we can use. I wouldn't mind having something else to choose from. The HK is nice at close range but the barrel on that thing is about nine inches. Courtney has a Mini 14 Rancher. She has a few 20-round magazines, but no 30-round mags."

"We've got plenty of AR-15s and plenty of 30-round mags. We've even got a couple AK-47s, with mags and ammo, of course.

"I don't know where you guys are, but Sarah and I have made up our minds. We want to survive, but not as slaves. And while a lot of the people who wanted to stand up to the Global Republic just disappeared, there are still a few other people like us around. If we happen to run into more like-minded individuals, it's nice to know that we've got the extra hardware to resist."

"Sure, it's good to have options." Everett was less comfortable with being on the front lines than feeding information to a militia, but he knew who Kevin and Sarah were before he invited them up to the cabin. Everett and Courtney also agreed that surrendering to the Global Republic was absolutely out of the question.

Kevin looked through his duffel bag on the bed. "Here's your satellite receiver box. Do you know how to hack it?"

"Between Courtney and myself, I'm sure we can figure it out. The satellite is constantly sending the signal in Mpeg2, but within the same signal, it's basically sending malware to corrupt the TSOP which is designed to disable a receiver that's been tampered with. Decrypting the signal is easy, the hard part is stopping that malware." Everett looked the box over.

"Sounds complicated. Wouldn't it be easier to

just catch whatever is being passed over regular local television?"

"All the stations around here are down."

"What about DC? I'm sure propaganda is a priority for the GR. They must have a local public station."

Everett set the receiver on the bed. "80 Miles is about the best you can hope for, in terms of receiving a television signal. We're about 90 miles from DC."

Kevin scratched his head. "You should give it a try. I'm sure the GR would be pumping out enough power to send the signal to at least Baltimore. And I doubt the signal tower is in downtown DC. It's probably a few miles outside of town, which could be in your direction, plus you're on the side of a mountain facing DC. On a good day, with just a little luck, who knows, it just might work."

Everett nodded. "Even if the signal was weak, we just need it to get information. Yeah, I'll give it a try. It would be easier. And I doubt I'll get any information from satellite that isn't available from the local station."

"Dinner is served." Courtney called from the kitchen.

Everett and Kevin made their way to the kitchen and sat down at the small table.

It had always been Ken or Lisa who prayed before meals. Now it was Everett. "Do you two mind if we pray before we eat?"

"Please, go ahead. Everyone else in our group prayed before meals." Sarah paused. "Obviously."

"Why do you say obviously?" Courtney asked.

"Because they're gone." Sarah bowed her head. "And we're not."

Everett didn't know what to say to her. He just bowed his head and said a short prayer to bless the meal. Afterwards, he looked around. "Where's the cat?"

Courtney giggled. "He ran up the ladder into the loft to hide."

"He'll come down when he gets hungry." Sarah smiled as she took some rice and passed the bowl.

"What about the dog?" Everett asked.

"Danger seems pretty happy to be outside," Kevin said. "He's a great watch dog."

"We bring him inside if it gets below freezing," Sarah said.

Everett mixed his stew into his rice with his fork. "I assume you didn't hit any checkpoints on your ride up today."

Sarah sipped her water. "Not today. We did see those large electric road construction signs announcing the location of various census stations along the way. There was one at every small town all the way up Interstate 81.

"At three different places, we saw facilities being constructed alongside the highway. Each of them, had construction teams clearing out massive areas of land and covering it with gravel. All of them had trailers which looked like temporary living quarters or possibly administrative buildings. And they were putting up fencing around the perimeters. We saw one near Johnson City where I-26 crosses I-81, another outside of Blacksburg, and one by Roanoke."

Kevin added, "The facility at Roanoke is colossal. They've got trailers and fence on each side of the road. Plus, it looked like they were in the initial stages of building permanent structures."

"How high was the fence? Did it look like it was designed to keep people in or keep them out?" Courtney took a bite of her stew.

Kevin finished chewing then said, "Probably twelve or thirteen feet. I didn't see any razor wire along the top yet, but I'm sure it's coming. I'm certain that the facilities are some type of detention centers. The Global Republic will probably be doing inspections on commuters, vehicles, and cargo. If anything isn't in compliance, you'll likely win a free vacation at one of the new state-of-the-art facilities."

The four of them proceeded to chat well beyond the time they spent eating. Courtney made a pot of tea and served it afterwards, as they continued to get to know each other. Everett felt confident that they would all get along just fine.

The next three days were spent driving back and forth to Sevier County, Tennessee. Everett and Courtney drove one truck, while Kevin and Sarah drove another pickup from the cabin in Tennessee. This was to help Kevin and Sarah load the supplies as well as provide additional security for the long trip.

CHAPTER 6

Some trust in chariots, and some in horses: but we will remember the name of the LORD our God.

Psalm 20:7

Boxes, bins and buckets were stacked all throughout the small living room of the cabin. More containers were stacked up outside on the porch and even more around the back of the house.

Everett looked between two stacks of plastic bins, and out the window at the falling snow after breakfast Friday morning. "Snowing in March."

Kevin sipped his coffee as he stood behind Everett, also looking out at the accumulating flurries. "Brother, you're in the mountains. You can get snow til May."

"Stop! Don't say that." Courtney voiced her opposition. "This is depressing enough without two more months of cold weather."

Sarah snickered. "I wish two months of snow is all we had to worry about."

Everett walked away from the window, around an island of five-gallon buckets, stacked floor to ceiling, and had a seat on the couch. "At least we got you guys moved before the snow came. I wouldn't want to be driving around the mountains in this weather. These roads are as crooked as they come. They're dangerous enough when they're clear."

Kevin sat on the hearth since the recliner was inaccessible due to boxes sitting on top of it. "I guess getting this stuff to the cave is out of the question for a few days. Sorry your place looks like a storage facility. We've done everything we can to make more room, but our bedroom is stuffed. We've got just enough room to get to the radio and the bed."

Courtney squeezed by Everett to make her way toward the front door. "A house full of supplies is a good problem to have. And it's your place too. Not just ours."

"Thanks." Sarah sat on the hearth next to Kevin. "You guys have been very hospitable. We weren't sure how that would go, seeing how we'd never met. But we're pleasantly surprised."

"Same here," Everett said. "You guys are great."

Courtney opened the door. "Cupcake, come on boy!"

The dog came in and shook himself dry. He'd

been on the porch, so he wasn't soaking wet to begin with. He walked over and sat on the floor next to the fireplace hearth beside Sarah.

"You'll spoil him, letting him inside all the time." Sarah petted him as she talked.

Courtney smiled and crossed her arms. "We're happy to have him. He does make a good watch dog. We used to have a person awake every night to stand watch. He hears stuff none of us ever would."

"And I've trained myself to listen for his growl. I get up at the least little sound to check it out. It's usually a raccoon, but better safe than sorry." Kevin leaned forward to give Danger a scratch. "Do you think Elijah will still come for dinner?"

"He'll be here." Courtney gave a slight nod. "He's made of pretty rugged stuff."

"I'm looking forward to meeting him." Sarah leaned back on the hearth and repositioned one log that wasn't quite all the way in the fire. "Is there any reason he didn't move down here with you guys for mutual assistance?"

A pang of guilt shot through Everett. He'd never even thought to offer. Everett furrowed his brow. "Umm, no, not really. He's been up there by himself for ages, and he's got a finely oiled machine running with his goats, chickens, rabbits, smokehouse, greenhouse, garden; it's some operation. I couldn't see him walking away from all that." All this was true, but Everett felt somewhat ashamed that he'd never, at least, extended the invitation. Then, another thought hit Everett. "And for whatever reason, he's never had any trouble up there, at all."

Kevin shrugged. "Old man, by himself on a hill with tons of supplies, and hasn't been bothered. Sounds lucky. But, if you want to ask him to move, we wouldn't mind if he were sleeping on the couch or something. After we get the stuff to the cave, of course."

"Yeah, maybe I'll ask him." Somehow, Everett knew it wasn't luck. And he knew Elijah wouldn't accept. Perhaps that was why he'd never asked.

Kevin said, "And even if he says no, we can give him a walkie talkie. We've got a few and they've got decent range if he's on the same side of the mountain. Then if he ever did have trouble, he could give us a call."

"Great idea." Sarah gave Kevin's leg a pat.

"Speaking of radios." Courtney walked toward the kitchen. "Let's see if we can filter any reliable information out of the GR propaganda being spewed over the airwaves today."

"Count me in." Everett got up from the couch. "But maybe we can listen at the kitchen table. The storage-closet feeling of the living room is a little too stuffy for me. Kevin, Sarah, will you join us?"

"Sounds like a plan." Kevin stood and offered his hand to help Sarah up as well.

Courtney switched on the power and turned up the volume.

The Global Republic Broadcasting Network reporter was covering the geopolitical news. "Former BRICS president and new Russian and Chinese Alliance Ambassador to the GR, Changlie Chau has vehemently denied allegations made by former IMF Director and new GR Prime Minister, Simon Alexander, that China and Russia have seized upon the recent period of instability to invade neighboring countries, such as Mongolia, Vietnam, Laos, Japan, New Zealand, Kazakhstan, Georgia, Belarus, and Ukraine. Chau insists that it is not an invasion but that the Alliance forces are there by invitation.

"Prime Minister Alexander has completely dismissed the fallacy, citing that Japan, New Zealand, and Ukraine are all signatories of the Global Republic charter. Absolute sanctions have been enacted on China and Russia, banning all international aid, commerce, and trade by GR signatories. Alexander expressed His High and Most Prepotent Majesty, Angelo Luz's desire for peace above all, but warned that the Global Republic had responsibilities to its signatories which could include military action if China and Russia refuse to remove their forces from those countries.

"In a statement this morning at the new GR General Assembly building, Prime Minister Alexander reiterated the Global Republic's initiative to reorganize the militaries of the individual signatories under the guide of Global republic peacekeeping forces and the Republic's Elite Guard. He is calling on all those with prior military service to enlist. Those applications can be made at your regional census station.

"In other news, Press Secretary Athaliah Jennings gave GRBN an interview last night. We will be re-airing the full interview tonight at eight o'clock. The highlights included her reminder to avoid pop-up markets, barter networks, and flea markets. She said that not only are all of these activities illegal, but they are also highly dangerous. Participants in such activities put themselves at risk to contract typhoid or other diseases, and there are widespread reports of theft and robbery in areas known to be hubs for illegal trade.

"Secretary Jennings pointed out that the currencies used in these markets are also illegal and possession of such currencies will carry stiff penalties after the amnesty period which expires on March 15th. Such currencies include all paper and coin issued by the former sovereign countries of the GR, including US dollars, Canadian dollars, and Mexican pesos. Gold and silver bullion are also on the list of prohibited currencies, and any jewelry which is caught being used for trade or barter will likewise be treated as contraband.

"Jennings repeated previous exhortations to operate within the confines of GR law, saying that while the GR has decriminalized prostitution and recreational drug use, those activities still must be transacted through government approved channels using the Mark for payment to prevent health risks and crime."

Kevin shook his head. "So it's okay to get a hooker and shoot heroine, as long as you pay for it with the Mark?"

"Well, it's not okay for you." Sarah gave him a stern look.

He hugged her. "That's not what I meant."

"As long as you pay for it with the Mark." Courtney rolled her eyes. "Otherwise, it's at-risk behavior."

They turned their attention back to the radio.

The reporter continued. "In North American news, typhoid inoculations are being administered at all census centers. The small injection contains a new vaccine which can be used to kill off an existing infection or give the recipient immunity from the disease. Those who are treated at the census stations will receive their implant at the same time, which will conveniently contain all of their health records, including their recent typhoid inoculation.

"While services could be paid for using the very same Mark, it will not be necessary as this is the first service provided by the new Global Republic Health Organization at no charge. As the administrative infrastructure of the GRHO is built out, all health services will be provided without cost to the consumer. The GRHO will incorporate elements from the World Health Organization, the former American Department of Health and Human Services, as well as all other health services administrative agencies from the former sovereign countries in the GR.

"In local news, electrical power is slated to be restored to the surrounding areas of the former District of Columbia, New Atlantis. These areas will include Winchester, Harrisonburg, Culpeper, and Fredericksburg as well as the smaller towns in the region. These regions may have felt somewhat neglected in having power restored. The delay has been caused by the massive requirement of power in the former DC area to get New Atlantis up and running. If you live in one of these areas, Minister to the Americas, Richard Clay wants you to know that your sacrifice is appreciated."

"Hold up! The news media is just releasing official statements on behalf of the government?" Kevin protested. "So much for the fourth estate."

"The fourth estate died a long time ago." Courtney pursed her lips.

"At least we're getting electricity." Sarah looked optimistic.

Everett shook his head and held up a finger. "Wait for it."

The anchor proceeded to relay the news. "All utilities have been absorbed by the GR. Water and electric services can be applied for at your local census office. Your Mark will be used to process your account for service connection, billing, and payment. Once essential services are restored, cable, internet and satellite services will be reestablished. Your Mark will also be your credentials for accessing emergency food rations. While the occupancy capacity of most census stations are already maxed out with administrators trying to get citizens registered, vaccinated, implanted and utilities restored, emergency relief food centers are being set up at nearby locations. Often times, food distribution tents are being set up in adjacent parking lots or buildings next door.

More populated areas have multiple census stations set up, usually at schools, post offices, county courthouses, police stations or firehouses. Smaller towns will typically have the census station at the facility which is most central to town out of that list. The exact location of census stations will be posted on the front door of all public buildings. If you still don't know where your nearest census office is, just stop by the nearest public building, such as a school, post office, courthouse or police station. If it's not there and there's no one there to ask, a list of census locations will be posted on the door. The lines are getting longer and longer, so don't wait until the last minute. People who do, may find themselves standing in lines for extended periods. As long as you are in line to register by March 15th, you won't be in violation, but why wait?"

Kevin turned off the power. "That's it. We need to hit one of those supply trucks to round out our seven years' worth of supplies."

Immediately, Everett's heart began racing. His eyes widened as he looked at Courtney to see her reaction. She looked as if she were caught off guard by the comment, but not as though she objected. He glanced at Sarah who acted as if she'd already thought of the plan. "Um, can we talk about that? Is there perhaps a more sensible way to acquire goods than knocking over a GR convoy of supplies?"

Kevin nodded. "I understand your apprehension, and I probably blurted that out without thinking about how I should have phrased it." He looked at Sarah. "I know you two don't know us very well yet, but we haven't survived this long by acting fast and loose. If we make a move, it will be well thought out. We'll have as much information as possible, and the mission will have an extremely high likelihood of success. If we don't like the odds of pulling a plan off, we absolutely won't execute it. I'm not a cowboy."

Everett smirked. That was funny because *cowboy* was exactly the term he would have used to describe Kevin. He felt somewhat easier about the situation, but Everett was in no hurry to start his career as a pirate. "So what did you have in mind?" he asked cautiously.

"I'm not sure. Can you still access the GR communication satellites?"

Everett shrugged. "It depends whether the GR is still using the old passwords for the intelligence databases. At some point, that will all end."

Kevin stroked his beard. "The data is still going to the same hard drives right?"

Everett tilted his head from side to side. "Yes and no. The Utah data center has been on line for a while, but everything, and I mean everything is being shifted to Utah. And at some point soon, government passwords will be replaced by biometric authentication that will utilize the Mark. It tracks your specific heartbeat which is more unique than your fingerprint."

"But there's a way around everything, right?" Kevin asked.

Everett shook his head slowly. "Not Utah. It houses a series of seven quantum super computers called Dragon."

Sarah seemed to catch on first. "You mean like AI?"

Everett sighed. "I mean like self-aware."

Sarah shivered as she hugged Kevin. Her face was wrought with concern. "Oh no. And that thing is running the whole Global Republic?"

Kevin seemed to be processing the implications. "Could we take it out? I mean theoretically, in a perfect world, if we had the right equipment."

Everett chuckled as he thought about how far from a perfect world they lived in. "No. Dragon is plugged into every computer on the web, every store surveillance camera, every traffic light cam, every keyhole satellite, and it has its own army of drones that are always watching over the data center and it can make its own decisions on when to attack. Trust me, if the Russians and the Chinese knew what I knew, they'd give up and sign the charter right now.

"So, no, you wouldn't stand a chance."

"Omniscient, omnipotent, and omnipresent." The totality of Dragon's ability seemed to be sinking in for Kevin.

"Well, Dragon holds a distant second place in all those things, but I think that's what the designers were going for." Everett sat back in his chair. "If you'd rather just sit back and try to ride it all out to the end, we have some gold and silver coins that we could use to buy more supplies if we can find a barter market that's still operational."

"That's a pretty big *if*," Kevin commented. "Besides, even if I can't win, I'd like to know I'm doing my part to cause the New World Order some problems. If we can take out some of their supplies, we financially set them back by the same amount we increase our own wellbeing."

Courtney giggled. "Kind of like double coupon day."

Kevin smiled at her. "Exactly. Does that mean you're on board?"

Courtney looked at Everett and smiled. "I don't know. Are we on board?"

Everett was hesitant, but he was obviously in the minority. "Believe me, I've got no love for the GR, but if we're going to make any moves, they have to be flawlessly devised."

"Sounds like it's unanimous!" Sarah said.

Later that evening, Everett answered the knock at the door. "Come in. Elijah, this is Kevin and Sarah."

The old prophet wiped his feet thoroughly. "I've heard so much about you. It's a pleasure."

"Nice to meet you, sir." Kevin shook Elijah's hand.

Sarah squeezed around the side of a stack of plastic bins to shake hands with Elijah as well. "It's a pleasure to meet you. Sorry we've made sort of a mess of the place."

Elijah smiled. "Most people in the world today would be delighted to have the problem of having too many supplies to be able to walk through the house."

Kevin followed the rest to the kitchen. "Everett says you can take us to a cave where we might find a little more storage space."

"I can do that." Elijah nodded. "Once the roads clear, that is."

Everett pulled a chair out for Elijah. "It supposed to be in the fifties tomorrow. Of course that's down in Woodstock. Still we should at least hit the mid to high forties. If it's sunny, that should get the snow off the roads."

"Thank you." Elijah sat in the chair offered to him. "I trust you had an uneventful move; no trouble from the authorities?"

"No, but we saw plenty of signs of the buildup for a total clampdown. The GR is building checkpoints and detainment areas up and down the highway." Courtney began plating up the sweet-and-sour chicken dish she'd prepared. John Jones had stored up several buckets of premium dehydrated food pouches. Since there was a lot more beans and rice than the premium long-term-storage foods, they were reserved for special occasions such as this dinner. She'd prepared three of the Asian sweet-and-sour rice packets, and added the home-canned meat from one of Elijah's chickens.

Sarah took a seat next to Elijah. "They're gearing up for a complete police state, totalitarian government."

Elijah nodded. "The enemy has always promised freedom and delivered bondage. I would expect nothing less of him."

As he helped Courtney set the table, Everett watched Kevin's reaction to Elijah's statement about the enemy. He didn't seem to think too much of it. After all, Kevin had said that they believed in

God's existence and understood why things were happening. Everett couldn't quite understand why Sarah and Kevin wouldn't come all the way over and place their trust in Christ. He said a silent prayer that God would not give up on them.

Once the food was served, Elijah prayed to bless it and they all ate together. Everett sat on a food-storage bucket as there were only four chairs at the small table. Nevertheless, they made do.

Elijah spread out his napkin in his lap. "Everything looks wonderful. This is quite a treat."

Courtney smiled. "Thank you."

Kevin glanced over at Elijah as he mixed the chicken into the rice on his plate. "Did you happen to hear the GRBN broadcast today?"

"Yes. With the snow, I had little else to do."

"Creepy stuff, huh?" Sarah said.

Elijah finished chewing then replied, "Yes, and it's only going to get worse. I'm sure you heard about the Temple of Baal archway that is being erected by the new Ministry of Religion."

"I guess we missed that." Courtney took another bite.

Elijah blotted his mouth with his napkin. "The Ministry of Religion is to be the last building, at the end of the National Mall. Between that building and the Washington Monument, the Temple of Baal archway will be set up. It is fitting, since the Washington Monument itself is a symbol of sun god worship."

Sarah sipped her water. "Cassie, one of the women in our group who disappeared said that Baal was the same god as the Babylonian god, Marduk.

She said that all occult religions and secret societies trace their beginnings back to Babylon; and that Babylon is the same as Babel which means gate of the gods. Do you think that's all true?"

"Absolutely." Elijah nodded. "And that is precisely what Luz is attempting to do in DC. Just as Nimrod, the founder of Babylon, attempted to open a gate to the heavens with his Tower of Babel, so is Luz trying to unlock the door to the abyss."

"But why would he want to do such a thing?" Courtney asked.

"For the same reason as all of those who have studied the mystery religions before him. To tap into the dark power of Lucifer's servants."

Everett hated this line of conversation and he almost said nothing. But, he couldn't resist one question that was eating at him. "Isn't God all powerful? How would Satan have power?"

Elijah held a finger in the air. "Yes, indeed, God is all powerful. But Paul writes in his letter to the Church of Ephesus, 'For we wrestle not against flesh and blood, but against principalities, against powers, against the rulers of the darkness of this world, against spiritual wickedness in high places.' So, the enemy does have power for a time. And this, my friends, is his appointed time. These are the days that have been allotted that Satan might rule upon the earth. We know the final outcome, but that is because we have faith in what the Word of God says. Those who do not share our faith will be deceived into thinking that Lucifer and his servant, Luz, will be the victors in this battle that we have just entered into.

"It is for the power to pull off this very deception, that Luz must breach the portal between this world and the next."

Everett sighed. He wasn't the type to be believing in black magic and interdimensional portals, but then again, it was his stubbornness that had landed him in the midst of the most devastating period of human history. He crossed his arms and reluctantly asked yet another question, that he was sure he'd regret. "So how is Luz going to open the door when this guy, Nimrod, couldn't?"

Elijah took a deep breath. "I'm going to have to give you a little background. Genesis 6 tells us of the Nephilim, which means fallen. It says that the sons of God procreated with the daughters of men, creating a hybrid race. Some of this race were giants and others were endowed with demonic power. It was because of this that wickedness increased to such a level that God had to wipe the slate clean with the great flood. Additionally, he had to annihilate the genetic corruption which was coming upon the human race and destroying the species through interbreeding. This genetic corruption was part of Satan's plan to block the coming of Messiah, as he had to be born of a virgin woman that he might be fully God and fully man.

"God destroyed the world with the flood, saving only Noah and his family. It is thought that either Ham, one of Noah's sons, or Ham's wife preserved the esoteric wisdom of the Nephilim, for it was their offspring, Nimrod who settled in Shinar to begin work on reopening the pathway that had been shut off by the flood. And it is Nimrod who came to be known as Marduk, Baal, and all the different manifestations of the sun god. Yet it is not the sun that the highest orders worship, but Sirius the Dog Star, which in the day is obscured by the light of the sun, that the highest order of the mystery religions worship. In Egypt, Sirius was considered to be the most evil of all the stars that were gazed upon in the night sky."

Everett relaxed his arms and let them fall to his side. "I'm enjoying the history lesson, but what does Sirius have to do with Luz opening a demonic doorway?"

"I'll get to that if you'll let me." Elijah gave him a stern look that showed his annoyance at being interrupted. "New Atlantis, or Washington DC rather, was designed by Masonic architects who had been trained in the esoteric wisdom. It was modeled after the vision of a New Atlantis which was developed by a member of the Rosicrucian Order, Francis Bacon and the founder of Enochian magic, Dr. John Dee. The streets of DC are designed to make an inverted pentagram, or upside down five-pointed star. This is the sign of the star, Sirius, and is the most powerful symbol in all of occult magic. It is within this symbol that demonic entities are summoned, and the largest single representation of this symbol is drawn out by the streets of downtown DC. It is here, that the gates of hell will be opened and all manner of evil will be released on this planet."

Kevin didn't look like he was buying it. His forehead was heavily furrowed as he listened. "And all of this is in the Bible? The gates of hell being opened?"

Elijah gave Kevin a graceful nod. "The fifth trumpet. Revelation 9 reads, 'And the fifth angel sounded, and I saw a star fall from heaven unto the earth: and to him was given the key of the bottomless pit. And he opened the bottomless pit; and there arose a smoke out of the pit, as the smoke of a great furnace; and the sun and the air were darkened by reason of the smoke of the pit. And there came out of the smoke locusts upon the earth: and unto them was given power, as the scorpions of the earth have power.'

"But let's not get ahead of ourselves. You've got a little time on that one and there are other, more immediate threats that you'll have to survive first."

Sarah put her fork on the table and sarcastically remarked, "Oh, that's a relief. With all of the death and destruction we have to face right now, we'll probably never live long enough to see the gates of hades flung wide open."

"I didn't mean to distract from this delicious meal. Let us speak of more pleasant things. I saw some building materials on the side of the house. Will you be building a greenhouse?"

Everett nodded. He was all for changing the subject. "Eventually, yes. But spring is right around the corner, so probably not until next fall."

Kevin joined the conversation, also seeming eager to talk about something else. "We scavenged those materials from the house where we were staying in Tennessee. The first thing we need is more storage space."

Elijah winked at Kevin. "And there's a man with

the fascinating ability to state the obvious."

Kevin began laughing and the others soon joined in for a brief chuckle.

Everett smiled as he thought what an uncanny ability Elijah had to take them to the edge of panic and then turn it all around in a second.

After the light-hearted lark, they all resumed eating and enjoyed the rest of the meal getting to know each other better.

Once they'd finished their meals, Everett asked, "Is everything okay, Elijah?" He could see the old man had something on his mind. "You don't seem quite as chipper as usual."

Elijah looked at the others sitting around the table as if he were weighing the thought of replying to Everett now or waiting until they were alone. He sighed. "I've received my instructions, at least for now."

"Oh." Everett had a sudden sense of loss. He'd quickly grown to admire the old man. "Will you be leaving?"

Before he could answer, Courtney placed a cup of tea in front of the prophet and asked in a distressed voice. "When are you going?"

Elijah put a hand in the air. "Settle down, both of you. Hear me out. At some point, I'll be leaving the country, to go to Jerusalem. When I leave for Israel, I won't be coming back. But I've not been instructed on that matter yet. Before the amnesty period ends, I am to go to DC. I am to stand before Luz and pronounce judgement against him and the Global Republic."

"Then you'll come back here?" Everett asked.

"I presume, but I can't be certain."

"Good, I feel like I have so many things to ask you before you leave." Everett was relieved that Elijah would be coming back.

"Yes, well, you may have more of an opportunity to pick my brain than you think." Elijah sipped his tea.

Everett chuckled at the remark. It sounded like another one of Elijah's absurd comments. Finally, curiosity got the better of him and he asked, "Okay, I give up, when will I have this opportunity?"

Elijah peered into Everett's eyes over the top of his tea cup as he took another sip. "You are to accompany me on my journey."

Everett shook his head without speaking. His stomach sank. He'd just finished dealing with Kevin who wanted to knock over a GR supply truck. Now the crazy old man had in mind to drag him into the belly of the beast. Everett was on this mountain to survive, to keep his head low, and to ride out the coming storm. Why was everyone insisting that he put himself in harm's way? In a flash, Everett's opinion of the old man had evolved from honor and respect to thinking of him as a complete lunatic.

Courtney grabbed Everett's arm. "That doesn't sound like a very wise thing to do. I understand that God has called you and you have a special mission, but what good would it do you for Everett to go along with you? I'm sorry Elijah, it just sounds like an unnecessary risk."

Everett put his hand on hers and smiled at her. At least Courtney hadn't lost her mind, too. He wasn't alone. "Yeah, I don't have any skill set that's going to increase your odds of success. I'd just get in the way." He gave the prophet a condescending smile, as if he were talking to a senile elderly man in a nursing home.

Elijah's heavy hearted expression changed to that of light amusement. He laughed as he pointed to Courtney. "Oh, you are to come along as well."

"Me? Why me? What does any of this have to do with me?" She shook her head adamantly. "Oh no, absolutely not."

Elijah stood up. "I should be going. I've caused enough anxiety for one night."

Everett didn't want him to feel bad. "Elijah, you're welcome to stay. We're not mad, but we're not going to DC or New Atlantis or anywhere else. We've put a lot of effort into making this cabin our fortress."

"Exactly." Elijah chuckled as he put his coat on. "The safest place you can be is in the center of God's will. We leave first thing Monday morning."

"Elijah!" Courtney called out to him as he walked out the door.

Kevin and Sarah said nothing during the entire exchange.

Courtney turned to them. "I'm sorry. He's not usually like this."

Sarah shook her head. "Don't apologize to me. You didn't do anything. Besides, I've had to raise the bar on what I consider *weird* these days." She pointed toward the door that Elijah had just left through. "And that, just barely makes the cut."

Everett took a deep breath and exhaled. He hated that Elijah had left without talking the disagreement over, but had the man gone stark raving mad? What possible good could come of Everett and Courtney tagging along while Elijah made some wild attempt to aggravate the most powerful man on the face of the earth? Sure, none of them liked Luz, but Antichrist or not, he had the full power of the New World Order at his beck and call.

CHAPTER 7

I will say of the LORD, He is my refuge and
my fortress: my God; in him will I trust.

Psalm 91:2

Late Saturday morning, Everett called out to
Danger who was barking. "It's okay, boy. It's just
Elijah." Danger ran to the porch but continued
barking. Everett walked out to pet the dog. "I know,
I know, he scares me too sometimes."

Elijah pulled the old truck into the driveway
which was now full with Everett's BMW, Ken's
Camaro, Kevin's green TWRA truck, and a Ford F-
150 which had belonged to a man from Kevin's
group who'd disappeared.

Everett walked down the drive to greet Elijah.
"Sorry about last evening, I . . ."

"Let us speak no more of it." Elijah put his hand in the air as he cut Everett off before he could finish. "Today is a new day. The road is clearing up. I should think the rest of the road down the mountain will be clear if you'd like to go see the cave."

Everett looked in the back of Elijah's truck. The old man had an extension ladder and some rope. "You must be figuring on some hard core spelunking."

"If you intend to put any of your supplies there, I'm sure you'd prefer them to not be overly visible nor readily accessible. Have you any coffee?"

Everett smiled. For a crazy old man, Elijah certainly thought of everything. "I think we've got time to put a pot on. Come on in."

Everett put on a pot of coffee then tapped on Kevin and Sarah's door. "Elijah's here, but we've got a little time before we roll out to the cave. He's going to have a cup of coffee before we go."

Kevin called out through the closed door. "Great, we'll be ready in about fifteen minutes."

Everett climbed up the ladder to tell Courtney. She was lying on the bed, reading her Bible and her face was as white as a ghost.

"Are you all right? Your hands are shaking." He sat down beside her and put his hand on her back.

She shook her head and tears began to stream down her face.

"Hey, what's wrong?" He lay down next to her.

She closed the Bible. "God, he's talking to me!"

Everett gritted his teeth. He remembered the feeling when Ken and Lisa had accepted Christ.

How he'd felt abandoned by them and left with only him and Courtney who were thinking rationally. Now he had that feeling again, but this time he was the only one left. "Are you sure? What did he say? Could it just be your imagination?"

"Everett!" She wiped the tear from her eye. "Don't talk to me like I'm crazy. I know what you're thinking. You have to quit being like that. You think you know everything and your reality is how it is. You think anyone who doesn't see things your way is a kook. I'm not a kook, Everett. This is me talking to you. You know me."

He sat up and gave her some distance. "Okay. Just explain to me what happened." She was right. It was that attitude that had guaranteed his reservation to the Great Tribulation; but still, he wasn't about to admit it. "What did God say to you?"

"Nothing, like I didn't hear a voice."

He wanted to say, *Work with me here. I'm trying*. But instead he just nodded. He'd learned the hard way that it was sometimes better to just nod.

"Everett, I know that look." She pointed at him. "Okay, you're right, that sounds even crazier." She took a deep breath. "So, I was reading my Bible, just straight through the New Testament, like we've been doing since we read Romans and John, I'm in Hebrews, right? Chapter 11, I think. Anyway, the whole chapter is about all these people who basically do something crazy because God told them to do it. By faith, Noah builds an ark even though it has never rained, by faith Abraham leaves his home to go wander off in the desert looking for some place he's never heard of, by faith Abraham is willing to sacrifice his son, by faith Moses chose to suffer with his people rather than enjoy the pleasures of Egypt. I read it over and over like five times. And do you know what else it says?"

Everett shook his head, not really wanting to know. He could feel it in his bones. While he didn't know the words she'd use, he knew exactly the meaning of what Courtney was about to say. A shiver ran up his back and he could feel the hairs standing up on his arms.

"It says without faith; it is impossible to please God." She began crying again. "We spent so much time not pleasing God, Everett." She took his hand. "I want to please God; I want to have faith. If he's calling us to do something, we have to do it."

Tears were streaming down Everett's face as well as he pulled his wife close to himself. "I know."

She pushed him back to look in his eyes. "You mean it, Everett? You're not just saying I know to shut me up?"

"No, the same thing happened to me this morning."

"What? The same thing? You were reading Hebrews 11?"

"No, different verse, but same type of experience. I wrote it off to my imagination, but after hearing you, I know it was God speaking. And he was telling me the same thing."

She dried her eyes. "Tell me about it!"

"Last night, I said something to Elijah, I told him we weren't going with him because this cabin is our fortress. And like he always does, he said something that made no sense. He said exactly. I mean, what kind of a response is that?

"This morning, I'm reading my Bible, Psalm. For whatever reason, I've been reading a few psalms every morning before I read the New Testament" He picked up her Bible. "I'm reading Psalm 18 this morning, and right away I read, 'The LORD is my rock, and my fortress, and my deliverer; my God, my strength, in whom I will trust; my buckler, and the horn of my salvation, and my high tower. I will call upon the LORD, who is worthy to be praised: so shall I be saved from mine enemies.'

"Right after I told Elijah that this house was my fortress, I read that the LORD is my fortress. It's the same thing that he's telling you. I have to trust him. What did you say? It's impossible to please God without faith? That's exactly what I was feeling when I was reading this psalm.

"But that's not all, the psalm goes on to talk about all of this calamitous stuff, it says the sorrows of hell compassed me, the earth shook and trembled; the foundations also of the hills moved and were shaken, because he was wroth. This is exactly what we are about to go through. It sounds like a description of the Great Tribulation. The earth shaking, that's the quake that's coming! It sounds like this was written just for me; like it's been in this book the whole time, for thousands of years, just waiting for me to read it. I thought I was just making something out of nothing, blowing it out of proportion, but then the same thing happened to you."

"Wow." Courtney just sat at the edge of the bed. After a few moments of silence, she turned to him. "Then we're going to tell Elijah that we're going with him?"

Everett huffed. "He didn't really ask. He basically just told us when to be ready."

"Okay, then. We'll be ready."

Everett took a deep breath. "I hope so."

An hour later, Everett and the others had the two trucks loaded with some supplies which they would attempt to stash and conceal inside the cave.

"If you have a dolly or hand cart, you should bring it." Elijah said as he got in the cab of his truck.

"Why? How far is the cave from the road?" Kevin asked.

Elijah rolled down his window and shrugged. "Maybe a half mile. First leg of the trip would be easy to use a cart. But the last hundred yards is pretty rugged terrain. It will require a fair amount of agility to get up a steep incline then a small cliff."

"Hmm." Everett furrowed his brow as he looked at all of the supplies they'd loaded into the back of the trucks. "How much of this stuff do you think we can get moved in today?"

Elijah put his truck in reverse and began slowly backing out of the drive as if to hurry them along. "It depends on how long you dilly dally."

Everett rushed to get a hand cart and returned to the truck. He started the engine. Courtney quickly got in the passenger's side and closed the door. "I have a feeling that we are in for a workout."

Everett pursed his lips. "I should have picked up the clue when he told us to pack a lunch and bring plenty of water."

"Elijah is always full of surprises." Courtney sighed.

Kevin and Sarah followed Everett closely in the green truck as he trailed along behind Elijah. The convoy climbed the winding road up past Elijah's home, on toward the peak of the mountain. They continued along the narrow pavement down the other side of the summit. As the caravan descended to a lower elevation, they crossed over into West Virginia. Another mile down the road was a mountain stream. Elijah pulled off the road and led the way toward the water. The stream was slow and calm with low cliffs where the water had cut through the rocks over the years.

Elijah got out and closed his door. He hung the coil of rope around his shoulder and took his ladder from the truck bed. "We shall have to make several trips, so let's get a move on."

Everett configured the dolly to be a low pushcart and stacked 2 five-gallon buckets on the flat surface. He then positioned two more buckets, one on top of the other next to the first two and secured them all with bungee cords.

Elijah smiled. "We'll see how far you get with that configuration. The narrow trail follows around the stream about an eighth of a mile then we leave the path and walk through the woods. You could probably push the dolly another 200 yards if you reconfigure it to roll upright."

Everett sighed and nodded. There was no use

arguing about it. Kevin and Courtney each took two buckets, one in each hand.

Sarah slung her rifle over her back, carried a bucket in one hand and a walking stick in the other. "If I'm traveling on uneven terrain, I have to have something to steady myself when I step onto my prosthetic leg."

"You won't hear any complaints out of me. People who have a lot more abilities than you find reasons to give up and do a lot less." Everett patted his back pocket to double check that his extra pistol magazines were where they were supposed to be, before starting the cart along the trail. "You are an inspiration to all of us."

"Thanks. I guess giving up isn't in my nature." Sarah cracked a faint smile as she followed behind Everett. She didn't seem the type that needed a constant barrage of accolades, but everyone likes a compliment now and then.

Everett stopped when he saw Elijah leave the trail. He removed the buckets, reconfigured the dolly to roll upright, and reloaded it with two of the four buckets. It wasn't the most convenient maneuver, but at least he wouldn't have to go all the way back to the truck for the two additional food-storage buckets. He continued to follow behind Elijah, Kevin and Courtney, with Sarah trailing in the back as the rear guard.

Just as Elijah had said, the utility of the dolly ran out in about 200 yards. The group paused for a break after carrying the heavy buckets and equipment this far. Everett unfastened the bungee cords and took off the buckets.

Elijah instructed them on the next leg of the journey. "We've got some steep situations between here and the entrance of the cave. I'd recommend each of you using one hand to carry a bucket and the other to maintain your balance. The higher we go, the more detrimental a fall would be. Don't try to be a hero. If you fall and injure yourself, you'll be a serious liability to the rest of the group. Slow and steady; we'll get it all moved. We have plenty of time. Sarah, I'd recommend that you leave your bucket here and focus on getting yourself up the hill. We can make a couple of trips back and forth, the cave isn't far now."

Sarah dropped her bucket next to the other spare buckets. "Roger that."

Everett gave her a smile. She appeared determined to do her part, but didn't seem to have anything to prove. He hoped that if he were in her position, that he'd have the wisdom to do the same, but knew that as a man, pride would more often cloud one's judgement on such issues.

They traversed the slope, made more treacherous by the moisture from the melted snow. Everett was careful to check the firmness of the ground before shifting his weight with each successive step. He would use the trunks of saplings to hoist himself up when they were available and he could be sure that they'd support his weight.

The group reached a narrow ridge and outcropping of rocks which jetted out from beneath the earth. Elijah pointed to a small crevice between two jagged boulders. "That's it."

Everett looked at the tiny space. It was not what

he'd pictured. "Where? That? It looks like a groundhog hole."

"I'm not going in there! It looks like a snake pit!" Courtney vehemently voiced her opposition.

Kevin helped Sarah up by the hand to the narrow landing above the short cliff. "Doesn't look like much of a cave."

Elijah grinned. "That's good. It makes it less likely to be discovered by others. But trust me, as soon as you get inside, it really opens up." He pushed the ladder through the small opening, shined his flashlight inside and crawled through the hole. "Come, come." Elijah's voice came from inside.

Everett grunted his disapproval, laid the bucket on its side so it would clear the mossy tree roots at the top of the crevice, pushed it through and crawled in behind. Just inside, the floor dropped down two feet, immediately making the space larger. The floor of the cave continued to go lower at a more gradual decline until the area opened up into what looked like a room with a low ceiling which was about seven feet high. Everett crawled until he got to a place in the room where he could stand up. "Wow!" He shined his flashlight all around the space. The light glistened off the shiny smooth walls of the limestone cave. The formations along the edges of the room resembled tiny stone icicles.

Sarah was the next to crawl through the low opening. "This is amazing."

Kevin and Courtney pushed through the other supplies then crawled through and joined the others.

Courtney shined her flashlight. "I don't see any

signs that other people have ever been in here."

Elijah called for them to follow. "Come along. We've got a lot of stuff to move." The old man led the way through what looked like a wide hallway with a low roof which slanted down and eventually hit the bottom of the cave. Everett and the others had to duck down as they traveled through the corridor until they came out into an open space with a high ceiling that looked to be nearly thirty feet tall at its highest point. "I call this room the cathedral."

Everett looked all around. The room had a level floor, and a vast open space, comparable to a school gymnasium. "This is fantastic. Is this where we should stash our supplies?"

"No, up there."

Everett looked over to the point where Elijah was shining his light. About ten feet up the wall of the cave was a ledge that seemed to go back only a few feet.

Elijah set his flashlight down and positioned his ladder up against the wall. "There is an opening that leads down another small crawl space then opens up to a chamber, roughly four feet high. It's only about five feet wide, but it goes back about fifty yards. It will make a good storage area, and you can't get to it without a ladder or something to get you up onto the ledge. Even if someone was to discover the cave, they'd be unlikely to find your supplies."

"Yeah, I guess most people don't go caving with a ladder. Except for you, of course." Everett looked at the old man.

Elijah handed him the rope. "You climb up and lower the rope down. Then we'll tie the buckets to the end and you can hoist up the supplies. Line them up along the ledge then I'll come up and help you transport them down the crawl space to the chamber."

Everett followed the instructions. "So how did you happen upon this place anyway?"

"Hiking, when I first moved here years back. I know there are lots of caves, so when I saw the opening, I assumed that's what it was."

Everett reached the top and lowered the rope down. "And when did you decide to bring a ladder here?"

Elijah tied the rope to the first bucket. "I'd explored the cave about three times. It doesn't go very far until it's not possible for a human to go further. I suppose I just got curious and wanted there to be more."

"It certainly paid off for us. Thanks for finding it." Courtney brought over the bucket she'd lugged up the hill and into the cave.

Once the buckets were up on the ledge, Elijah climbed the ladder and helped Everett move the buckets into the chamber which was just a few feet down the crawl space. Moving three buckets wasn't too cumbersome of a task, but they still had many more at the bottom of the hill, and even more in the truck. Getting two truckloads of supplies up to the cave, through the corridor, up to the ledge, down the crawl space and in the storage chamber would be an all-day job.

Once the first three buckets were in position, they made their way back toward the entrance to complete the tedious chore, leaving the ladder and rope in place.

When they reached the inside of the cave entrance, Sarah said, "Since I can't move buckets up the hill, why don't I stay here and ferry the buckets from the entrance to the back wall of the cathedral. You guys just keep them coming and I'll keep taking them to the back."

Kevin shined his light around the cave. "I don't know if it's safe for you to be in here alone."

She pushed him toward the opening. "I'm perfectly safe. Now let me be part of getting the supplies in position."

Kevin kissed her on the cheek. "Okay, but stay alert."

Everett climbed out of the cave. He had to squint his eyes. The bright light of the sun burned his eyes to the point of watering. As the others came out, they also had to allow for a period of adjustment before continuing down the hill to the trail. Finally, they finished moving the supplies at the bottom of the hill up to the cave entrance and fed them through the opening to Sarah.

After a short break to eat lunch, they worked out a new system. Kevin would move the buckets with the dolly to the bottom of the hill. Elijah, Courtney and Everett would move them up the hill, and Sarah would relocate the buckets from the cave opening to the back wall of the cathedral.

It took all day, but once the process started moving, they began moving faster and faster. Other than one bucket being dropped by Courtney, which had to be moved back up the hill a second time, the project was completed without incident, and not a moment too soon. By the time they'd returned to the trucks, with the ladder and rope, the sun was down and the last glints of daylight were fading.

Everett knew he would sleep well after such a physically demanding undertaking. As they got back into the vehicles, Everett said, "I suppose we can make another run tomorrow."

Elijah held a finger in the air. "No. Tomorrow, we rest. We can finish moving the rest of the supplies when we return from DC." He closed the door of his truck and led the way back to the road.

Everett followed Elijah back up the mountain then down to his house where he turned off. Everett gave a light honk and waved as he continued on down the road to the cabin. When they arrived, Kevin and Sarah pulled in the drive behind Everett and got out of the green truck.

Everett opened the door, lit a candle for light and toppled over on the couch. Elijah was right, he certainly needed a day of rest.

Courtney took her holster off and sat down next to Everett. "We put a pretty good dent in the supplies."

Kevin sat down in the recliner which was now freed up by the buckets that had been relocated to the cave. "We'll have the living room cleared up before you know it."

Sarah sat on the hearth and stirred the hot coals, putting in some tinder and blowing on it to get a flame. "So, I thought you guys weren't going to DC. Elijah seems unconvinced by your decline to his invitation."

Everett sighed. He was entirely too tired to think

about going to DC to help Elijah confront the Antichrist. "I suppose we're going. You two can just keep an eye out around here. We'll help you move the rest of the supplies when we get back on Tuesday. I hope to be back Monday night."

Kevin scratched his beard. "Would you want a little extra security?"

Everett sat up on the couch. "Are you offering your services?"

"Our services," Sarah said.

Everett couldn't quite imagine why they'd want to tag along. "Elijah is planning to crawl straight into a pit of vipers. I'm going because . . . I feel like God is telling me to go. I know it sounds weird, and trust me, I don't usually talk like this."

Courtney added, "If you'd have known us before the disappearances, you'd have never believed we'd be saying we hear from God. It's kind of hard to explain."

"We're used to it," Sarah replied.

Kevin stood up and walked over to where Sarah was. "But we wouldn't mind coming along. I'd like to see what type of security setup they have for the perimeter, where the supplies are coming in, how hard it is to get in and out."

"Oh, recon." Everett looked at Kevin. "You should know, we don't have any plan, and I don't think Elijah does either."

"But you think God is going to protect him. And you think God is going to get him in and out of DC, right?" Kevin sat on the hearth next to Sarah.

"Yeah, I guess so." Everett gently nodded. He was confused. For people who weren't willing to accept the free gift of salvation, they sure had a lot of faith in God.

"Then if you don't mind, we'd like to come also," Kevin said.

"It's fine with me, but it's Elijah's decision." Everett still couldn't get his head around Kevin and Sarah wanting to go.

"Great. It will be a group outing." Courtney stretched out her hands in dramatic fashion. "To the New Atlantis, a mystical land where nightmares come true."

Sarah giggled. "It will be interesting to see what they've done to the place."

Everett resumed his reclined position on the couch and fought to keep from falling asleep. He wanted to wash up and get something to eat before bed, but he just had to rest for a few more minutes.

Courtney woke him from his short nap half an hour later. They ate a quick meal of leftover stew and cornbread. Afterwards, Everett took a quick cat bath and went straight to bed. He was back to sleep within seconds of his head hitting the pillow.

CHAPTER 8

Elijah was a man with a nature like ours, and he prayed earnestly that it would not rain; and it did not rain on the land for three years and six months.

James 5:17 NKJV

Everett stretched out on the bed and ran his fingers through Courtney's hair. She lay next to him on the bed, opened her eyes and smiled softly. As instructed by Elijah, Sunday morning was spent resting and recuperating from a tough week of getting Kevin and Sarah moved to the cabin and the previous day's mission of taking supplies out to the cave.

Sox meowed and scratched the sheets at the foot

of the bed. Courtney sat up and picked up the cat to pet him.

"I think he's hungry," Everett said. "As a matter of fact, I could use something to eat myself."

"You relax; I'll make breakfast this morning." She put Sox down and got up.

"Wow. We should have got a cat a long time ago."

Courtney whacked him with the pillow. "Shut up! I've made breakfast before."

"Not since I've met you." Everett took cover in case of another assault by the pillow.

Courtney just rolled her eyes and put her jeans on.

Everett watched her as she finished dressing. "Isn't Sarah going to get mad about you abducting her cat? He's slept up here every night since they moved to the cabin."

Courtney pulled her hair back into a ponytail. "No. Cupcake is her pet. Sox belonged to the little girl that disappeared. I think Sarah said her name was Lacy."

"Okay, then I guess it's a good arrangement for everybody." Everett reached out to give Sox a scratch.

"Do you think Elijah will let Kevin and Sarah come to DC?" she asked.

"I haven't the foggiest idea." Everett continued to scratch the purring feline.

"I suppose we should walk over to his house and ask after breakfast."

"Okay. Plus, we never asked him what to bring."

"What do you mean?"

"You know, guns, packs, water, food, maybe some coins."

Courtney furrowed her brow. "Now you're making me think about it too much. It's going to make me want to back out."

"By faith." Everett winked.

She began climbing down the ladder. "Yeah, by faith."

Everett and Courtney managed to accomplish very little else, besides eating, resting and stopping by Elijah's for a few minutes Sunday afternoon. Despite doing nothing, the day flew by and it was soon time for bed.

Monday morning, Everett heard Elijah's knock at the door downstairs. He stared at the contents of the safe before closing it. Elijah had been very vague when they'd asked what to bring the day before, but Courtney, Kevin, Sarah and himself had determined to bring the essentials for a worst-case-scenario. Everett brought his Sig pistol because it was easily concealed. He still had his CIA credentials. He doubted that they would do him any good at all if he were caught in DC with a weapon and no Mark, but it couldn't hurt. They'd be driving in Ken's Camaro, which was fast, had a trunk to conceal the long guns they'd be traveling with and couldn't be directly connected to any of them if they had to ditch it. Packs were stowed in the back of the Camaro with three days of food for the entire team, in case they had to lay low for a while or travel back on foot. Everett opened the tube of one-ounce gold American eagle coins and dropped five in his pocket. Anyone who would be in the position to provide any type of black-market service they may need, such as hiding them in a safe house or giving them food or transportation, would recognize the value of the coins.

"Elijah's here. It's time to go." Courtney called out from downstairs.

"I'm almost ready." Everett closed the safe, spun the dial and looked toward heaven. "God, please keep us safe. I know I'm supposed to trust you, but I'm a little new at this, so please, be patient with me."

Fifteen minutes later, they were in the car and on the road. Everett drove, Kevin rode in the passenger's seat, Courtney, Sarah and Elijah rode in the back.

"How far is it to DC?" Sarah asked.

Everett glanced at the rearview. "Two hours if we were going straight in on I-66, but we're cutting around from the north. It adds a half hour to the trip, but it reduces our odds of hitting a checkpoint before we get to the fence."

"Do you have a place near the fence where we can stash the packs and rifles in case things go south?" Kevin asked.

Everett looked at the keys dangling from the ignition. "My old apartment is in Ashburn, which is right outside of the first fence, but everything in that area was looted, vandalized, and generally destroyed after the attacks in November. My building could have been burnt to the ground for all I know."

"Is it out of the way?" Kevin turned toward Everett.

"No. We'll go right by there since we're taking the scenic route." Everett adjusted his visor to shield his eyes from the bright morning sun.

"It's worth a shot. We can keep our pistols with us, in case we have to shoot our way back." Kevin turned to watch the passing countryside out the passenger's side window.

"Sure." Everett didn't want to consider his odds of shooting his way out of DC, the hub of the new one-world government.

An hour later, they drove by the first series of electronic road signs.

Kevin read them aloud. "Winchester Census, next exit. Follow signs to Shenandoah University."

Sarah's voice came from the back seat. "Should we drive by and have a look at the setup? It might be a good place to hit a supply truck."

Everett gritted his teeth, but saw no point in objecting. If they were actually going to pull it off, Winchester was the perfect distance from the cabin. "Elijah, do you mind if we take a quick detour?"

"Please, do what you like. You're driving and it's your car. You certainly don't need my permission."

Everett wouldn't have minded if the old man had opposed the suggestion. He was half-hoping for an excuse to skip driving by the GR facilities. "Well, it's your mission, and it's not really my car."

"Thank you for your consideration, but I'm in no hurry. We'll get there when we get there."

Everett took the exit and followed the signs. The university was just off I-81. He turned onto the road and drove slowly past the area which was marked as a census station. There were several large up armored vehicles. He counted three near the census station, and three more near a large fenced-in enclosure where food was being distributed to a long line of people. The line snaked back and forth between poles with lengths of chain which were used as dividers. "Looks like a line in a theme park."

"Yeah, Apocalypse Land." Courtney scoffed.

"Four Hummers and two Maxx Pros." Kevin placed a large magazine in his Glock that stuck out several inches from the bottom of the grip. "These guys are pretty well armed for a small town."

Everett glanced at the pistol as he continued to drive, hoping that there'd be no need for a confrontation with the GR troops just yards away. He continued to drive down University Drive.

"We're getting some looks from those guards. We should probably keep moving," Sarah said.

Everett's heart beat faster. He came to an intersection where University Drive ended. "Think I should turn around?"

Kevin shook his head. "I'd follow Shockey Drive, to the left, and see if we can get out without driving back past the GR troops."

Everett followed his suggestion and kept driving. The road ran beneath I-81 and Everett was soon able to circle back to the same street he'd been on when he exited the interstate. He re-entered the highway, keeping a constant eye on the rearview to see if they'd been followed. Once they were safely back on their way, Everett looked over at the pistol in Kevin's lap. "That's a big magazine."

"It eats through those seventeen-round mags pretty quick when it's on full auto. A 33-round mag buys me a little more trigger time."

"Full auto?"

"Yep. It's a Glock 18C clone. A gunsmith built it out of a Glock 17. You gotta be a little higher up than a sheriff's deputy to get your hands on a real Glock 18. Sarah's got one too, a clone I mean."

"Wow! Can I see it?" Courtney asked.

"Sure," Sarah answered.

Everett could hear the sound of a magazine coming out of a pistol and the chamber being cleared in the back seat.

"I've got to shoot this when we get back!" Courtney exclaimed.

"You bet." Sarah laughed.

Half an hour later, Everett was breathing a little easier. He saw no one tailing the car, however, he did keep looking up at the sky to see if he could spot any drones that might be surveilling them. He doubted that a suspicious car driving by would warrant the dispatch of a drone. Not long after, they arrived in Ashburn. "This was a nice place, lots of young professionals but not congested, clean, and not much crime." Everett sighed. "But those days are over."

Kevin looked out the window. "It doesn't look all that bad. A few broken windows and little fire damage, but I was expecting a lot worse."

"I guess it looks worse when it was your home."

Everett continued toward his old apartment building.

Courtney put her hand on his shoulder from the back seat. "You've got a new home now."

Everett smiled. She was right. Most people had nowhere to go; he was very thankful for the cabin, Courtney, and his new friends. "That's my place. It looks like the security gate didn't last long. Not many cars, I suppose most of my neighbors found somewhere else to go." He pulled into his old parking spot and got out. "Let's check it out before we cart any supplies in."

The others followed Everett up the stairs and to his door. It was unlocked. The front window had been smashed and the intruders had left through the front door. Everett pulled his pistol as he entered. "We better make sure no one is here."

Kevin drew his Glock in which he'd replaced the short magazine to make the pistol concealable. "I'm right behind you."

Seconds later, Everett called out. "All clear."

Courtney walked through the apartment and stuck her Glock 21 back in her purse. "They didn't really tear anything up. It just looks looted."

Kevin looked at the broken window. "We'll have to figure out a way to secure that, if we're going to keep anything here. Do you have a tool box?"

"I probably have a screw driver and maybe some pliers in the car." Everett said.

"I was thinking more like a saw, hammer, nails, screw gun, that sort of thing."

"Oh, no. Maintenance handled all the repairs."

Courtney put her hands on her hips and looked at

Everett. "You don't even have a hammer to hang pictures?"

Everett glanced up at the ceiling as he thought. "Yeah. Somewhere." He walked back to his old bedroom and rummaged through the closet. "I've got a small hammer and a box of odds and ends; screws, washers, a few small nails." Everett handed the box and the hammer to Kevin.

"Can you grab that screw driver and the pliers out of the car?" Kevin asked. "If I can get them off the hinges, I think I can use your bathroom door and your bedroom door to secure the window."

"Be right back." Everett looked around to make sure there were no signs of danger before sprinting down the stairs and to the car. He hurried to retrieve the tools from the glove box and ran back up to the apartment.

Once back in the apartment, Everett helped Kevin get the doors off the hinges and positioned in front of the window.

Kevin held up one of the nails from the small plastic box. "Way too short. These are for like hanging pictures. Are you sure you don't have anything else?"

"No." Everett shook his head.

Sarah looked at the doors. "These doors are basically two sheets of paper thin cardboard stapled on a wood frame. Why don't you just bust holes out of the backside where you need to run the nails? But you better lay them on the floor when you do it, or the hammer will go all the way through the other side."

"Good idea, let's lay them down." Kevin grabbed

one side of the first door.

Everett took hold of the other side and helped him lay the door down. "If these doors are that thin, it won't be very secure."

"They're just for looks, but I've got an idea for a good deterrent. Let's get these done first." Kevin easily punched out the first hole in the back of the door with the hammer. "How many nails do we have? I need to know so I can figure out how far to space the holes."

"Looks like about ten." Courtney fished the nails out of the small box of odds and ends.

Elijah made a suggestion. "Perhaps we can pull a few nails out of the walls. I noticed Everett had several pictures hanging around the apartment."

"Good idea. Bring them to me when you get them pulled out." Kevin continued bashing holes out of the door with the hammer.

Everett took down the picture over his couch and handed it to Elijah. He then began pulling the nail out with the pliers, being careful not to bend it. He stepped down from the couch, handed the nail to Sarah to take to Kevin and took down the picture near the door to retrieve that nail as well.

"Nobody move a muscle!" A raspy female voice called from the other side of the broken window. "You people are looting in the wrong complex. You've got one minute to clear out or we'll kill you dead where you stand! And come out with your hands over your heads, single file and if you've got weapons, you better leave them on the floor. If you place any value on your life, you'll do exactly what I say."

Everett held the hammer over his head and slowly turned to look out the window. A monster of a man was holding a pump action shotgun, pointed right at Kevin. The man looked to be well over six feet tall and nearly obese. Next to him was another man, slightly shorter and very muscular leveling a rifle at Everett. Behind and between the two men was the source of the voice. An extremely thin woman with an exceptionally short black skirt and a midriff tight white shirt, long black hair, blood-shot eyes and a nickel-plated .45 automatic pistol that moved from person to person with her eyes.

"Vanessa?" Everett said cautiously.

"Everett? No way!" the woman who was much too young for such a raspy voice lowered her pistol. "It's okay Tiny, you and Ronny wait for me downstairs."

The two men on either side slowly lowered their weapons. "You sure?" the enormous one asked.

"No Tiny, I need to think it over for a while." Vanessa said sarcastically.

Tiny huffed and led the way down the stairs. "Come on, Ronny."

"So can I come in?" Vanessa asked.

Everett cracked a smile and unlocked the front door. "You're still here."

Vanessa walked in and ignored the others. Her eyes looked Everett up and down. "Yeah. What are you doing here? You look really good."

Courtney cleared her throat and crossed her arms.

Vanessa, still holding the gun rolled her blood-shot eyes toward Courtney and said with a hint of a snarl. "Healthy, I mean. Anyone who isn't dead is doing above average." She walked over and sat on the couch, letting the shiny 1911 pistol lay at her side. "All that banging woke me up, and I was sure it was looters up here. It's been crazy, you know. We've been trying to keep them scared off, maintain some type of order until the GR can get this area secured. Sorry I look a little crazy, we had a party last night. I'm having another one tomorrow night; you're welcome as usual. Bring your friends, but they have to bring something. Either booze, party supplies or something to trade for them.

"Enough about me, where have you been?"

Everett glanced at Courtney's scowl then back to Vanessa. "My Uncle had a cabin out in the country. I've been laying low." Everett continued with the cover story they'd devised beforehand. "We just came back to look for work."

Vanessa sat up on the couch. "Are you going back to accounting or whatever you did for the old government?"

Since Everett wasn't supposed to disclose that the CIA was his employer, he'd generally told most people that he worked for the GAO. There was nothing like telling people that you were a bean counter to get them to quit asking you questions about your job. "We'll see. I hear there's tons of jobs in Washington."

"Yeah, maybe if you know someone. My real estate gig is over, since the GR is handling all housing requests. I applied to the government agency that is over assigning living quarters, but I haven't heard anything back. If you still know some people with the new government, put in a good word for me.

"For now, I'm working at a club on H Street. It's changed a lot, but H Street is still the entertainment district. It looks more like Amsterdam, Vegas or Ibiza than DC. It's pretty cool, you guys should come check it out tonight after you're done job hunting."

Vanessa flicked her right wrist and a phone interface lit up on her skin. She slid her finger across the screen and selected her contacts. "Did you get your Mark implant already? What's your number?"

Everett shook his head. "No. There were no census stations out where I've been staying. We'll probably get them in DC, if the lines aren't too long."

She flicked her wrist again, turning off the pico projector just under the skin on the back of her hand. "You'll have to get them before you apply for a job, even if you worked for the old government. They're not bending on that one."

Vanessa stood and gave a slight tug to the edge of her skirt, which didn't do much. "Well, I better let you guys get back to whatever you were doing. I've got to get a little hair of the dog; I've got a nasty hangover coming on."

"Good seeing you again." Everett waved.

Vanessa gave him a hug and a kiss on the cheek. "You, too."

"Before you go, can you tell me where the soft perimeter runs? I'm trying to get by as many checkpoints as possible. I just don't want them to give me any grief over not having my Mark yet." Vanessa had always run with a seedy crowd. Everett had been to enough of her parties to know that if anyone would know how to get around the authorities, she would.

Vanessa stuck the gun under her arm pit and pulled a pack of cigarettes out of the waist of her mini skirt. She looked at Elijah, Kevin, Courtney and Sarah with a glare of mistrust. "Come outside. I need a smoke."

Everett understood that he was the only one invited. "I'll be right back." He closed the door behind him and walked out to the landing above the stairs.

Vanessa lit her cigarette and handed the pistol to Everett. "Hold this for me." She took a long deep drag and held the smoke while she flicked her wrist. She pulled up her map application and zoomed in on New Atlantis. "I freakin' love this thing. I would either get so high that I'd lose my phone or I'd spill a pitcher of margarita on it and ruin it at least once every other month." Smoke poured out of her mouth like a dragon as she spoke.

She held her arm close to Everett so he could see. "The fence only runs to Leesburg Pike. So if you take Georgetown along the river, you can get all the way to the beltway before you hit a checkpoint. But you can't get a vehicle past the beltway."

"What do you mean? Is it possible to get by with no vehicle?"

"You can walk under the beltway, along the river. They watch for boat traffic, but if you wear dark clothes and stay in the tree line, you can get in and out through there at night." She pointed to the place where I-495 crossed the Potomac. "There's some traffic moving through there all the time. Obviously, the GR outlawed guns, but then they don't provide security, so what are we supposed to do?"

"Yeah, I hear you. Your secret is safe with me."

She took another long deep draw from her cigarette. "And what about your crew? Are they cool?"

Everett gave her a nod. "Yeah, they're cool."

"Okay, I trust you. If you vouch for them, I believe you. Anyway, back to what I was saying. The new government legalized drugs, but things were a lot better when they were illegal. Now it's more expensive, they're rationed like everything else, and for the people who depended on the previous illegal status of drugs for their second income, it flat out sucks." She had a look of disgust as she exhaled the next puff of smoke.

Everett knew she was referring to herself. Her late night get-togethers functioned similarly to a Tupperware party, only instead of Tupperware, she'd offer cocaine, pot, molly, and ecstasy, always offering generous discounts to anyone who was looking for sufficient quantities to join her multilevel marketing network. He had never been into drugs, and he certainly had no interest now, but knowing someone with connections to the underground had an unquestionable value in the new world. "Where one door closes, another door opens."

"Whatever." She swiped her finger across the

projected screen on her arm and held it up for Everett to see the details of the map. "If you can stay in the woods until you get to Potomac Heritage Trail, take that along the river, cross over Chain Bridge to the tow path. That will run right into the Capital Crescent Trail, you'll be able to take that all the way into DC."

"Good call. I didn't realize the trail went so far up the river. Is it heavily patrolled?"

"Hardly anybody uses it, especially that far out. And then by the time you get downtown, it's full of joggers and walkers." She sucked the last drag of the cigarette and flicked it out into the street. "Come on by tomorrow night if you're still around." She started down the stairs. "Bring your friends if you like." She stopped to turn and gave him a wink. "Or come alone. Whatever."

He chuckled and waved. "Okay. See you later."

When Everett walked back in the apartment. Kevin and Elijah were nailing the second door to the inside of the window.

"Did you get her number?" Courtney's arms were crossed tightly and her jaw clenched even tighter.

"Seriously?" Everett let his mouth hang open in utter surprise. "That chick is a total crack head. You must be joking!"

"She's a total hooker is what she is." Courtney turned her back to him.

"Whatever she is, she has a line on the underworld and that's an asset we might need to exploit. You worked in intelligence. You were a profiler. Never in a million years would you think that I'd hook up with somebody like that if your mind wasn't being clouded by emotion."

Courtney still wouldn't look at him. "You seemed to know each other pretty well. You never told me about her. There must be something to hide."

"If you're wondering if we ever hooked up, the answer is no. She had parties all the time downstairs, and sometimes on the weekends, I'd go hang out. It was better that going to a bar and driving home. But like you, I'm a different person than before I knew Jesus."

Courtney softened her stance at that statement. "Okay, I don't want to talk about it anymore."

Everett started to say something else, but saw Sarah out of the corner of his eye. She was shaking her head and seemed to be whispering, "Let it go."

He walked away to check on the progress with the door. Kevin had removed his bracelet and was taking it apart.

"Paracord?" Everett asked.

"Yep. I'm pulling it apart. I'm going to use the inner strands to rig up a little surprise for anyone who wants to come through the window. I'll run the string from the door knob, up over the curtain rod then around the leg of the coffee table and on the trigger of one of the ARs. I'll brace the AR to the coffee table with the other strands from the paracord."

"And you think the AR will hit the potential intruder?" Everett considered the basic design of the booby trap that Kevin had just described.

"Maybe, maybe not. Either way, if you were

breaking in and heard a gunshot, would you keep going or retreat?"

"Point taken," Everett said.

"What if it's a kid trying to break in, just being curious? Won't you feel bad?" Courtney inquired.

Sarah's voice was despondent and dark. "There are no kids. All the children disappeared."

Everett lowered his head. This was something that Sarah had talked about several times. It was obvious that of all the people who disappeared, it was the two little girls in her group, Lacy and Lynette that bothered her the most. It wasn't like she was sad for them, after all, they'd been spared much misery, but it was like Sarah didn't want to live in a world without the laughter and purity of children.

Kevin continued running the line around the curtain rod and to the weapon on the coffee table. "Do you think your little friend will have the good sense to not try breaking in here after we leave?"

"I hope so. If not, she'll either get a bullet hole or a good scare." Everett looked over his shoulder at Courtney who was obviously trying to hold back a smile. He smiled and shook his finger at her as a lighthearted disapproval of her somewhat sadistic nature.

"What? I didn't say anything." She now had an ear-to-ear grin.

He put his arms around her neck and pulled her in for a quick kiss. "No, but you thought it."

"Let's try to get the stuff in the apartment before the hooker completely sobers up and starts eyeballing our gear." Sarah headed toward the door.

Everett, and Courtney followed her while Elijah and Kevin finished putting the final touches on the booby trap.

All of the gear was in the house in one trip, since there wasn't much. Everett broke open one of the packs and began handing out MREs. Between what Kevin had brought from Tennessee and several cases stashed by John Jones, the group had plenty of them. Everett and Courtney sat at the small table in the kitchen. The others sat on the stools at Everett's breakfast bar.

Over dinner, Everett explained what he'd learned about the smugglers passage along the river bank and it was decided that they would wait until nightfall and sneak past the checkpoint in the early morning hours rather than risk being detained for not having the Mark. They still had one more week of the amnesty period, but this was the belly of the beast, literally.

As they were discussing the plan to get past the beltway, there was a knock at the door. Everett pulled his pistol and got up to check the peep hole. He shook his head. It was Vanessa again. She was cleaned up, dressed and evidently ready to go to the club where she worked. He opened the door. "Hey."

"I forgot to mention. We keep our curtains closed at night. Light is a good signal that there's something worth stealing. They won't turn your electric service back on until you get registered and take your Mark, but even candles will let looters know you're here. And where there's people, there's probably stuff worth robbing. Anyway, be safe, and pop by tomorrow night if you can." She waved as she turned to leave.

Kevin pulled his shirt tail back over the handle of his pistol. "She's got street smarts. I'll give her that."

"Hmm." Everett locked the door. "I suppose people like that have been operating on a more surreptitious level for years."

"Says the guy from the CIA." Sarah smiled. "It's true, certain people are able to adapt to a covert lifestyle faster than others. The girl in our group who disappeared, Cassie, she saw all of this coming. We listened to enough of her crazy conspiracy theories to drop out of the system just in time."

Sunrise was around six-thirty, so they'd leave the apartment at three. That would give them time to find a good spot to stash the car and work their way up the river bank in the dark. The group stayed in the apartment and rested until just before the time they'd decided to leave. They took turns keeping watch while the others slept.

Everett got a few hours of sleep, which was better than nothing, but his mind wouldn't turn off. Even as he slept, he was haunted by the anticipation of sneaking into DC and the ghosts of the past which came roaring back with his visit to his old apartment. He remembered his days at the CIA, the clandestine meetings with John Jones, who'd warned him of the coming tribulation and the New World Order.

Finally, it was time to leave. Everett got up from the couch, laced up his boots and tapped Courtney on the shoulder. "Let's get rolling." Everett walked back to his bedroom to tell Elijah it was time to go. He opened the door to find the old man lying face down on the floor. "Elijah!"

"What is it?" The old man turned over quickly.

"Oh, I thought . . . I thought something had happened to you."

"No, no. Nothing will happen to me until the appointed time."

Everett helped him up from the floor. "What were you doing on the floor?"

"Praying."

"With your face on the ground?"

"Yes. I want to make sure I am ready to confront Luz when I see him."

Everett was somewhat confused. Both by seeing Elijah praying like that and by wondering how the man intended to get an audience with the supreme leader of the New World Order. "Okay, well, it's time to go."

Elijah brushed the front of his shirt and pants to straighten them. He grabbed his jacket and said, "Then let us go."

Half an hour later, the team was in the car and driving down Georgetown Pike, which was quite rural.

"How far til we hit the beltway?" Kevin asked.

"It should be about two miles from here." Everett continued to observe the roads on the left, looking for a good place to leave the car and access the river bank.

"Then we need to be finding a spot quick. Headlights can travel a long way, especially if the

GR has an observation post up high. The last thing we want to do is run out of space and have to turn around. That would be very suspicious."

Everett dropped his speed so he could get a better look at the signs as they drove by. A white split-rail fence ran along an open pasture for horses. "Madeira School, it looks ritzy. I doubt that place is up and running yet. Even if it is, there shouldn't be anyone there this early."

Courtney leaned forward from the back seat. "But if it's open, we might get towed when the administrators show up and find a car with no parking pass."

"Good point." Everett began to drive on by.

Kevin pointed down the side road which displayed the sign. "Why don't we take a spin down the road and see. I'm sure we'll be able to tell if it's open. If it's full of broken windows and the grass hasn't been cut since the collapse, it's probably safe to say it's not functioning."

Everett turned sharply to avoid missing the entrance. They saw no signs of other people as they proceeded down the long path. They passed the school grounds and Everett saw yet another sign. "Camp Greenway. It looks like a separate summer camp. I'm sure that place won't be up and running. Plus, it puts us closer to the river. I'd say we've found our spot. Elijah, what do you think?"

"It's your car and you're driving. You make the decisions."

Everett did not want to be responsible if something went wrong, but there was no use having the same conversation over and over with the old man. As badly as he wanted to remind him that it was Elijah's mission, he simply found a secluded spot at the end of the road to park the car.

They quietly got out of the car, and began working their way down toward the bank of the river.

Sarah took a long drink from the jug of water they'd brought. "Everybody hydrate. We've got some water and we have a good filter so we can resupply straight from the river, but that's pretty suspicious activity, so we don't want to, unless it's our only option."

Courtney took the jug next, had several drinks, and then passed it to Everett.

Kevin looked up at the sky. "We've got a crescent moon, so not much light. We really have to avoid using flashlights unless we absolutely need them. I've got one light with a red filter, which won't travel as far, so if we get stuck and have to use it, I'll lead the way then shine the light for each of you to follow over to me.

Everett and Kevin carried two small packs with food and water for the trip. While they had less than two miles to the beltway, they'd still have another twelve miles into DC proper.

The first leg of the journey was fairly smooth. Sarah walked next to Kevin who was accustomed to helping her navigate uneven terrain. Many places they had to traverse were rather steep. They approached a small water fall which required using rocks for stepping stones. Sarah used her walking stick to support her weight with one hand and Kevin steadied her with the other hand. Soon, they could see the I-495 bridge crossing the Potomac and moved deeper into the tree line. The checkpoints were only on the exits, but they did not want to be spotted by a chance patrol that might be on the beltway.

They passed through without incident.

"We made it!" Courtney whispered excitedly.

Everett gave her hand a squeeze. "Let's celebrate when we make it back out."

It had taken more than an hour to traverse the rough terrain. They had only another couple hundred yards before they would hit the Potomac Heritage Trail which would allow them to follow the river, cross over Chain Bridge to the Chesapeake Tow Path and finally connect with the Capital Crescent Trail, a paved foot path which would take them straight into downtown DC. It was roughly a thirteen-mile trek, but having an even walking surface would greatly speed up their time.

Moving at a slow steady pace which allowed for occasional breaks, they reached Washington circle at 10:30 AM.

Elijah lifted his arms in the air. "And here we are. This very spot marks the lower left point of the pentagram formed by the streets of Washington DC." He pointed down K Street. "The convention center, fourteen blocks down, marks the lower right point." He pointed toward the northeast. "Connecticut Avenue and Vermont Avenue converge at the White House, to create the lowest point, or the mouth of the Goat of Mendes. Quite fitting if you think about it."

Sarah looked around the circle and pointed

toward a red brick building. "Wouldn't a street have to intersect Washington Circle right here to make a pentagram?"

"Very astute." Elijah laughed and nodded his approval. "Rhode Island Avenue terminates at Connecticut Avenue, leaving the only opening in the perfect inverted star."

"So it's not a complete pentagram." Sarah looked at Elijah as if he were making up something that wasn't really there.

"In deep pagan mysticism, the pentagram, which represents the star, Sirius, is a gateway for summoning vile spirits. The single broken arm, acts as a door and allows them to leave the control of the conjuror, free to enter into our world, unrestrained." Elijah waited for Sarah's reply.

She shivered and turned away without challenging his explanation.

"Come. Let us find this malignant creature that we might not weary ourselves in this God-forsaken city any longer than need be." Elijah began walking south on 23rd Street.

Everett held Courtney's hand as they followed. He was pleased, both because Elijah was taking the lead and telling them where to go, and because he seemed determined to get this field trip over with. Everett felt a sense of nostalgia and loss as they continued down 23rd, past the buildings of George Washington University, where he'd attended college. He considered what he'd learned about the world during his time there and how wrong most of those notions were.

Elijah turned toward the left, and followed

Virginia Avenue. The elderly man seemed to have found a renewed source of energy, marching steadfastly in the direction of the Washington Monument.

Everett was in good shape, as was the rest of the team, but they all found themselves breathing heavily to keep up with the much older man.

Once they reached Constitution Avenue, Elijah headed east, quickening his pace to almost a jog. He finally slowed down when they reached 14th Street, but kept walking toward the new GR Ministry of Religion Building, which was being erected on the National Mall, directly across from the Washington Monument.

Elijah pointed out the newly erected replica of the archway to the entrance of the Temple of Baal which sat near the base of the Washington Monument. "Yet another passage way for every unclean spirit. And what a fitting place, at the bottom of an obelisk, the ancient phallic symbol of sun god worship."

Everett looked over the archway and then turned around. He stared at the new Global Republic General Assembly Building, which now occupied the field that he'd once looked across for an unobstructed view of the Capitol Building. It seemed surreal. He'd always thought of the National Mall as sacred, a place no one would dare construct a building, particularly this hideous architectural nightmare. The thirteen-story building was stepped as it ascended toward the sky, like a ziggurat from a lost city of ruins, deep in the jungles of South America. There were few other buildings in DC which clashed with the other buildings of the city which were modeled after Greek or Roman temples.

Courtney seemed to know what he was thinking. "They have a glass pyramid at the Louvre. It's not really any worse than that."

Everett pursed his lips. "It's worse."

Kevin was less concerned with the heinous crime against aesthetics and pointed at a trench where the footer of the new Ministry of Religion building was being prepared. "Look at those."

Everett turned his attention to where Kevin was pointing. "Giant rubber separators, why would anyone put those under a building?"

Kevin continued to stare at the devices being installed in the footer. "Those are called seismic isolators. They're layers of rubber and layers of metal with a lead cylinder core. The lead is soft, so it can bend without breaking if it needs to. When a quake hits, the ground can move independently of the rest of building, so less destructive energy is transferred into the structure. The isolators basically act as shock absorbers for the building."

Sarah crossed her arms as she looked at the series of devices which were mounted with heavy steel plates on top and bottom. "So the Antichrist and the designers of this building actually believe what the Bible says about the coming earthquakes, yet they're going to keep fighting against God? That makes no sense."

Everett said nothing as he looked at Sarah, wondering if she saw the irony of the statement she'd just made.

Sarah looked up from the area being prepared for the foundation of the building. "I don't believe it!"

Everett turned to see what she was looking at. His heart nearly stopped. Angelo Luz was walking with an entourage of his staff, including Former President Clay, the new Minister of Religion, Jacob Ralston, and a host of other dignitaries, flanked by several GR elite guards wearing their black helmets with the red shield and black dragon insignia. The group seemed to be looking over the progress of the new building.

Elijah stared at Luz with a piercing glare. "You there, son of hell, offspring of perdition, thou child of damnation. Hear what the LORD thy God will say to you and the judgment which he has pronounced against your unholy kingdom."

Luz turned slowly and looked at Elijah as if he recognized him. "A foolish old man who thinks he hears from God, I'm always looking for some comical amusement. Go on then, let's hear what you have to say, you troubler of Babylon."

Elijah pointed at Luz with disdain. "I have not troubled Babylon nor the earth, but it is you and your father's house, in that you have forsaken the commandments of the LORD, and have followed in the footsteps of your father, to exalt your throne above the stars of God to say that you are the most high. To you, man of iniquity, God says 'Thou shalt be brought down to hell, to the sides of the pit. They that see thee shall narrowly look upon thee, and consider thee, saying, is this the man that made the earth to tremble, that did shake kingdoms; that made the world as a wilderness, and destroyed the cities thereof; that opened not the house of his prisoners? Thou art cast out of thy grave like an abominable branch, and as the raiment of those that are slain, thrust through with a sword, that go down to the stones of the pit; as a carcase trodden under feet.

"And to the kingdoms and people over whom you rule, God says, 'You have waxed fat, and kicked: thou art waxen fat, thou art grown thick, thou art covered with fatness; then you forsook God which made you, and lightly esteemed the Rock of your salvation. You provoked him to jealousy with strange gods, with abominations provoked you him to anger. You sacrificed unto devils, not to God; to gods whom you knew not, to new gods that came newly up, whom your fathers feared not.

"'And now a fire is kindled in mine anger, and shall burn unto the lowest hell, and shall consume the earth with her increase, and set on fire the foundations of the mountains. I will heap mischiefs upon you; I will spend mine arrows upon you. You shall be burnt with hunger, and devoured with burning heat, and with bitter destruction: I will also send the teeth of beasts upon you, with the poison of serpents of the dust. The sword without, and terror within, shall destroy both the young man and the virgin.

"'See now that I, even I, am he, and there is no god with me: I kill, and I make alive; I wound, and I heal: neither is there any that can deliver out of my hand. For I lift up my hand to heaven, and say, I live forever. If I whet my glittering sword, and mine hand take hold on judgment; I will render vengeance to mine enemies, and will reward them that hate me. I will make mine arrows drunk with blood, and my sword shall devour flesh; and that with the blood of the slain and of the captives, from the beginning of revenges upon the enemy.'

"And now wilt the LORD shut up the heavens over this place that there be no rain over your throne until the times are fulfilled."

Luz laughed hysterically. "Old prophet, the number one rule of comedy is that you have to be quick on your feet. The sky is turning black; it's getting ready to pour at this very minute."

Everett looked up at the clouds that had formed since Elijah began his speech. They had completely blocked out the sun and darkness was falling on them as if it were night.

"If a single drop of rain falls from these dark clouds, then I am no prophet at all." Elijah turned and walked away.

Suddenly lightning struck the Washington monument, and was followed by a tremendous clap of thunder which made Everett duck his head. Courtney clasped his arm.

Just then another lightning strike hit the archway from the Temple of Baal. That was immediately followed by yet another lightning strike which hit the new GR General Assembly Building. Two loud booms of thunder trailed the lightning.

"Rain or no rain, we need to take cover, that was really close!" Kevin held Sarah's hand as he began walking very quickly back towards the Smithsonian.

"No. Not that way, follow me." Elijah walked in

the direction of the Washington Monument, cutting across the lawn towards Virginia Avenue.

Everett held Courtney's hand as they followed Elijah. Kevin and Sarah trailed along behind.

Luz yelled as Everett and the others ran, "You should take heed of the book the old man so zealously espouses, bad company corrupts good character. And the companion of fools suffers harm."

Everett knew the comment was intended as a threat. He glanced over his shoulder to see if any of the guards were pursuing them. None were, but one was talking on his radio, and Everett was sure he knew why. He had to sprint hard to catch up with Elijah. "I think we're going to have company. We should look for a place to lay low."

Elijah turned to look at Everett. "Yeah, maybe so."

The team continued a quick pace as they moved up Virginia Avenue. Everett took a quick turn onto 20th and called out to the others who were all within earshot, "If we can get back to the university, we can at least duck into the yard. It will be tougher to spot us from a vehicle."

It was a three-block sprint back to George Washington University, Everett led the way through a narrow walkway and into a courtyard where they wouldn't be visible from the street. They'd arrived in the nick of time. Sirens from New Atlantis Police cars could be heard just blocks away. Everett bent down, putting his hands on his knees and fighting to catch his breath, just as the others were doing.

"We can't stay here long. As soon as campus

security gets an alert, we'll be made." Sarah scanned the handful of students walking through the courtyard.

Everett thought fast. "They've probably only recently resumed classes and I can't imagine they've got a ton of people enrolled since the collapse. If we can tail someone with a security card in a door, we can go up to one of the upper floors where no classes are being held. Who knows, we might even find an unlocked door."

Kevin knuckled his brow. "I don't like it, but I can't think of anything better."

Everett replied, "Elijah looks like he could be a professor, and the rest of us aren't much older than the average student. Plus, we're wearing backpacks. I think we can pull it off."

"Then let's strike while the iron is hot." Courtney began walking. "There's my mark."

Everett looked at the slightly overweight young man walking toward the door that Courtney had nodded at. "What is she doing?" Everett watched as she sped ahead of everyone else, timing her arrival at the door to coincide with the boy she'd labeled as her mark. He observed her as she smiled at the boy and said hi, walking in the door behind him. Everett saw the boy acknowledge her, return the salutation, and bashfully turn away. Everett guessed that Courtney was roughly four leagues above any girl that had ever smiled at the boy, much less spoken to him.

Kevin patted Everett on the shoulder as he headed toward the door. "Operation honey pot is a success."

Everett forced a smile, as he didn't appreciate the comment. Seconds later, Courtney held the door open so the rest of the team could come in. They quickly located the stairs and made their way up to the third floor. Kevin took out his knife and unlocked the door to a vacant classroom. They stood near enough to the window to watch the police cars driving by, but far enough to not be spotted standing there.

"Now what?" Sarah asked.

Everett shrugged. "I don't know. I guess we wait and hope they call off the search."

Kevin walked around the room and took a seat at a desk. "I say we stay here until nightfall. And then break up into two teams, so we don't look like the group of five people the police are looking for."

Courtney sat down as well. "What if we just space ourselves out several yards? You guys take the lead as a couple. Elijah could follow fifty yards behind you then Everett and I can trail behind another fifty or sixty yards. Two separate couples and one man by himself. Then if we run into trouble, one of the other team could assist."

"Good idea." Everett looked at Kevin. "What do you think?"

Kevin nodded. "Yeah, but if we get into a firefight, we need a rendezvous point."

Sarah said, "The car. If we can get all the way back to the Camaro, it's probably safe to say we weren't followed."

Elijah nodded his approval. "Does everyone agree?"

Each of them gave some gesture to let it be

known that they concurred with the proposed course of action.

CHAPTER 9

And the third angel followed them, saying with a loud voice, If any man worship the beast and his image, and receive his mark in his forehead, or in his hand, The same shall drink of the wine of the wrath of God, which is poured out without mixture into the cup of his indignation; and he shall be tormented with fire and brimstone in the presence of the holy angels, and in the presence of the Lamb: And the smoke of their torment ascendeth up for ever and ever: and they have no rest day nor night, who worship the beast and his image, and whosoever receiveth the mark of his name.

Revelation 14:9-11

The next few hours passed very slowly for Everett. He listened for footsteps in the hallway then returned to monitor the street below. After repeating this motion several times, Courtney finally said, "Everett, can you please sit down? You're making me nervous."

He frowned, but complied with her request, for a while. As the sun began to set, he resumed walking back and forth to listen for footsteps and look out the window.

Minutes later, Kevin stood up. "It's pretty close to dark, and I'm not hearing anymore sirens. I say we move now."

Everett nodded. He'd had enough of the anticipation. Everett led the way out the door and down the stairs. When they hit the first floor, they ran into a security guard coming out of the stairwell.

"Can I see your pass?" he asked. Fortunately, he was armed only with a radio.

Everett restrained the panic he felt inside. "Sure." He smiled and reached toward his back pocket as if he were going for his pass. Everett quickly drew his pistol and leveled it at the guard's head. "Place your radio on the ground. And be super quiet. I'll kill you if you make a sound." Everett's face fell hollow. "You guys go ahead and start moving. We'll walk him back upstairs and restrain him. We'll catch up."

Kevin, Sarah and Elijah nodded and proceeded out the door.

Everett and Courtney hurried the guard up the stairwell to the classroom which they'd left unlocked in case they had to return. Everett held the gun on the man. "Strip down to your underwear."

The man complied without argument.

"Take his boots and pull his laces out. You can use those to secure him to a desk."

Courtney nodded and began removing the laces. Next, she began tying his hands behind his back. Once he was secure, Everett turned the desk toward the window and draped the guard's shirt over his head. "You better count to a thousand before you start yelling for help. I'm going to be quietly waiting right outside this door for the next five minutes. If you start yelling before I'm gone, I'll put a bullet in your head. Understand?"

The guard nodded.

Everett nodded to Courtney to walk out the door. Everett stuck the guard's radio in his backpack and the two of them headed back down the stairs. Once they were out the door, Everett pulled the radio back out to turn up the volume then returned it to his pack. He and Courtney walked quickly in the direction of the river.

Everett surveyed the street. Elijah, Kevin and Sarah were nowhere in sight. "They'll probably go back to K Street to get back to the river. We'll go up G, hit the river at the Watergate, and try to catch up with them at Washington Harbor."

Courtney looked nervous. "Okay. You know your way around better than me. I'm following you."

They kept moving fast. Soon, they'd passed the Watergate apartments and crossed Rock Creek Parkway. The foot path ran parallel to the parkway, which wasn't optimal for not being spotted by a police officer who might still be looking for them. Suddenly, the radio in Everett's pack sprang to life. "Denis, did you get your zone locked down? I need you back up front."

Everett paused to look at Courtney. "I'm betting they'll be looking for Denis real soon. The clock is ticking."

"Then we better keep moving," she said.

Everett followed the pedestrian bridge across Rock Creek. "That's Washington Harbor. I would imagine most of the restaurants in the complex have reopened to service the global citizens of the great New Atlantis. It would be a good spot to blend in and watch to see if Elijah and the others might pass by."

"Whatever you say."

The radio sounded again. "Denis, can you read me?"

"Boss, this is James."

"Go ahead."

"The police were looking for some fugitives earlier today, I . . ." The feed cut out.

Everett stopped to take the radio out of his pack. He fiddled with the antenna and looked up at Courtney. "I think we're out of range."

She pursed her lips. "We've heard all we need to hear. I'd say they're about thirty seconds from calling NAPD."

Everett turned the radio off and tossed it over the bridge into Rock Creek which flowed into the Potomac. "Then we better move and trust that God will get the others back to the car safely."

She nodded in agreement.

Everett looked in the other direction. "There's a boat rental place on the left. Let's see if we can cut a deal with someone."

"It's bound to be closed," she objected.

"Even better, come on." Everett moved quickly toward the docks. He soon spotted a worker who was rinsing the boats with a hose. "Hey! How's business been?"

The young man's arms were covered with tattoos, his nose, ears and eyebrows were riddled with piercings, but he was quite cordial. "We just opened March 1st. It's still too cold for people to be getting out on the water, but the boss said he's expecting the best season ever. All these people moving to DC with the UN, or GR, or whatever they call it. And you've got all the construction workers coming in, they've got money. Things were tough all around during the crash, but we bounced right back. I feel bad for the people in the rest of the country, but I think this guy Luz is going to get it all put back together. He's done a heck of a job here. He's a little heavy handed with the cops, but people were killing each other over a can of soup. I'm sure he'll lighten up when things get back to normal."

Everett hid his disappointment in the man's deception. Things would never be normal again, and Luz would be tightening the screws at every turn, he'd never lighten up. Everett wanted to ask the man what he thought about the disappearances; what he thought about Christ, but he could see the telltale blemish on the back of the man's hand where his Mark had been implanted. As Elijah had explained, once someone took the Mark and had renounced Christ, all hope was lost; their souls were damned.

Everett had to make some more small talk, after all, he was getting ready to put in a big request. "Did you get any business today?"

"Ha!" The man rolled his eyes. "Are you kidding? It looked like it was going to be an absolutely beautiful day. We had a few people take out some kayaks late this morning, first warm day since winter. Then, out of nowhere, a massive storm rolled up. Thundering, lightening, but then it never rained, not one drop. But the clouds hung around and that was the end of it for us. I've been doing busy work all day, just finishing up. I'm rolling up the hose and heading over to the harbor for a beer and a bag of weed. It's all legal now, if you can afford it."

"So you're here by yourself?"

"Yep, I get all the grunt work."

Everett pulled one of the gold American Eagles out of his pocket and handed it to the man. "Ever seen one of these?"

"Yeah, yeah. That guy from 24, he was selling these. My grandmother used to watch Fox News all the time, and he'd be on there all the time saying, buy gold. He was always in a helicopter, or on his ranch or something, talking about inflation and financial crisis." He tossed the coin gently in his hand as if to get a feel for the weight of it. "Huh. I guess he was right. I probably should have bought some. But I never really had much money. The only reason I ever paid attention to those commercials was because I liked 24 when I was a little kid. What's this thing worth?"

"It was over seven grand when they stopped valuing it in US dollars last November. Of course hyperinflation had already taken off at that point. But it was close to four thousand, even before the attacks." Everett could see the man making calculations in his mind about what he could do with it. "That's the new underground currency, gold and silver. Since Luz can track and tax every transaction with the Mark, people looking to do something outside of the system are using gold and silver coins."

The man nodded. "Yeah. My buddy gets some silver coins. He's got one just like this, only silver. He's also got some of the old quarters and dimes; they used to be silver. He uses them for . . . whatever."

Everett winked. "You can get a lot of . . . whatever with what you've got in your hand."

"Yeah, I bet." The man tossed the coin. "It's heavy. Is it pure gold?"

"22 Karat. That's a little better than 90 percent. They put some silver and copper in them so they don't scratch so easily. Pure gold is super soft and it'll dent if you drop it. Minted by the US government, which doesn't exist anymore, so it's a collector's item on top of everything."

The guy looked up at Everett with untrusting eyes. "And you're telling me all of this because?"

"We'd like you to take us on a boat ride." Everett could hear the sirens in the background.

The man looked at the coin then at the boat

house. "Hmm."

Courtney squeezed Everett's arm and smiled at the man. "It's a special night for us. It would be so romantic. Please?"

The man looked at the coin again then looked back toward DC, in the direction of the sirens. He seemed to have made the connection.

Everett waited to see the man's reaction, and mentally rehearsed how he'd abduct and restrain him if he didn't agree to the request. He focused on not showing his determination.

"Romantic river cruise, huh?" The man stuck the coin in his pocket. "I don't want to know anything else. If we get caught, I can't get in much trouble as long as I don't know anything. I don't want to know your name; you don't need to know mine. I'm just being a nice guy and taking you for an evening ride on the river. And, if you get caught, I did it out of the kindness of my heart, no mention of a coin, right?"

Everett nodded.

"And don't try to pull anything on me. I've been around." The man gave them both a very serious look.

Everett held his hands in the air. "Your boat, your rules."

The man pointed toward one of the small power boats toward the middle of the dock. "Get in that one right there, and sit real low. The cops could be here any minute. I'm going to grab the keys and I'll be right back."

Everett nodded and held Courtney's hand as they made their way to the boat.

She stepped off the dock and into the small boat. "Do you think he'll turn us in?"

"You're the profiler, what do you think?"

"No way. He wants that coin. And he doesn't want to risk that we'll say something about it if he turns us in. Plus, this ain't his first rodeo."

"Then why are you asking me?"

She shrugged as she positioned herself in the back. "I suppose I'm a little less confident about my skills when it's our lives at stake."

He kissed her and put his arm around her. "You've still got it."

Seconds later, the man came jogging toward the dock. He tossed in a plastic bag. "I brought you some chips, soda and candy bars, in case you're hungry." He untied the rope securing the boat to the cleat on the dock and pushed off. He started the engine and asked, "Where to?"

"Up the river, past the beltway bridge." Everett took two sodas out of the bag, handed one to Courtney and opened the other. It had been months since he'd had a soda in a can. And it wasn't likely that he'd have another anytime soon. He hated that the man's soul was doomed for eternity and that it was too late for Everett to do anything about it.

POP! POP! POP! . . . Crack, crack. An exchange of gunfire could be heard nearby as the boat passed by Georgetown Waterfront Park.

Everett looked at Courtney. "That's them."

The man driving the boat shook his head as if he were wondering what he'd gotten himself into.

Everett climbed up toward the front. "Any chance I could get you to slow down for a second and pull over?"

Gunfire rang out again. The people on the waterfront began scattering in panic.

"No way, bro. I didn't sign up for all of this."

Everett held out another coin.

The man glanced at the coin. He was less insistent, but he was still shaking his head. "This is too serious for me, man."

Everett pulled out yet another coin.

"Seriously?" The man slowed down. He looked at the two coins for several seconds, and then finally took them from Everett, and stuck them in his pocket. "Listen, if we get caught, I'm going to say you told me you had a gun and that I had no choice."

"I completely understand. If we get caught, I'll say I forced you, and threatened to kill you." Everett was glad that the man was coming around.

A long barrage of pops and cracks mixed with automatic gunfire rang out and it was obvious that it was coming from just ahead of them, on the other side of the Francis Scott Key Bridge. Everett pointed forward. "Start making your way toward the bank once we get under the bridge. The man increased the speed to go under the bridge.

Courtney pointed. "Look! There they are!"

Sarah and Kevin were walking slowly, close together. Sarah seemed to be assisting Kevin as if he were injured. The boat was between the Bridge Boathouse and the Washington Canoe Club.

Everett patted the man on the back. "Pull up next to the second dock."

The man did so.

Courtney waved her hands, but Sarah didn't see her.

"Stay with the boat." Everett said to Courtney as he leaped onto the dock. He got Sarah's attention and ran to help her with Kevin who was bleeding badly from his torso. Everett wrapped his arm under Kevin's armpit to help him to the boat. "Come on man, we've got a ride. You'll be okay."

By the time they'd gotten Kevin in the boat, it was apparent that he might not be okay. He was squirming in pain and seemed to be close to losing consciousness.

The second Sarah was in the boat she shouted, "Go, go, go!"

The man sped off quickly, still shaking his head as if he was really regretting his decision.

Sarah took the pistol still gripped in Kevin's hand. She placed it with her own into the pack and retrieved a small first aid kit. She pulled out a pair of EMT shears and began cutting Kevin's shirt off. She handed some gauze to Courtney. "Press against the wound with this."

Courtney followed her instructions.

Everett held Kevin's head in his lap. Blood was coming out of his mouth and his eyes were beginning to roll back. "Come on, buddy, you're going to be just fine. Stay with me."

Sarah blotted the continuing flow of blood from Kevin's body with the cut up shirt. "Oh, no! He's been hit three times. He's got two in the gut and one in the chest."

Everett wiped the blood from Kevin's mouth with the sleeve of his jacket. Kevin had completely lost consciousness and his breathing was growing more shallow.

Sarah pointed to the spurts of air coming out the hole in Kevin's chest. "His lung has been punctured." She took a circular bandage from the kit which read ACS on the packaging. It had a short rubber flange in the middle. Sarah centered it over the hole in his chest. Air and blood continued to come out of the tube with each breath, but the tube closed to prevent air from going back in.

"See if you can lean him up, so I can wrap this around his gut wounds," Sarah said.

Courtney helped Everett lift Kevin into an upright sitting position. Sarah then opened another package which said The Emergency Bandage. It looked like an Ace bandage with a large piece of gauze and a compression cleat. She strategically attempted to cover both wounds with one bandage. "Okay, lay him down."

Everett looked up and saw the I-495 bridge. He pointed to the left. "You can drop us off on the bank about a mile up."

They soon reached the shore, close to where they'd parked the car. Normally, Everett wouldn't have been dropped off so near the vehicle, but they were not going to be able to move Kevin very far. The needed to get him to the vehicle immediately.

The man pulled up to where Everett had instructed. They fireman carried Kevin's limp body out of the boat then Courtney gathered the backpacks from the small craft.

Everett handed the man yet a fourth coin. "Take this for your time and head on up river another few miles before you turn around to go back. That's the best thing for you and for us. Sorry about all the blood."

The man gladly accepted the tip. "Don't even worry about. I'll wash it out when I get back to the dock. And trust me, I'll take my time about getting back. I hope your friend makes it. Good luck."

"Thanks." Everett waved as he pushed the boat off from the shore.

Everett held his flashlight with his teeth as he carried Kevin by the feet. Courtney and Sarah supported him by one arm each as they made their way through the woods and back to the car. Once they arrived, they laid Kevin out in the back seat. Sarah sat in the rear with his head in her lap. Everett shined the light one last time back towards the bank. "I don't see Elijah. We've got to get Kevin back to the apartment. I'm sure he can find his way back from here."

"I agree." Courtney gave a short nod and got in the passenger's side.

Everett started the engine and drove at a steady clip back to the apartment, being careful not to do anything that would attract the attention of a police car. They arrived back at the apartment without incident. Everett and Courtney quickly jumped out and opened the back door to help Sarah get Kevin out of the vehicle.

Sarah sat silently, stroking Kevin's hair with tears streaming from her eyes. "He's gone."

Everett's heart sank. Unwilling to accept what he'd been told, he said, "Let's get him upstairs. Maybe we can revive him with CPR."

Sarah stayed still. "It's no use. Even if we could revive him, he'd need serious surgery at a fully staffed, fully stocked trauma unit. We can't take him to the hospital. It would jeopardize us and if they could save him, he'd be a prisoner. He wouldn't want that." She stared at his lifeless face. "He never had a chance with those wounds."

Courtney put her hand on Sarah's shoulder. "I'm so sorry, but we can't stay here. Let's get him upstairs. We can at least get him cleaned up. We'll take him home and find a peaceful place for him to rest."

Sarah seemed to have no energy, no will to go on. "Okay."

Courtney wiped the tears off of Sarah's chin. "You just get yourself upstairs. Everett and I will get Kevin to the apartment." She motioned for Everett to pull Kevin by the arms as she took his feet.

Everett walked backwards up the stairs while Courtney followed. Everett had to rest him on the ground when they reached the landing, so he could open the door. Next, they carried his body to the bedroom and laid him on the bed. Sarah was still sitting in the car. Courtney went back to help her out and up the stairs. Everett grabbed the bags, locked the car and followed the girls to the apartment. As he climbed the stairs, he went over the day in his mind. How had this happened? Wasn't God supposed to protect them? Why had God allowed Kevin to die? He was on the verge of placing his faith in God. Now, not only was Kevin's soul lost for eternity, but Sarah would never trust in him. And why should she? Everett had gone from not believing in God, to wondering if he existed, to believing, to trusting, to anger. As he thought through how they'd come to go on this asinine quest, he shook his head. "Why did I listen to this idiot? This crazy old man who thinks he's a prophet? Why am I blaming God? I'm the moron that believed this old fool."

Immediately, Everett felt bad for blaming Elijah. He found the larger packs they'd brought and fished out some clean clothes and wondered where Elijah was. "It wasn't his fault. He can't help it if he's insane. Kevin is dead because I didn't have the good sense to tell the old man no."

Everett took the cleaning bucket from under the kitchen sink and walked downstairs to the service water faucet that the landscape crew used. He filled the bucket and took it to the bathroom to clean himself up by candlelight. As he emptied his pockets, he looked at the last gold coin. He wondered what mind easing substance he could buy from Vanessa. Anything that would take away this sense of self-hatred and guilt.

He stared into the mirror as he rinsed his face with the cool water. He continued to wash up. He knew he wasn't going to get high or drunk. As tempting as it sounded, that wasn't the answer. He felt a strange peace coming from somewhere deep inside and he wondered if that could possibly be coming from God. This was all new to him. He wiped his face with the damp cloth and looked up. "God, even after I'd blamed you, even after I've been angry with you, would you still try to comfort me?"

He began to cry and the tears seemed to cleanse his soul, just as the washcloth wiped away the grime from his face. "I'm sorry, God. I'm trying to trust you but this isn't easy and it's not what I expected."

Once he'd finished washing and changing into clean clothes, he walked into the bedroom with Courtney and Sarah. Sarah was holding onto Kevin's hand and weeping. He was the only person she had left in this brutal world.

Minutes later, Everett said, "I'll get him washed. If you girls want to go freshen up. We'll give Elijah a few more hours to get back, but we should probably try to get home before sunrise."

Courtney held Sarah's hand as she led her away to get cleaned up. Everett went back downstairs, drew a bucket of water to fill the bathroom sink for the girls, and then filled his bucket to wash Kevin's body.

Afterwards, Sarah and Courtney helped Everett put clean clothes on Kevin's cold stiffening body and wrapped him in a fresh white sheet. Once that was finished, Sarah laid her head on the corpse and cried.

Everett and Courtney sat next to her, but she refused to be comforted.

Everett patted Sarah's back. "Do you think you can eat something? We'll need our energy if we hit any trouble on the way home."

Sarah shook her head, but said nothing.

Everett tilted his head toward the door, signaling to Courtney that they should leave her alone to grieve for a while.

Courtney nodded. She gave Sarah a hug. "We'll be right back. If you get hungry, come on in the living room."

Courtney and Everett retrieved some food from the packs, ate together, and then took turns taking naps. Even without the toll on their emotions, the stress, and physical exertion of the day, they'd been up for nearly twenty-four hours and both of them desperately needed some sleep.

At 2:30 AM Everett lightly shook Courtney to rouse her from her slumber. "Time to wake up."

She rolled over, rubbing her weary eyes. "Is Elijah back?"

"No, we'll give him another half hour, but we've gotta go."

Courtney sat up. "Are there any instant coffee packets?"

Everett handed her a plastic water bottle filled with a dark liquid. "I already thought of that. It's cold, but it's coffee."

Courtney gave it a shake, unscrewed the cap and took a long swig. "Thanks. How is Sarah?"

"She's lying on the bed, next to his body. I think she fell asleep."

"That's good. Just let her sleep until it's time to go." Courtney took another drink.

Two taps on the door were followed by a series of two more taps.

"That's him, that's Elijah. I know his knock." Everett stood up from the couch.

"Check the peephole, just to be sure." Courtney was excited.

Everett peered out the small aperture, unlocked

the dead bolt, and opened the door. "Hey, you made it!"

Courtney walked over and hugged him. "We were so worried about you!"

Sarah walked into the room, her eyes swollen from crying and fatigue. She didn't smile. "Your God let Kevin die. He was all I had. Ask God why he doesn't just kill me, too."

Elijah's face lost the tender smile he'd had while hugging Courtney. "That is between you and him. You should ask him yourself. But, I'm sorry for your loss."

Sarah broke down in a fit of sobs and anger. "You're sorry for my loss? You? Man of God?" Her voice grew louder as she vented. "I'm sorry! I'm sorry we came on this idiotic quest of yours. I'm sorry I ever met any of you."

"Shhh." Elijah walked over to put his arms around her.

She fought him at first, but finally relented and let him hold her in his arms. She cried, "It's not your fault. I didn't mean that."

Elijah sat her on the couch and motioned for Everett and Courtney to come sit by Sarah. They did so and Elijah walked to the bedroom, closing the door behind him.

Ten minutes later, Sarah was calming down and her sobbing had subsided. Everett stood and checked his watch. "I'll start taking the packs and the rifles to the car."

Courtney nodded and continued to comfort Sarah.

Everett completed the task in two trips. He

walked to the door to knock and tell Elijah that they needed to go. But as he put his ear to the door, he heard him praying. The old man's voice grew in volume slightly with each sentence. Everett walked away.

Courtney stood. "What's he doing?"

Everett shrugged. "Praying, I think. I can't understand the language he's using. It might be Hebrew."

Courtney pursed her lips. "But we've gotta go. And we still need to put Kevin's body in the car. Have you thought about where you'll put him?"

"We have to put him in the trunk. I know Sarah isn't going to like it, but we can't be driving around with a dead body visible to passersby."

Courtney crinkled her nose. "It sounds so rude, but you're right. I can't think of any alternatives. Anyway, tell Elijah we should get going. He can pray in the car if he wants."

Everett nodded, and pecked on the door. "Elijah, we have to leave. Every second counts." Everett could hear through the door that the old man was still praying in what sounded like his native tongue. He seemed to be ignoring Everett. Everett rolled his eyes and shook his head.

Courtney walked over. "He's not listening?"

"No." Everett crossed his arms and leaned against the wall. "What should I do?"

"Give him a few more minutes, I guess." She leaned next to him.

Suddenly, the prayers stopped and the old man's voice fell silent.

Everett looked at Courtney. "You try knocking."

She did. "Elijah, sweetie, we have to go."

The door opened and Elijah stood in the doorway. "Bring him some water."

Everett was getting anxious to leave. "We cleaned him up before we wrapped him in the sheet. We need to get him to the car so we can get on the road."

"No!" Elijah's eyes were filled with fire. "Water to drink!" Elijah slammed the door closed.

Everett was taken back by Elijah's sudden change of demeanor, and even more so by his peculiar request. He looked at Courtney. "I don't even know what to say to that. We've got to leave now."

"Just get him some water. Elijah is probably really thirsty. He walked the whole way back from DC."

Sarah was up from the couch. "What's going on in there? What is Elijah doing to Kevin's body?"

Everett shook his head and went to retrieve a bottle of water from the small pack next to the door.

Sarah wasn't waiting for him to come back. She barged into the bedroom.

Everett returned with the water just in time to see Sarah's expression of extreme confusion as she fell unconscious and dropped to the floor. Everett and Courtney rushed to her side to wake her up.

Everett looked up at the bed. Elijah was sitting next to Kevin's body. The old man had removed the sheet and had Kevin sitting upright next to him on the bed. Everett fought to process what was going on. Was this some type of morbid prank? No wonder Sarah had passed out.

"The water. Give him the water!" Elijah stretched out his hand.

Everett looked at Kevin. His eyes were open. "He just blinked!" Everett's heart nearly stopped as he pointed at Kevin.

Elijah stood and grabbed the water bottle from Everett, handing it to Kevin who took it and proceeded to drink. Everett was dumbfounded.

Courtney just stared at Kevin, with her mouth open.

Kevin handed the bottle to Elijah and knelt on the floor next to Sarah. He shook her gently. "Wake up. Sarah, it's me. Everything is okay."

Everett watched in amazement as Sarah came back around, slowly realizing that Kevin was alive.

"Kevin?" Sarah's face was filled with confusion, as if she thought it might be a dream.

"It's okay. I'm here . . . I'm . . . alive." He pushed her hair back out of her face and kissed her.

"But, how did . . ." Her hand gripped his arm as he pulled back from the kiss.

"We were wrong. I was wrong." Kevin shook his head. "I've been so proud, I stood in judgement of God Almighty. I had no right. He's sovereign, I don't have to like everything he does, I don't even have to agree, but he is God of all and I'm just a man. And hell is real. It's a place of unfathomable misery and suffering, a place without hope. I can barely remember, thank God, but I was there. And I never want to go back. I've been given a second chance, we've been given a second chance, Sarah. We have to commit our lives to him, right now. Don't risk going there for one more second."

Tears of joy now streamed down Sarah's face, replacing the tears of sorrow. "Okay. So you believe in heaven and everything, right?"

Kevin nodded. "I've seen hell, so yes, if it's true, heaven must be also."

Sarah sat up and looked at Elijah. "What do we do? What do we say?"

Elijah pointed up. "Tell him. Tell him you're sorry for your pride, and all your sins. And tell him, where he leads, you will follow. Tell him that he is the God of your life, and it is no longer you yourselves. Then live according to that commitment." Elijah stood. "Come, this is between them and their father. Let us go, we must leave soon."

Everett and Courtney followed Elijah out of the room, leaving Kevin and Sarah alone to speak with God. Everett tapped his finger against his forehead. "Could Kevin have been merely sleeping? No, his skin was cold, his body was stiff. That man was dead, but now he's alive." Everett muttered to himself as he walked, contemplating all that he'd just witnessed.

A few minutes later, Elijah walked back to the bedroom. "Come along, we must go. You have the rest of eternity to commune with your father, now that you have become his children."

Kevin and Sarah finally emerged, both smiling.

Kevin looked at Everett as he struggled to get up from the couch. "I don't want to weird you out or anything, but I'm . . . really well rested. I don't mind driving back. You guys look beat."

Everett smiled with one side of his mouth.

"Yeah, I'll take you up on that. If you see any trouble, give me a nudge and wake me up."

Indeed, it was strange to have a man who'd just returned to the land of the living driving them home, but Elijah, the man who'd resurrected him, was the greater source of Everett's uneasiness. Never again would he wonder whether the man was a lunatic or a true prophet of God. And neither would Everett question why they'd been summoned to accompany the old man on the bizarre expedition. Not only had his and Courtney's faith been strengthened, but it had been a monumental awakening for Kevin and Sarah, who probably wouldn't have come along, had he and Courtney not followed Elijah in his adventure.

The team loaded into the car expeditiously. Within minutes of getting back on the road, Everett was out.

He awoke when Kevin turned onto the winding mountain road which led up to the cabin from Woodstock. Upon their arrival, they were greeted by the loyal tail wags of Danger who had faithfully guarded the cabin, even though he'd not been left enough food for a forty-eight-hour trip. Sarah made feeding him a priority. Sox was less forgiving over not being adequately provided for as evidenced by his loud protests and his persistent weaving in between Everett's and Courtney's feet as if he wanted to trip them, until his food bowl had been filled.

The animals were fed, the car unloaded and the team was exhausted; all except for Kevin who said he wanted to stay up and read the Bible for a while before turning in. Elijah waved as he left in his truck, and Everett, Courtney and Sarah made their way to their respective sleeping quarters.

Minutes later, Everett was fast asleep.

CHAPTER 10

In all thy ways acknowledge him, and he shall direct thy paths.

Proverbs 3:6

Everett scratched his head as he woke from his deep hibernation. He tried to process why the sun wasn't brighter. It felt as though he'd been out for several hours, it certainly couldn't still be early morning. He stretched his arms and legs under the blanket. He was stiff from the mission, and very hungry.

Courtney roused and rolled over to face him. "Hey." She smiled with eyes half-open.

"Good morning. It must be raining outside. The light is so dim, but it has to be way past sun up."

She giggled. "Yeah, the sun is going down silly.

It's like six o'clock."

"At night?"

"Yes, it was almost five when we went to bed. You didn't wake up to go to the bathroom that whole time?'

"No. But I've gotta go now."

"Okay. I'll be here." Courtney rolled back over in the bed.

Everett put on his sweats and a hoody and made his way down the ladder. He went out back to answer nature's call and quickly returned. Kevin was sleeping on the couch, with Lisa's old Bible open and turned face down on the coffee table. Everett thought about the familiar scene when it had been Ken sleeping on the couch and Lisa in the back bedroom. Now he had another set of sanctified lovebirds sleeping in separate rooms. He chuckled at the thought. "Here we go again," he whispered.

Kevin awoke at the sound of Everett building a fire to make some rice. "How did you sleep?"

"Good, thanks." Everett arranged the tinder and took out one of the homemade fire starters that Ken had made before he disappeared. It was a cotton ball which had been soaked in a bit of leftover candle wax. Once lit, just a small piece of the cotton ball would act as a wick, burning the wax for several minutes, which was plenty of time to get the tinder burning. Ken had made them for starting fires when all the tinder from outdoors was damp, but Everett was hungry and wanted to get the fire going as quickly as possible. Since there was no newspaper, and he didn't want to take the time to go scrounge up dried leaves from outside, this was the method he chose to use. "Did you sleep?"

"Yeah. I read the Bible until about 11:00 AM. I've been out since then."

"That's great." Everett blew on the tinder to get it burning faster.

"I suppose you've figured out who the old man is, right?" Kevin sat up on the couch.

Everett turned toward Kevin. "I know he's a prophet. But I guess that's stating the obvious."

"I read I and II Kings last night."

Everett nodded. "You know, he told me to read that, but I didn't get around to it."

Kevin lifted his eyebrows. "You're going to want to read that when you can. There was prophet in those books, his name was Elijah. Through the power of God, he brought some woman's child back to life . . . just like me. He confronted the evil king back then. He prayed for a drought and it came. When it was his time to go, he was taken away in a chariot of fire. He never died."

Everett remembered the curious explanation Elijah had given him when he'd asked why he hadn't disappeared with the rest of the Christians. "Hmm. So, you think he's the same guy?"

Kevin nodded. "Then I read Revelation, to get an idea of what to expect next. Did you know it says there will be two witnesses? And they have power to make it not rain, turn water to blood and release plagues on the earth."

Everett listened closely. "He said something about his mission being to bear witness against the evil of the earth. I didn't know what he was talking about. And he told me there was someone else."

"So that's him, right?"

Everett nodded. "I guess so. What else did it say about him?"

"It said he'll wear sackcloth; what's that shirt he wore to DC made out of?"

Everett shrugged. "I don't know. It looked like burlap. Believe me, of all the crazy stuff he's said and done, that shirt doesn't even rank in the top 100. I didn't think to ask him about it."

"But it could be sackcloth, right?"

"I suppose. I can't say as I'm not that well acquainted with the material." Everett stood up from the hearth to retrieve the water for his rice. He returned and placed the pot on the cooking grate.

Kevin was reading from the Bible. "It also says he's going to be killed then come back to life in three days."

Everett's heart sank. Resurrection or not, he'd grown fond of the old man and did not want to see him suffer. "Does it say how he'll die?"

Kevin looked over the page. "No. It just says the beast will kill them, and the whole world will see their bodies lying in the street for three and a half days. Then they'll come back to life and ascend into heaven."

"Does it say where all this is going to happen?"

"It says where our Lord was crucified. So Jerusalem, I guess."

"Yeah, he said he'd have to go there eventually." Everett was saddened by the thought of Elijah leaving.

Courtney came down the ladder and into the living room. She hugged Everett and looked at

Kevin. "Hey, how'd you sleep?"

"Like the dead." Kevin winked.

"That's not even a little bit funny." Courtney tried to keep a straight face. "Okay, maybe a little, but I wouldn't try that joke on Sarah. She might send you right back."

She lifted the lid from the pot in the fireplace. "Rice?"

"Yeah. I thought I'd make a big pot. I want a bowl with a little sugar for now. Then I figured we could eat it with some smoked venison later," Everett said.

"Sounds good." Kevin reclined back on the couch. "What are your thoughts on hitting that census station up in Winchester?"

Courtney's mouth hung open. "Seriously? Boy! You're in a hurry to get killed again aren't you?"

"Not really, but I'm not afraid. I know I'm not going back to where I was. I don't know what heaven is like, but the simple fact that it ain't that place makes it good enough for me."

Everett looked at Kevin for a while, wondering if the man was brave or fool-hearty. "I don't know, Kevin. I'm pretty busted from that last mission. We've only got four more days of amnesty. We still need to get the rest of these supplies to the cave."

"We can get theses supplies moved in one day."

Everett pursed his lips. "We don't even have a plan. We did one quick drive by."

Kevin sat up and leaned forward on the couch. "Can't you get back in the comms satellite to get the delivery schedule for the facility? We really just need to know when a supply truck is coming in so we can hit it."

"I really doubt it. Passwords have been replaced with bio-authentication which is done through an individual's Mark. And even if I could create a workaround for the bio-authentication, which I can't; Dragon is up and running. You're talking about hacking into a system that is self-aware. It could literally triangulate the location of a hacker then locate and destroy him via drone. The only reason we got out of DC was because of the low hanging clouds, which prevented the drones from spotting us."

"Then we work around the technology. We go old school, human intelligence."

Everett rolled his eyes. "Ha! How, pray tell, do you recommend we do that?"

Kevin held his hands palms up. "We go hang around some bars, or wherever the truck drivers and guards are hanging out."

"We've got no Marks. We can't even buy a soda pop in a bar."

"We've got stuff to trade. There's an underground economy in Winchester. Guns are illegal and this is good-ol-boy country. I guarantee there's a well-established network of black market arms and ammo dealers. Come on, Everett, you're an intelligence analyst. You should be telling me this stuff."

Everett crossed his arms. It was one thing to know what to do, and quite another to know if it should be done. "Let's focus on getting the rest of these buckets out to the cave, and then see how much time we've got left."

Kevin nodded. "Great. We can get that knocked out tomorrow then we can go into Winchester on Friday to feel out the temperature around town. If it's too hot, we'll melt away and never come back."

Courtney shook her head. "We've got to get the garden going. The mountains have a really short growing season. I don't want to miss it. A few fresh vegetables can make a world of difference in extending our stored food and putting some better nutrition into our diet."

"Then Everett and I will go into Winchester on Friday, while you and Sarah get started on the garden."

The man with all the answers. Everett adjusted the pot on the cooking grate so the rice wouldn't boil over. He was not looking forward to another adventure.

The sun was down soon after they'd all gotten up, so there wasn't much that could be accomplished. When Sarah finally woke up, the four of them played cards until it was time to go back to bed.

Thursday's job of moving supplies progressed quite efficiently and much quicker than their first trip out to the cave. The team had developed something of a system for lugging the buckets from the trucks, to the cave, through the cavern, and up the ladder, into the long narrow storage corridor. Everett was glad to have moved the excess supplies out of the living room, both because he hated the state of disarray in the cabin, and because he understood the value in having their supplies diversified. He'd been able to deal with the last bunch of looters that had come to the cabin, but there were no guarantees that he'd have the same success in the future. In addition to the food, Kevin had brought a small arsenal of weapons and ammunition to the cave for safe keeping. They'd also taken some extra clothing to the cave. Some of it had been Ken and Lisa's. Not only would it be there for an emergency, but Kevin and Sarah needed the space.

Kevin gave Everett's shoulder a squeeze. "Look at that. We're finished before sunset. We'll be rested up and as right as rain to go to Winchester tomorrow."

Everett half grinned. "Lucky me."

Once again, the tiring day's work insured Everett and the rest a good night's sleep.

Everett was up early Friday morning, as was everyone else in the house. The girls would be working on the garden, while he and Kevin were heading to Winchester to see how much trouble they could get into, at least, that's the way Everett saw it.

They all had breakfast together. And since it was to be a long day for everyone, they had a huge breakfast. Grits, eggs, pancakes, and smoked venison, which lent itself to the morning meal.

Everett cut into a stack of pancakes, piled three high on his plate. "Lots of carbs and protein, exactly what we need."

"Your butt is going to be sitting in a car all day, we're the ones who'll be working." Courtney chided.

Everett wasn't amused. "I doubt that. We'll be walking around, looking for mischief, which could very well end up in running for our lives. Just like DC."

Courtney's face grew more somber. "I know. I was trying to lighten the mood. You be safe. And if it looks sketchy, you guys get out of there. Promise me you won't take any unnecessary chances, Kevin!"

Kevin finished a bite of grits and took a swig of coffee. "Cross my heart."

Sarah looked concerned as well. "Yes, please don't put me through that again, Kevin. I really don't think I can handle a repeat."

Everett saw no point in belaboring the issue, so he changed the subject. "Silver and gold coins seem to have emerged as the predominant black market currency. The guy in DC with the boat knew all about silver coins, and didn't need much convincing to believe gold trumped the white metal. We've got a little of each."

"Our team had a king's ransom in silver and gold coins, but they spent most of them on the mountain retreat. But we've still got a few coins left." Kevin cut into his smoked venison.

"Obviously, the reason you're going to Winchester is to try and secure two more years' worth of storable food, so you won't be offering any of that for barter. If no one is interested in coins, what's your back-up plan?" Courtney looked at Kevin.

He answered, "We brought enough guns and

ammo out here to start a war. Most of our group worked for the Sevier County Sheriff's Department or were prior military."

"Or both." Sarah crossed her arms.

Kevin leaned over to kiss her. "Or both. Anyway, that adds up to lots of battle rifles, pistols, shotguns and ammo. We could let go of a few firearms and still have more than we could ever shoot. We stashed four AR-15s, four 9mm Glocks, four shotguns and ammo for all of them in the cave yesterday."

Courtney rubbed her head as if she were thinking. "We got hit on the day of the disappearances. Aren't you worried you could be arming people who could end up attacking us?"

Kevin shook his head. "Winchester is a pretty long drive from here. I'd say the odds of someone from there assaulting us are pretty slim. The amnesty period expires on Monday. After that, traveling with firearms is going to get increasingly risky. A potential hostile would be taking a big chance to move firearms that distance, only to come up here on the mountain to shoot it out with us.

"Most of the people looking for weapons at this point are going to be causing problems for the Global Republic, and that's exactly the people I'd like to see have our extra guns. So, If I can use them to trade for information, I'd say it's a good deal."

Everett considered Kevin's reasoning. "Yeah, that makes sense. I agree with your plan. But we've got two more days besides today before the amnesty expires. I think we should just take a couple spare weapons for trade. We can sniff around town, and if we see the need for more guns, we'll make another trip."

"I can go along with that." Kevin smiled.

"What vehicle are you taking?" Courtney asked.

Everett looked at Kevin. "I recommend we take the F-150. A truck will blend in better in Winchester. But you don't want to drive the green truck, with government insignia on it."

"The F-150 is going to burn a lot more gas than the Camaro or the BMW. Plus, you've got no trunk to hide weapons," Sarah commented.

"The back seat flips up. We can get some guns and ammo under there," Kevin said.

Courtney echoed Sarah's concerns. "And your gear. You guys are taking packs with food and water, right? Are you going to leave those sitting out in the seats while you're walking around?"

Everett thought about the conundrum. "We'll put our gear in the floor of the backseat. The windows are tinted. No one can see in the back floorboard unless they're pressing their head up against the glass. We'll try to stay close to the vehicle at all times."

Kevin put his hand on Sarah's leg. "Would you let Everett take your Glock?"

"My 18C clone? That's asking a lot."

Kevin winked. "It increases my chances of coming home."

She got up and went to the back bedroom. She returned with the ordinary looking pistol and several 33-round magazines. She handed Everett the gun, pointing to a lever on the back of the slide. "Here's your select fire. It's set for full auto, because if you need it in a hurry, that's where you want it. If you need it for single fire, you'll probably have time to hit the lever. Bring my gun back! Even if you need to leave Kevin."

"Ha, ha! You're a real riot." Kevin gave her a sarcastic smile.

Everett took the pistol. "I'll take good care of them both."

Sarah sat in Kevin's lap and put her arms around his neck. "Even better."

Courtney reached across the table to put her hand on Everett's arm. "How are we going to know if you get in trouble?"

Kevin answered, "We've got radios. We'd be able to receive anything you girls transmit over the ham, but we won't have enough juice to transmit all the way back here, unless we're already on our way back up the mountain."

"That doesn't do us much good." Courtney wrinkled her forehead.

Everett thought for a while. "Maybe if we could reach a local ham, we could have them relay a message to you, so if we're not back by dark, keep the ham turned on and listen. I know the frequency it's set at right now, so don't change it."

Sarah lifted her eyebrows. "It's better than nothing."

Once breakfast was finished, Everett and Kevin loaded up the F-150 with the supplies they'd be taking along with a few silver coins, three pistols that had come from the sheriff's evidence room, two shotguns, and an AR-15 for potential barter items.

Elijah pulled into the drive, just as they were about to leave. He stepped out of his truck. "You boys are running off and leaving me here to work the land with the women, are you?"

Everett chuckled. "We've only got three days til the amnesty period ends. We have to strike while the iron is hot."

"Yes, yes, I know. But come, let me pray for you. Let us ask God to watch over you and bring you home safely."

Everett wasn't about to question the value of a prayer of protection from Elijah. And he was certain that Kevin needed no further convincing either. He walked over and took the old man's outstretched hand. Kevin took the other.

Elijah said a quick prayer and lifted his head. "Be wise, and hurry home."

Kevin looked up. "That's it? That wasn't very long."

Elijah was already walking toward the house. "It' not the length of the prayer, but the fact that you sought God's blessing in your endeavor."

Everett was also suppressed by the brevity. "I suppose if you want a longer prayer, you'll have to do it yourself. Let's hit the road. I'm ready to get this quest over with."

Kevin tossed the keys to Everett. "You know the area better, you drive."

The two of them were soon on the road and headed toward Winchester, which was about a one-hour drive. They listened to the local GRBN radio station, since it was the only one playing. It streamed a persistent flow of propaganda, telling of the wonders of Angelo Luz and his new utopia that would radiate out from the New Atlantis to the four corners of the world. Very little actual news was disseminated and none of it was new to Everett or Kevin. They saw very few vehicles on the road. Despite the promises of the New World Order, fuel was still hard to come by, and even for those with the Mark, it was prohibitively expensive.

Everett turned off the highway. His intention was to take Valley Pike into town. Valley Pike ran parallel to the highway. They were more exposed driving through the suburbs of Winchester, but it would allow them to get a better feel of what was going on in the town. As soon as he exited I-81, he pointed up Valley Pike. "We'll drive by the Gander Mountain store where we stocked up, right when everything was falling apart last November." As they approached the intersection to turn off for Gander Mountain, Everett pointed at the abandoned Citgo Station. "I bought gas from a crazy old man, right there. By then the pumps were empty from the attacks, but he was selling it for $50 a gallon. He was selling it out of an old rusted-out white van."

Kevin pointed at a white van in the run-down motel parking lot, next to the gas station. "Like that one?"

Everett looked over his shoulder. "Exactly like that one." Everett pulled a sharp U-turn. He slowly pulled into the lot of the seedy little hotel, which other than the old white van, was completely abandoned. Between the disappearances and the massive die-offs from starvation, typhoid, and violence, there were plenty of unoccupied homes, making a resurgence in demand for such unsavory establishments as this dirty little motel, highly unlikely.

An old man emerged from the door of one of the rooms, carrying a cardboard box toward the van. "Scratchy!" Everett pulled up next to the van.

"You know this guy?" Kevin sounded surprised.

"That's the guy I bought my gas from." Everett rolled his window down. "Hey, old-timer."

The man wore dingy overalls, and a faded ball cap. He had shifty eyes and stood near the back door of the van, with one hand concealed behind the door as he looked at Everett and Kevin. "I don't want no trouble, but I got somethin' for you if n' want some."

Everett smiled. "Let me guess, you've got a big shiny cowboy gun, a revolver with an eight-inch barrel behind that door."

"Maybe I do and maybe I don't. Who are you? State your business!"

Everett was having fun with the old man, but he was still careful not to make any sudden moves that might make the man nervous. Few people still around had come to live this long without having to kill someone. "Seriously? You don't remember me? I bought gas from you right there, in the parking lot next door."

The old man walked out from behind the van, sticking the long-barreled revolver in a shoulder holster that looked like he'd fashioned it himself from a regular holster, and a series of belts. "You're that city slicker ain't you?" The old man chuckled, revealing two uneven rows of heavily stained teeth. "Boy, I didn't recognize you in that truck. You're a fittin' in right nice. What'd you do with that smart-aleck hot rod you had last time?"

"Hot rods are great for the city, but a man needs a truck around these parts." Everett grinned.

"He might, he might. What cha lookin' fer? I bet you still got a pocket full of them dead presidents, but they ain't gonna do you a bit a good round here. If you want to trade, you need somethin' nice."

Everett cut the engine. "What do you have?"

"What do you have?" The old man pointed at Everett.

Everett knew Scratchy had something in the box he'd just loaded into the back of the van. And if he was still driving around, he had access to fuel. He decided to lay a card on the table, but not show his entire hand. He pulled four one-ounce silver American eagle coins out of his pocket and held them out the window for the old man to see.

"These real?" The man took two of them and clanked them around in his hand.

"You tell me." Everett held his hand out for the man to return the coins.

He dropped them in Everett's hand. "Yep. I can tell by the sound. That's what they made money out of when I was a boy. Then they came out with them government slugs. Never did get used to the sound of that funny money a janglin' around in my pocket. I'll give ya a quart of liquor for one of them. Best liquor to ever come out of these hills here. It was my grandpappy's recipe, and his grandpappy's before him."

Of course Everett had no need of moonshine, they had a bottle and a half of whiskey at the house, for medicinal purposes. But, he'd broken the ice with Scratchy who had turned out to be just the sort of person they'd hoped to meet. "What about gas?"

The old man adjusted his ball cap. "Gas is a tight commodity round here. I don't know if I could get any or not. Probably need something besides silver for that."

"I might have something. Do you have anywhere more private we could talk?"

"Let me get another box then you follow me around the corner." Scratchy went back into the motel room and came out with another box, which he put in the back of the van.

As they waited, Kevin stared curiously at the van. "So, that's his name? Scratchy?"

Everett shrugged as he followed the white van out of the lot. "I don't know. That was the nickname Courtney gave him when we bought the gas."

Everett followed the van up the street several blocks then turned off onto a side street, passing through a small neighborhood, and then driving past a sign, which read *Kearnstown Battlefield*. They continued up the narrow one-lane road.

"I guess this is an old Civil War historical site." Kevin looked out the window as they approached a three-story antebellum brick house.

"Jackson fought here." Everett continued following Scratchy's van, past the house and down another path which was not paved. They drove by another, more recently constructed farmhouse, several out buildings, a large barn, and stables, all empty. Everett considered what must have happened to the horses. "Well, it's a delicacy in France," he muttered to himself. After another two hundred yards down the dirt road, they arrived at a rustic barn, tucked back in the middle of a thick clump of trees. Five, or maybe six other vehicles were parked back amongst the trees.

Scratchy got out and walked up to Everett's truck. "This here is the new Grey Fox Saloon. The fellow who ran the old Blue Fox in town took his followin' over here. Y'all grab one of them boxes out the back of my van, and come on in."

Everett surveyed the area before getting out and complying with Sctratchy's request. "I'm Everett, by the way."

Scratchy held out his hand. "Lloyd. Much obliged."

Kevin shook his hand next. "I'm Kevin, pleased to meet you."

"You think the boys in here will be all right with you bringing company?" Everett took the cardboard box that Lloyd handed him. He could hear the distinct sound of glass jars clanking against each other.

"They better be. I ain't never had no problem getting' rid of my liquor. If they don't like the company I keep, they can find somebody else to sell em' the liquor." Lloyd handed another box to Kevin to carry and led the way, empty handed.

Lloyd slid the door open. Inside the barn was a rudimentary wooden bar lined with a row of stools, and four men sitting on them. Another man stood behind the bar. Several tables of various styles, made of diverse materials, and surrounded by mismatch chairs filled the open area adjacent to the bar. A small, battery-operated AM/FM radio playing the news from the local GRBN affiliate constituted the establishment's sound system.

Lloyd closed the door after they were inside. "Put them boxes over yonder on that table in the back."

The bartender gave Lloyd a nod and gave Everett and Kevin a suspicious look. "How y'all?"

Everett smiled uneasily. "Hey."

"This here's my friend, Everett. He's from the city, but he's good folk." Lloyd patted Everett on the back without introducing Kevin.

Kevin stuck his hand out to the bartender. "I'm Kevin."

The bartender appeared reluctant, but finally stepped forward to shake his hand. "Devon. Good to meet you."

"Is Tommy around?" Lloyd looked around the bar.

"He said to tell you he'd be back in an hour. He had to go pick up a BBQ pit smoker. One of them big devils, mounted on a trailer."

"All right, give us three Cokes."

"They ain't cold. You know we don't get no ice til after six. Tommy said it's a waste."

"They ain't hot, is they?"

"Cool, I reckon."

"That'll be fine."

The bartender placed three Coca Colas in cans on the bar. Lloyd picked them up and carried them to a table against the wall, and out of earshot of the rest of the people inside. He handed a can to Kevin and another to Everett.

Everett took the can, sat down, and popped the top. "Thanks. This is a rare treat."

"I appreciate it." Kevin did the same.

"I don't see no Mark on neither of you boys' hands." Lloyd sipped his Coke.

"I don't see one on you either," Everett replied.

Lloyd sat back in his chair and took off his dusty old ball cap. "I ain't never been the conformin' sort."

Everett feigned a look of surprise. "You don't say?"

Lloyd chuckled. "I didn't have much endearment for the old government. I plum detest this new one, this Global Republic, or whatever they are. Some of these old boys round here ain't taken too kindly to 'em neither.

"Some folks took the Mark to get their free money, but couldn't hardly buy nothin' with it cause they've got the darn prices jacked up so high. Other ones took it and got themselves reassigned to work farms out west. 'Course they won't tell ya that on the radio.

"I reckon this snake in DC, or New Whatchamacallit has gone and confiscated most all the farm land across the country. He's takin' anyone he sees fit to, and sendin' 'em out to work them farms."

Lloyd chuckled. "Hee hee! Serves 'em right. They thought they was a gonna sit round here and do nothin' but cash checks like they did when this last bunch of snakes was runnin' the show. Ain't never had no time for nobody who'd sit around and leech off the rest of us, paying taxes."

Everett laughed. "You paid taxes?"

"Dern right! I had to pay taxes on everything I bought. Taxes on my farm, taxes on my van, taxes on the gas, taxes, taxes, taxes. I might not've paid much to them devils at the IRS, but I didn't sit around with my hand out neither. I got up and made my own livin'.

"Anyhow, some of these ol' boys round here ain't plannin' on takin' no Mark. Some thinks it's of the devil, and other ones, like Tommy and me, don't have no hankerin' to be relocated or have them up in our business, tellin' us how to live. And I reckon all of us together can make our own way."

"What do you think about the disappearances?" Everett asked.

"I couldn't tell you. Radio said the aliens got em', other ones says Jesus got em', and other ones says Jesus is an alien."

Everett rolled his eyes. "It was Jesus. This was all prophesied of in the Bible. It even tells what's coming. The next major event is a global earthquake."

Lloyd rubbed his head and put his hat back on. "That's what Preacher says. We got to callin' him Preacher long time ago. He'd be in the Blue Fox chuggin' down the beer with the rest of em', a goin' on about this, that, and the other, what the Bible said. After all them folks disappeared, he quit drinkin'. He got ol' Stewart to quit drinkin', too. Reckon he practices what he preaches now. They still come around some nights, tellin' the rest of us to repent. He's claimin' there's a big quake comin'. If it comes, I might believe him. I might quit drinkin' too, or I might not.

"Anyhow, Tommy will be along directly. If anybody can get gas, it'll be Tommy. Course the only things anybody'd want to trade would be either, liquor, drugs, food, or guns. He might take silver. Folks who've got more than they need are usin' it for money, but most folks are lookin' for things they can use. Now them boys who drive for the new army, they'll take your silver. Couple of em' come in here from time to time. We do a lot of tradin' with them.

"If you ain't got nothin' else to trade, we might work out something with them army boys for your silver then swap that with Tommy for your gas. But I'll tell you, gas ain't cheap."

Everett pointed toward Lloyd's large revolver hanging under his coat. "You need something a little more discreet. Once the GR gets a good foothold in town, they'll be ramping up patrols. And that cannon is pretty easy to spot."

Lloyd tugged at the bottom of his coat to better conceal the tip of his holster. "Like I said. Guns is a top commodity these days."

"Top, like better than gas?" Everett asked.

Lloyd grimaced. "Yep."

"So if I could help you out with something a little more discreet, you think it'd get me a fill up?" Everett put his elbows on the table and leaned forward.

"Well a fill up may be askin' a might much, but let's see what you have in mind." Lloyd's face showed his excitement.

Lloyd was a great networker, but Everett was sure that poker wasn't his game. Everett stood up. "Come on out to the truck."

Kevin and Lloyd followed Everett back outside. Everett dropped the tailgate. "Wait here." He walked to the back door, retrieved the duffle bag with the three pistols and brought it back to the tailgate.

Kevin unzipped the duffle bag and took out a small semi-automatic pistol. "This is a Berretta Cheetah, .380."

Lloyd smiled. "I like it, but it is a little small, you got anything else?"

Kevin pulled out the Springfield XD. "How about a 9mm?"

"Now you're talkin'. You got ammo for all these?"

Everett nodded. "Yep. We've got ammo."

Kevin pulled the last pistol out. "Now this one is similar to what you have, but a shorter barrel. This barrel is just over four inches."

Lloyd took the revolver. "357?"

"Yes, sir." Kevin pulled a box of shells out of the bag and set them on the tailgate.

Lloyd held the revolver like a baby. "I believe we can work something out."

"Full tank?" Everett asked.

Lloyd seemed anxious to close the deal. "How many shells can you give me?"

Kevin pulled out two more 50-round boxes and stacked them next to the first box. "150, if you can fill us up."

Lloyd grinned, showing his grubby teeth. "I reckon we got ourselves a deal."

"So you'll work it out with Tommy?"

"Oh yeah. He swaps me gas for liquor all the time. He owes me for this load. That'll be a full tank. We'll settle up just as soon as he gets here."

Kevin put the shells back in the duffle. "Sounds great."

Everett held his hand out for the pistol and winked. "It's just good business."

Lloyd looked as though it pained him to hand the pistol back, even for a short time.

Everett and Kevin followed their new friend back into the make-shift saloon and returned to their table.

Everett looked at the nearly empty bar. "You said something about drivers for the new army. What do they drive?"

"Supply trucks. They don't want no 'mericans havin' guns so they put 'em to work drivin' food, medical supplies, or whatever. Anybody recruited as a gun-totin' soldier for the new government is shipped out, assigned overseas. All the soldiers brought in to this country is from somewhere else. I reckon they think that'll keep the soldiers from sidin' with the rebels in the case of a revolt. It's a mite easier to shoot somebody that ain't from your country; 'specially for 'mericans."

"So the GR drivers who come in here, they're all American?" Kevin asked.

Lloyd finished the last sip of his Coke. "Yep. And they ain't got no love for these sons-a-bucks neither."

"How well guarded are the supply trucks?" Everett inquired.

"Depends what they're haulin'. If it's guns or ammo, they're in a full military convoy. Drugs and alcohol shipments have armed escorts."

Everett furrowed his brow. "The government is shipping drugs and alcohol?"

"Oh yeah, pot, heroin, cocaine, they sell it all. 'Course, like everything else, it ain't cheap. Some of Tommy's boys, they grow the marijuana, and they got all upset about the government sellin' it. But I told 'em, my grandpappy went through the same thing when they ended prohibition. You know, it didn't hurt us one bit. Ain't never been a day in my life when there wasn't somebody wantin' my liquor over what they could get at the package store."

Everett half-smiled. He was quickly getting a feel for who this guy Tommy was. Prior to the War on Drugs, a loose organization of marijuana producers, known as the Cornbread Mafia had operated all through the Appalachians of Virginia, West Virginia, Kentucky, and Tennessee. They'd funded candidates in most all elections in the small towns, insuring they were free to operate without harassment of the local police or courts. Everett was deeply apprehensive about getting any more involved with this lot who hung around the Grey Fox Saloon. He glanced over at Kevin and thought to himself about how he'd been heavily involved with the militia movement and the uprising against the old government. Kevin and his crew of conservative constitutionalists had been termed by the liberal media as Y'all Qaeda, a derogatory term painting them as hillbilly domestic terrorists. Everett had come around to their way of thinking, despite his heavy indoctrination by his schooling, and his time at the CIA. And while they'd been viewed no differently than the Cornbread Mafia by the former government, Everett knew there was a vast difference between the patriots and the drug runners. But to borrow a morsel of wisdom from Muslim extremists, he also knew that his enemy's enemy could be his friend.

Minutes later, Everett heard the sound of a dog barking outside. He turned to Lloyd to see his reaction.

Lloyd stood up. "That's Genghis, Tommy's Rottweiler. Come on outside."

Everett stopped at the doorway. Genghis snarled and barked, daring him to breach the threshold.

A voice called from outside. "Genghis! Get over here!"

The dog retreated and Everett carefully made his way outside. He and Kevin followed Lloyd over to a towering man, with long hair, and a long beard. Yet, very well-manicured. He wore a plaid shirt, boots, and jeans; all of which were exceptionally clean. In an era without the conveniences of stores to buy laundry soap nor electricity to run washers and dryers, it was rare to see a man so impeccable.

Everett instinctively held out his hand for Genghis to sniff. Kevin did likewise, following up the introduction with a rough pat on the head, and scratch of the neck.

Lloyd introduced them. "Tommy, this here is

Everett and Kevin, acquaintances of mine."

Tommy looked them over and seemed more trusting than the bartender had been. He offered a warm smile with his hand. "Tommy Boone. It's a pleasure."

Everett shook hands with the man. "Nice to meet you."

"Likewise." Kevin also shook his hand.

Lloyd adjusted the straps of his overalls. "I need to settle up with these boys. I owe them a tank of gas."

Tommy worked the crank on the BBQ trailer, to raise the stand so he could unhitch it from his truck. "Tank of gas? That's big money, Lloyd. I hope you didn't lose it in a poker game."

"Now you know I gave up poker, Tommy."

Tommy laughed. "After losing for three years straight. I just want to make sure you didn't fall off the wagon. It ain't none of my business no how. You can follow me in their truck on out to the house." Tommy looked up at Everett. "We'll be back in twenty or thirty minutes."

Everett stuck his hands in his pockets. "I'd rather not be separated from my truck."

"Take Lloyd's keys. He ain't going nowhere with your truck. I'm sure you understand, we just met and I can't have you comin' out to my place."

"I fully understand, but I'm sure you appreciate my position," Everett replied.

"I do, but I ain't the one wantin' gas."

Lloyd held his hands up. "I reckon the problem is you don't want to let your cargo out of your sight. How 'bout I give you my keys to the van and you keep your belongin's there 'til we get back?"

Kevin looked at Everett and nodded. "I think that sounds fair."

"Good enough." Everett smiled.

Tommy rested his arm on the back of his truck bed. "Now y'all have done got me curious as to what ol' Lloyd here could want so bad. I've never seen him try so hard to put a deal together."

Lloyd began walking toward his van. "We can discuss that when we get back. Let's get movin', Tommy."

They soon had everything from the F-150 loaded into Lloyd's van. While all the weapons had some type of case, it was obvious that the cargo consisted of guns and ammo.

Tommy whistled and Genghis jumped in the bed of the truck. He then pulled away, followed by Lloyd, who was driving the Ford.

"Think we can trust them?" Everett asked.

Kevin started walking back toward the sliding door on the barn. "If they wanted to rob us, we'd already be dead."

They returned to the table inside to wait for Tommy and Lloyd to come back.

Everett looked at the men sitting at the bar. "I bet this place is hopping at night."

"Hottest place in town." Kevin adjusted his hat and leaned back in his chair.

Everett leaned in close to whisper. "I'd like to meet some of these guys driving the supply trucks."

Kevin also kept the volume of his voice low. "We might not have to. Let's see where the conversation goes when Tommy gets back. I say the less people we meet, the better. And I think Tommy could be pretty close to the top of the food chain around here."

Everett nodded. "Okay, let's see how it plays out."

Lloyd and Tommy were back in less than a half an hour, just as they'd said. Lloyd walked in and tossed Everett the keys to the F-150. "Mind if we settle up?"

Everett stood. "Sure thing."

The four of them walked outside. Everett checked his gas gauge then retrieved Lloyd's revolver. He and Kevin returned the rest of their items to the truck.

Tommy leaned against the F-150. "You willing to trade for the rest of your merchandise in there?"

Everett rubbed his chin. "That's why we brought it."

"What are you lookin' for?" Tommy inquired.

"We need two years of storable food for five people," Kevin said firmly.

Tommy's mouth was hidden by his thick black beard, but his eyes showed that he was smiling in amusement. "You fellas got some prized products from what Lloyd tells me, but that's a tall order. Most folks, least the ones we come by, have got some form of defense. But, nobody is willing to give them up, and everybody seems to want just one more, creating a very high demand on an extremely scarce commodity. Now, that's good for you. But, as it happens, food is also hard to come by, especially if you ain't willin' to take the Mark.

"Would you mind if I had a look at what you

have? I doubt I can help you out that much, but I'd sure love to make you an offer."

Everett dropped the tailgate. "Sure."

Kevin pulled the cases back out of the truck and brought them to the bed to open them up. "I didn't mean to insinuate that we thought these few little pieces would be worth two years of food for five people."

Everett first presented the two remaining pistols to Tommy, since Lloyd had, no doubt, already told him about them.

Tommy looked the Springfield XD over. "You got extra magazines for this?"

"Nope, but I got plenty of ammo for it." Everett stacked up five boxes of ammo with fifty rounds each.

Kevin unzipped the soft rifle case and took out the two pump-action 12 gauge shotguns. "We've got ammo for these also."

Everett waited for Tommy to hand him back the XD before opening the hard rifle case. He flipped the tabs and lifted the top, revealing the AR-15. Kevin had installed a flashlight, forward grip, reflex sight, and back-up sights to make it look more appealing than a stripped down model. Five extra magazines were also laid out next to the rifle.

Tommy picked it up and held it up to check the reflex site. "So I think I understand where you're driving with what you're lookin' to get, but bein' the cautious fella that I am, I'd just as soon let you spell it out."

Everett looked at Lloyd who was loading his new pistol. "If we could get solid information about the location of that amount of food that was relatively easy-to-access, say on a Global Republic truck, or a Global Republic warehouse, I think that information would be worth a gun or two."

"Hmm." Tommy laid the rifle back down on the foam padding inside the case and picked up one of the magazines to examine. "And you'd be doing all the work yourself?"

"Yep, we just need the when and where." Everett took the magazine as Tommy handed it back to him. "Unless . . ."

"Unless I'm interested in a joint venture?" Tommy stroked his beard.

Kevin nodded. "Exactly."

Tommy looked up at the sky as he continued to stroke his beard. "Let's say I could get information on an unescorted semi, and let's say y'all came along and I had a few boys with me. Suppose we stop the truck and you carry off two pickups full of goods, and suppose me and my boys carry off the rest. You think that'd be worth all these guns here and the ammo you've got there?"

Everett looked at Kevin. "I think it'd be worth a rifle. You seem to like that black one. And maybe a pistol."

Kevin added, "And the ammo and magazines for the rifle."

Tommy looked at the two shotguns, seeming to not want to leave any money on the table. "Let's suppose we could provide a safe location to load your groceries. Somewhere away from the place where we actually, shall we say, commandeered the tractor trailer. Would that add enough value to the deal for the shotguns, the other two pistols and the rest of the ammo?"

Everett looked at Kevin again. "Would we have first dibs on which groceries we took?"

Tommy slowly agreed with a slight nod.

Kevin looked pleased with the agreement. "I like it, but I'd like to be clear. We're not looking for two pickups full of beans and rice. That could be part of it, but that's not my ideal diet. And like we said before, it has to be storable food. Canned food, MREs, dry goods."

Tommy stuck his hand out. "I understand. We'll make it happen. I'm having a BBQ tomorrow night for all the folks who have been coming out to the Grey Fox. I'm going to announce that we're moving the Fox to a place out on Cedar Creek Grade. I want to put some distance between the Fox and town before the amnesty period is up. Why don't you boys come on back out tomorrow?"

Everett asked, "Do you think you'd have some details for us tomorrow night?"

"No, I'm hopin' the right fellas will be here tomorrow night and I can start workin' on 'em. I can have it all ironed out by this time next week."

Kevin crossed his hands on the back of the truck. "Then would it be all right if we come out to the new location, say next Friday?"

Tommy nodded. "That would be just fine. Lloyd, do you think you can draw these boys a map to the new place?"

"Sure thing, Tommy."

Once it was finished, Everett looked over the map that Lloyd had drawn for them. Everett wanted to make sure they understood his less-than-perfect representations of roads and landmarks. Then they headed back to the cabin.

CHAPTER 11

And when he had opened the fifth seal, I saw under the altar the souls of them that were slain for the word of God, and for the testimony which they held: And they cried with a loud voice, saying, How long, O Lord, holy and true, dost thou not judge and avenge our blood on them that dwell on the earth? And white robes were given unto every one of them; and it was said unto them, that they should rest yet for a little season, until their fellowservants also and their brethren, that should be killed as they were, should be fulfilled.

Revelation 6:9-11

It was early evening when Everett and Kevin returned home. Courtney, Sarah, and Elijah all came around, from the back of the cabin, to greet them.

Courtney brushed the dirt off of her hands and the front of her jeans then gave Everett a quick hug. "You're home early. How did it go?"

He gave her a peck on the cheek. "Better than we could have ever expected. You'll never guess who we ran into."

Courtney paused for a moment, as if she were trying to think of who it could possibly be. She shook her head slowly. "I haven't got a clue. Tell me."

"Scratchy!"

"Who?"

"Scratchy! The guy we bought gas from, in Winchester. Well, his name is actually Lloyd."

Courtney put her hands on her hips. "No way!"

"Yeah. Turns out, he's a moonshiner and seems to be pretty well connected with the Winchester underground. He took us to meet the guy."

Courtney lifted her chin to glare at Everett. "Now there's a term you don't hear every day, Winchester underground. Is this a formalized crime syndicate, or just a loosely associated smattering of ne'er-do-wells?"

Kevin chuckled. "I didn't see any insignia or logos. The latter is probably the more accurate description. Either way, they're all opposed to the Global Republic and are willing to do whatever is necessary to avoid taking the Mark."

Sarah leaned against the truck. "They don't

sound like they miss the old government too badly either."

Elijah chuckled. "Do you?"

Sarah shrugged. "I guess the GR is just the natural progression of the old guard. So, let's cut to the chase. I don't see any supplies. Were you guys able to cut a deal?"

Everett nodded then proceeded to catch them up on the proposed agreement they'd hammered out with Tommy.

Courtney looked concerned. "Next Friday? The amnesty period ends on Monday. That sounds very risky."

Kevin opened the back door of the truck and began unloading. "We'll listen to the local hams that are still talking. We can gather enough information to figure out how heavy the patrols are after the amnesty period. If it's not safe, we won't go. But I agree with Everett. I think this is our best shot at rounding out our food storage."

Courtney looked over at Elijah. "What do you think?"

"Times are about as easy as they are ever going to be. The GR isn't going to lighten up, and supplies are not going to become any more readily available than they are now. If you feel reasonably comfortable about these people, you should probably make hay while the sun shines."

"So, is that like your prophetic seal of approval for the mission?" Courtney crossed her arms.

"I'm not a fortune teller, nor do I have a crystal ball. When the Lord speaks, he speaks, and when he is silent, you must depend on wisdom, prayer and providence. I think what Kevin has suggested is wise. Listen to the radio and see what the situation is with the patrols. And pray. Ask God to direct your path. You have to learn to hear from God for yourself. I will not always be with you. Besides, he wants you to come to him directly. He doesn't want you coming through me. Many sheep have been led astray by false shepherds. Oh, the heartache that could have been spared if the children of God had learned to draw near and listen to the Good Shepherd himself."

Everett understood what Elijah was saying. God wanted Everett and the others dependent on him alone. And that was their true test of faith.

Saturday was spent working on the garden beds and constructing the storage shed addition for the remaining items that Kevin and Sarah had brought, which were not being taken to the cave. Since the entire property was sloped, they used logs as low retaining walls to terrace the garden, providing an even surface, so the rain wouldn't wash away the top soil and seeds. Elijah provided them with seeds to plant. They focused on lettuces and things that would produce with minimal sunlight, in the event that the anticipated ash cloud should darken the sky for a prolonged period.

With Elijah's instructions, Everett put together a rudimentary compost bin, filling it with the leaves from the forest floor, as they were already in the process of decomposing and had the necessary organisms to decompose other organic material the group would add to the bin. Once fully broken down, the dirt from the compost bin would be used to keep the garden beds topped off, providing the optimum nutrition for the plants that might be struggling to grow in low sunlight.

On Sunday, they rested. Elijah came by the cabin to lead a Bible study. Kevin and Sarah decided to tie the knot, but had no desire to make a fuss over the ceremony. Elijah facilitated an exchange of vows between them and pronounced them man and wife. Afterwards, Everett and Courtney pulled out all the stops to make a nice dinner in celebration, and Courtney made a cake from their dry storage food.

Everett woke up early Monday morning, feeling rested and renewed. He and Courtney had breakfast, letting the newlyweds sleep in. After breakfast, Everett and Courtney went outside to work on the garden. Low clouds hung over the mountain.

Everett began making rows of shallow holes with his finger then filling them with the various seeds from the heirloom spring mix. "I just felt the first drop of rain."

"Then I guess we better hurry." Courtney was following Everett, covering each hole and patting the dirt down so the seeds wouldn't wash away or be an easy meal for birds.

"I'm glad we're far enough from DC to not be under Elijah's curse."

Courtney continued diligently covering the holes and patting the dirt. "Yeah, I wonder how large of a radius isn't going to get rain?"

Everett moved faster as he felt more drops of rain, coming more frequently.

Twenty minutes later, the rain had grown to a steady drizzle. Courtney stood. "I give up. I'm getting wet, let's go inside. We've finished everything but that last small section."

Everett followed her toward the house. "Okay, let's go."

Once inside, the two of them climbed up to the loft to put on dry clothes then returned down to the kitchen to find Kevin making coffee.

"You guys want a cup?" Kevin measured out the grounds into the old blue speckled percolator.

"No thanks. Looks like it's going to rain all day. I can't get much done, so I was planning to take a nap." Everett took a seat at the kitchen table.

"Sarah and I could go over some maneuvers with you guys that could up your combat game. We can train with empty weapons, so we could do it inside. It would keep the day from being a complete waste and you'd be better prepared when we go back to Winchester, or whenever the need arises." Kevin held the coffee pot in his hand as if he were waiting for Everett to change his mind.

Courtney stuck her finger in the air. "I'll take you up on that."

Kevin turned toward her. "The training or the coffee?"

"Both."

Kevin put another scoop of grounds in the top chamber. "Everett? Last chance."

"Okay, put me down for one of each, also. Cup of coffee, and a round of training."

Everett turned on the radio. "I want to see what the propaganda machine has to say about the end of the amnesty period. Today's the fifteenth."

The broadcast was mixed with heavy static. Between the distance and the weather, the signal wasn't strong, but they could make out what the reporter was saying.

". . . midnight tonight, all persons will be required to be implanted with the Mark. Those who are found to have not yet registered will be escorted to the nearest census station to be implanted. Please be advised that any such person will be responsible for getting themselves home after they have been implanted. This one-way-ride policy is designed to create a significant inconvenience to those who have still not complied with the mandatory program. Census administrators hope this inconvenience will be an adequate deterrent to keep people from continuing to procrastinate their civil responsibilities of taking their pledge and getting their Mark.

"Despite the many benefits that go along with a person's new Global Citizenry status, some are still holding out. Prime Minister Alexander has made a temporary provision for what has been termed conscientious objectors. For the present time, they will be relocated to personal betterment facilities where they'll be educated about the new policies of the Global Republic and have opportunities to be part of society through work programs such as manufacturing, and farming.

"The conscientious objector program is only

available to those who are caught without the Mark and refuse to be implanted or take the pledge of citizenship in a non-violent manner. Violent offenders as well as those caught with contraband, such as firearms, illegal currencies, unregistered food, or goods bought on the black market will be incarcerated at high security camps and held until they have served their time for their particular offence. At that time, they may be reintegrated back into society through a personal betterment facility.

"As His Prepotent Majesty, Angelo Luz has stated many times before, the Global Republic will, at all costs, seek to bring the lost sheep into the fold, but those who continue to hold bigoted notions that those who believe differently than them are somehow evil, will not be tolerated. All branches of the GR government have confirmed His Majesty's executive order authorizing euthanasia for those who will not renounce these tremendously dark convictions, such as those held by the cult-like offshoot sects of Christianity.

"Former megachurch Pastor, and recently appointed Minister of Religion, Jacob Ralston stood side by side with His Holiness Pope Peter at a press conference in New Atlantis today. They issued a joint statement to professing Protestants and Catholics, reminding them that hatred was never a teaching of Christ.

"In Ralston's speech, he read from Romans 13 reminding attendees that those who stand against Angelo Luz are standing against God himself and pointing out the scriptural authority for the Global Republic to institute its euthanasia policy.

"Pope Peter reiterated Ralston's comments, and warned followers that rebels of the Global Republic risked being cut off from the mercies of God.

"In their respective speeches, both Ralston and Pope Peter individually cautioned listeners against keeping company with those who are still spreading the pernicious rumor that the disappearances were caused by the mythological rapture. Both religious leaders spoke to the absurdity of such poisonous hearsay, pointing out that had Jesus came to steal away all Christians, neither of them would be present."

Sarah had come out of the back bedroom while the others were listening to the radio. "Aren't there any country stations?"

Everett shut off the radio. "I'm afraid not."

Courtney sat next to Everett. "Are you sure you guys should go back to Winchester? You're going back for a meeting to find out if the guy is even going to be able to set something up. Then you'll have to leave again to hit the supply truck. Don't even get me started talking about all the things that can go wrong with that."

Everett put his hand on hers. He wished there was another way, also. "I know, but you heard Elijah. It's not going to get any easier than it is now."

"We'll be safe. And I don't think we have that much to worry about just yet. The GR is going to have their work cut out for them, getting the cities locked down before they can start allocating resources to patrolling the boonies." Kevin walked back into the living room to check the coffee.

Courtney huffed and pursed her lips. "I just don't like it."

Kevin returned with the coffee and served four cups. "You guys grab your gear and empty out some magazines. We'll drink our coffee and do some training. Nothing quells the anxiety quite like being prepared."

They finished their coffee and the rest of the afternoon was spent doing maneuvers and learning to change magazines faster.

The next three days were spent monitoring the ham radio to listen for reports of GR patrols. A few single GR Humvees had been spotted in the area but there were no reports of checkpoints or heavy activity, except for in the immediate vicinity of the various census stations.

Everett listened to the small AM/FM radio Friday morning as he finished his breakfast, with Courtney, Kevin, and Sarah. "So I guess the mission is a go."

Kevin nodded. "I'll listen in on the ham while I finish getting ready. It seems like we should be able to pull it off if we act now, but the window is closing." Kevin slid a hand-drawn map to Sarah. "This is a copy of what Lloyd drew for me, so it's not very accurate, but this is the place where we are supposed to meet Tommy."

Courtney looked over Sarah's shoulder. "This is the exit, where Gander Mountain is?"

"Yep," Kevin answered.

"Okay, I think I can find it if I have to."

Courtney stuck her hands in her pockets.

"Good. If we're not back by morning, there's a problem. Either Tommy double crossed us or we got picked up by the Global Republic." Kevin looked at Courtney. "If you have to come looking for us, follow Sarah's lead. Trust her, she knows what she's doing."

Courtney frowned as she nodded. "Okay. But you guys be safe, and don't get into trouble in the first place."

There was a knock at the door. Everett recognized it as Elijah's, so he wasn't startled by it. Also, Danger would have never let anyone else make it to the porch without barking. Everett opened the door. "Good morning."

"Good morning to you my friend. I see you haven't left yet." The prophet removed his wide brimmed hat.

"Yeah, the people we're going to meet aren't exactly early risers." Everett raised the left corner of his mouth.

"Very well, very well. Call the girls. I have a project to keep them busy today so they don't spend all of their time worrying."

"Thanks, Elijah. That was nice of you." Everett put his hand on the old man's shoulder.

Courtney walked into the living room. "So, you've planned some busy work for us today?"

Sarah followed her in. "Good morning, Elijah."

"Good morning. Yes." He put one finger in the air. "Today, we will build an outdoor stove. I've brought some bricks and a steel grate. It will soon be too warm to be cooking over your fireplace comfortably. And the stove we are going to build is very efficient. It's called a rocket stove. It channels the air flow to burn your wood or kindling more quickly, producing the maximum amount of heat for cooking, and the least amount of smoke. Which in these dark times, is of utmost importance."

Courtney gave him a hug. "Thank you, Elijah."

"I've also brought some materials. Plywood, cardboard, aluminum foil, and a plate of glass from an old window to build a solar oven. I fear it may not be of much use when the sky is darkened, but you'll have it if by chance you do have a few sunny days."

Kevin emerged from the back bedroom, carrying his pack and his weapons. "Good morning, Elijah."

Elijah waved him over. "You and Everett come. Let me put my hand on your shoulder."

Both of them complied and the old prophet bowed his head. "May the Lord keep you and bless you and make his face shine upon you."

Everett waited to see if he was finished then looked up. "Thank you."

Elijah patted him on the back. "You boys hurry back. Next Saturday begins Passover and the following Tuesday is the Feast of First Fruits. We'll have a special time of worship and celebrate the death, and resurrection of Messiah."

Courtney tilted her head to one side. "But isn't Easter in April this year?"

Elijah sighed patiently. "Yes child, but you are not a pagan that should be celebrating Easter, which is named after the Babylonian goddess, Ishtar. Christ was crucified on Passover and resurrected on the Feast of First Fruits, not Easter. God has an important symbolic message for us through the celebration of Passover. The Jews had to slay a lamb without blemish and smear the blood on the sides and the tops of the wooden door frame, so the angel of death would pass over them. Likewise, Christ, your Passover Lamb was slain, and his blood smeared on the wooden beams of the cross, that you might live and be spared from the angel of eternal death and separation from God. It's a real tragedy if we miss that, due to celebrating on the wrong day.

Passover is determined by the Jewish calendar. Easter, however, comes on the first Sunday after the full moon following the spring solstice. The first full moon after the spring solstice was a day to celebrate the Babylonian goddess, Ishtar. This queen of heaven was worshiped throughout many different cultures using many other names, like, Eastra, Astarte, Aphrodite, and Venus, but she is always the goddess of love, sex, and fertility. Her sexuality and fertility are represented by rabbits in pagan cultures, and celebrated by the coloring of eggs, a common theme for Easter, even today."

Courtney threw her hands in the air. "Then why have churches been celebrating Good Friday and Easter instead of Passover and First Fruits?"

Elijah pursed his lips. "This insidious Babylonian system has been working its way into the Church since the reign of Theodosius. When he made Christianity the official religion of Rome, the pagan practices and gods, most of which stem from Babylon, were mingled together; the holy and the profane."

Sarah crossed her arms. "Didn't Constantine make Christianity the official religion of Rome?"

Elijah shook his finger. "No, no. Constantine legalized Christianity, ending the persecution. That wasn't what forced together the abominable practices of the pagan with the pure worship exercised by God's saints."

"Thanks for opening our eyes to that. I never knew. Not that I ever went to church on Easter anyway," Courtney said.

Elijah winked. "At least we won't have any bad habits to break."

Kevin looked at his watch. "Everett, we need to get going."

Everett nodded, kissed Courtney on the lips and gathered his gear. After a quick round of good-byes, the two young men were on the road. They took the back road rather than I-81, in hopes that it would reduce their odds of coming across a GR patrol. And indeed, they reached the small farm on Cedar Creek Grade without incident, or encounter. As they pulled up to the small farmhouse Everett spotted three armed men. He made eye contact with the one nearest the house and the man waved. "I suppose Tommy told them to expect us."

Kevin surveyed the surrounding area before opening his door. "I doubt we would have received such a warm reception if he hadn't. Still, let's save the celebration until they let us leave."

Everett smiled at the guard and waved as he stepped out of the truck. "Hey, we're here to see Tommy."

The man motioned toward the door. "Go on

inside."

"Thanks." Kevin gave the man a wave, also.

Everett locked the door to the truck and followed Kevin up the stairs to the quaint front porch. The old two-story farmhouse was very well kept. It had a newer metal roof, and had been painted recently. The landscaping was well-maintained, and a wooden swing hung from the roof of the porch. It was not at all what Everett had expected Tommy to be hiding out in. "Think they've relocated the bar in here?"

"Nope. He's probably running his bar in that barn, back by the woods." Kevin tilted his head to the left, indicating that Everett should look that way.

Everett turned to see what Kevin was referring to. A rugged old barn sat on the other side of an open field, butted up to the tree line of heavy woods. "Hmm." Everett knocked on the door.

Tommy's voice rang out from inside. "You boys come on in here."

Everett opened the door and let himself in. He walked into a beautiful living room with country lace curtains, wood floors, crown molding and thick baseboards. The furniture was new, built for comfort, with several antique pieces scattered about.

"Y'all come on in the kitchen. We're tryin' out Lloyd's latest batch." Tommy was sitting at the raised counter with Lloyd when they walked in.

Everett looked around at the kitchen. It had all high-end appliances, granite countertops and glass paneled white cabinets. He noticed the gas stove. "Nice place."

Tommy stood to grab two short glasses. "You like the stove?"

"Yeah. I wish we'd had time to get a gas stove and put in a tank. That would have made things a whole lot easier."

Tommy smiled. "You boys look like you're gettin' along better 'n most. Come on over here and have a shot."

"No thanks," Everett said politely.

Lloyd pointed at Kevin and Everett. "They think like Preacher; reckon Jesus is the one who made all them folk disappear."

Tommy opened his fridge. "How about a Coke then."

"Sure. You've got electricity?" Everett was happy to be getting a cold soda.

"I've got a generator for my fridge, water pump, water heater; just the essentials." Tommy handed them the sodas.

"Thanks." Everett marveled at the home and all its modern conveniences. Six months ago, it would have been a very nice home, but nothing to write home about. But now, it was comparable to a king's palace.

"Have a seat." Tommy motioned toward the bar stool next to his, at the counter.

Kevin sat down. "Were you able to line anything up?"

"Yep, I did. I wished I'd had some way to get in touch with you boys." Tommy poured a couple ounces of crystal clear liquid from a Mason jar into a short glass.

"I can give you a radio frequency if you have

access to a ham radio." Everett sat next to Kevin.

"I could probably find one if I needed to." Tommy sipped his glass.

"So, what did you find out?" Kevin seemed anxious to get down to brass tacks.

"There's been a slight change of plans." Tommy looked at Kevin as he said it.

Kevin turned to Everett. He said nothing, but his face showed his displeasure.

Everett's face also showed his concern. He didn't comment, but hoped things weren't getting ready to turn south.

"Now don't you boys go getting' your feathers ruffled. Just hear what I have to say. If you're in the position to accept the bargain, I believe you'll be much happier with the new arrangement."

"Okay, let's hear it." Everett was pretty sure that Tommy wasn't going to try to kill or rob them, so barring that, the worst case scenario was that they go home empty handed.

"The good news is, I've found a delivery driver who is going to let us blindfold him, drive his truck over to Lloyds' and unload the truck. Afterwards, we take him back to the position where he was and set him free with his truck."

"Okay, so no risk of a firefight. That's good. Now what's the bad news?" Everett inquired.

Tommy took another sip of Lloyd's finest. "Bad news is, we're gonna have to rough him up a bit, make it look good. Even so, he may lose his job over it, so we have to make it worth his while."

"And what is the fine gentleman requiring for this venture?" Kevin ran his fingertips over the small beads of water on the outside of the Coke can.

"Hundred ounces of silver. And it needs to be somethin' recognizable." Tommy finished the glass in one large gulp. He winced, closing his mouth and eyes tightly. Afterwards, he slammed the glass on the counter, took a deep breath, and blew as if he were trying to cool his throat.

"So the silver is instead of the guns?" Kevin asked.

Tommy's face slowly lost the reddish color and returned to normal. "In addition to. Guns and ammo are my cut for lining it up, silver is the drivers."

Kevin crossed his arms. "So you get the guns, ammo, and depending on the size of the trailer, way more than half of the supplies."

Tommy shook his head. "Don't get greedy boys. Y'all get first dibs on which supplies you want. You get two pickup truck beds full of food, which is exactly what you asked for. More than that, you have no risk whatsoever. I'd think a hundred ounces of silver would be well worth the price of not risking your lives. That's fifty ounces a life. Don't tell me you can't see the value in that.

"As for us, I'm taking the guns and ammo, might do a deal with the driver for one of the shotguns for some silver, but that's between us. Y'all get the first two loads of food, then I'm splitting the rest between me, the driver and Lloyd here. After all, it's his barn we're usin'. He's got to get something out of the deal.

"I understand that it might seem like a high price, but the Piggly Wiggly's done been closed for a good while. I ain't tryin' to be a hard nose, but times is tough. Y'all let me know what you want to do. It don't make me no difference, and ain't gonna be no hard feelins, least on my end of it."

Everett looked at Kevin. "What do you want to do?"

"I don't have a hundred ounces of silver. Maybe twenty-five, tops." He was too close to Tommy to avoid being overheard, but Kevin still spoke low.

"I've got the silver, and it's not doing us any good sitting in the safe." Everett just hoped they weren't being set up.

"Okay." Kevin extended his hand to Tommy. "You've got a deal."

"Good. Everything'll be just fine as frog's hair." Tommy shook Kevin's hand firmly. "Lloyd'll draw another map. Y'all be over to his place tomorrow round lunch time. Hope we can do some more business when this is all said and done."

Everett stood and shook Tommy's hand. "Great. We'll see you then."

"I am gonna need a deposit. Did you happen to bring that silver you showed Lloyd last week?"

"No. Didn't have any idea that we'd need it." Everett turned back around to face Tommy.

"How about the guns then." Tommy smiled. He looked like a highly reputable used car salesman or a trustworthy politician, a walking contradiction; just as friendly as could be, but capable of killing a man without a second thought.

Everett hoped they could keep the gentle horse of a man in good spirits. "How about we leave you with everything except the AR-15, and the magazines and ammo for the AR?"

"You sure know how to break a man's heart." Tommy patted Everett on the back.

Kevin laughed. "Well, we know you'll make sure everything goes smoothly so you can get your prize. Remember, the toy is always at the bottom of the Cracker Jack box."

Tommy followed them out to the truck. "I reckon it is."

Lloyd walked outside and handed a new map to Kevin. Then he helped Tommy pack the firearms and ammo into the house.

Everett and Kevin got in the truck. Everett started the engine and waved. "See you tomorrow at noon."

Tommy threw one hand in the air. "See you then."

Everett and Kevin returned via the same back roads they'd taken to get to Tommy's. Everett glanced over at Kevin. "Why don't you pull that map out and see if Lloyd's place is on the way back. I wouldn't mind getting a look at where he lives. It will make it easier to find tomorrow."

"Smart thinking." Kevin pulled the hand-drawn map out of his back pocket. "It looks like he's out near the West Virginia border on US 48. That might be out of the way."

"Unless 48 meets up with Trout Run, then we'd come straight in from the other side of the mountain. That would take us right past the cave. It would be very convenient if it connects."

"And very inconvenient if it doesn't. I miss the days of having Google maps on my phone."

Everett winked at him. "Get your Mark, and

you'll never be without a map again."

"No thanks. I don't miss it that bad. We can give your idea a shot. I'm sure the two roads connect. One is east-west and the other north-south."

"Okay let me know if you see any signage for US 48."

Minutes later, Kevin pointed. "There it is, up ahead."

Everett turned on the road and followed it for several miles.

Kevin studied the map and looked up. "If his map is right, it should be pretty close. Start watching for a trailer on your right."

Everett slowed down as he approached a turn off on the road. He saw a decrepit old trailer that looked like it had seen its share of wind storms. "You think that's it?"

"Blue trailer. I'd say that's about right. And there's the pole barn, back near the woods behind it. This is the place. I'd imagine we'd find a still if we were to go looking up in woods on that hill."

Everett chuckled as he sped up. "It's the polar opposite of Tommy's place."

"Just as I would expect," Kevin said.

Soon, the two men were home. Courtney, Sarah, and Elijah had a big meal waiting for them which they'd cooked on the new outdoor rocket stove. After dinner, Everett turned in early. Saturday would be a big day and he needed his rest so he could be sharp and ready for anything.

CHAPTER 12

And I beheld when he had opened the sixth seal, and, lo, there was a great earthquake; and the sun became black as sackcloth of hair, and the moon became as blood; And the stars of heaven fell unto the earth, even as a fig tree casteth her untimely figs, when she is shaken of a mighty wind. And the heaven departed as a scroll when it is rolled together; and every mountain and island were moved out of their places.

Revelation 6:12-13

The next morning, Everett awoke to Courtney's gentle kiss.

"Wake up sleepy head." She ran her fingers down his arm slowly.

"Good morning." He rolled over and smiled.

"You probably want a big breakfast today, right?"

"Yes. You never know what can go wrong. I might not get a chance to eat. Better to be full and hydrated than not."

"Okay, I'll make you breakfast."

"Thanks. I'll get the fire going."

"Great. Build a fire in the new rocket stove. You'll never believe how fast it gets hot enough to cook on."

"It's still pretty cold. We need a fire in the house anyway." Everett quickly grabbed a sweatshirt as he came out from beneath the covers.

"True, but the stove is just so awesome for cooking." She sounded excited. "Can you believe today is the first day of spring?"

Everett put on the cargo pants he'd be wearing to make the exchange for the supplies. "Still feels like winter."

"Yeah, but knowing spring is here makes me feel more alive. I'm ready to not be cold all the time." Courtney finished getting dressed and followed Everett down the ladder.

Everett found some tinder and started a small fire in the new stove. He admired the physics behind it. The simple design allowed air to flood into the bottom, across the fire pit, and push the heat up to the grate where the pots, or pans for cooking would sit. He added some larger pieces of wood, and was surprised at how quickly they caught fire.

Courtney joined him minutes later, placing the coffee pot on one section of the grate, and a skillet for pancakes on the other.

Kevin and Sarah were up and at the table by the time breakfast was ready to be served.

"What did you think of the stove?" Sarah asked.

"I love it. We made breakfast in half the time." Everett took another bite of his pancakes.

Kevin drew yet another map for the girls, explaining the landmarks and pointing out how US-48 connected with Trout Run. "We should be back, no later than 3:00 PM. It would be great if you girls could meet us at the cave. It will reduce the risk of us raising suspicion by driving around in a truck loaded with supplies."

"So you're just bringing one truckload today?" Courtney asked.

"Two trucks full of supplies would be a certain red flag if we drove by a patrol." Kevin drank down his coffee.

Sarah said, "But if a patrol sees one truck full of stuff, you know they're going to pull you over."

"I know. But we've still got a better chance to evade them, one vehicle at a time," Kevin replied.

Sarah pushed her eggs from side to side with her fork. "You don't want us involved. That's why you're going with one truckload at a time."

"I just gave you a map and told you where to look for us if we're not back in time." Kevin put his hand on hers. "But you're right. I don't want anything to happen to you."

Courtney asked Sarah, "Would it be okay if we go in your room to listen to the ham radio? I'd like to hear if anyone has seen patrols around the area this morning."

"Sure, give me a second to straighten up. It's a mess in there." Sarah finished her plate and went to her room.

Courtney joined her a few minutes later while Everett and Kevin loaded up the truck with the goods that they would be trading.

Everett peeked into the back bedroom once they were ready to go. "No news?"

"Lots of chatter about this, that, and the other, but I haven't heard anything about patrols between here and Winchester," Sarah said.

Courtney added. "But in town, they're saying the Global Republic peacekeepers are all over the place. Stay away from Winchester, whatever you do."

"The new back route should keep us far from town. We have to go through Wardensville, but it doesn't even have a stop light. And there's no census station there." Everett walked over to the radio. "Keep the radio on and take your walkies when you come to meet us at the cave."

"We will." Courtney stood to hug him.

"Ready to go, cowboy?" Kevin stuck his head in the room.

"Ready when you are." Everett walked out.

Sarah joined up with Kevin and kissed him as he reached the door. "Be safe."

"I will." He ran his hand across her cheek.

Everett and Kevin got in the truck and headed off to meet up with Lloyd and Tommy.

The trip to Lloyds' was uneventful, but when they turned into his drive, they saw no sign of a tractor trailer, nor delivery truck of any kind.

"Remember what I told you. Don't hesitate if we get in trouble. Shoot first, take cover second, and then keep shooting and moving." Kevin looked over at Everett as he pulled into the drive and over to the barn.

"I remember. Don't wait for you to shoot first. Start shooting the second I know things are going south." Everett cut the ignition.

"Your Glock is still on full-auto, right?"

"Yep. And I've got three extra magazines."

"Good. Use it to lay down cover fire so you can get back to the truck and retrieve your HK rifle." Kevin looked out the window as they waited. A half an hour inched by and no one showed up.

Everett looked at his watch. "How long should we give them?"

"I don't know. If you start feeling uncomfortable, we can leave. I'm okay to sit around for another half hour or so."

Just then Everett saw a van coming around the bend. "Look. That looks like Lloyd's van."

"Yep. That's it." Kevin sat up straight. "And there's a semi right behind him."

The van pulled into the drive and the tractor trailer slowly followed.

Everett saw Lloyd give him a wave as he drove past and back, toward the barn. Next, he identified Tommy as the driver of the truck. "Huh. Looks like he's not afraid to get his hands dirty. I figured he'd have one of his guys doing all of this for him."

"Yeah, I guess you have to respect that." Kevin watched as the semi pulled around to the back of the barn. The front door of the barn opened and Lloyd walked out, pushing both doors all the way back so Tommy could pull through. Afterwards, Tommy cut the engine and jumped out.

"Looks like he's doing everything as planned," Everett said.

Kevin opened his door to get out. "Just keep your head on a swivel and double time back to the truck if we get in a mess."

Tommy walked up to greet them. "Mind if we settle up real quick before we unload?"

"Not at all. Do you mind if we have a quick look in the back of the trailer?" Everett was careful to sound courteous but firm.

Tommy turned around and started back toward the barn. "You been in the city too long. You're gonna have to learn to trust me sooner or later." He led the way past the truck and pointed at the cab. "The driver is still in the passenger's seat. He's listenin' to some Merle Haggard, but don't say no names. The less he knows, the better it is for everybody. We blindfolded him so he can pass a lie detector if they ask him where we took him." Tommy proceeded to walk down the length of the trailer and opened the back.

Everett stayed cautious as he peered inside, knowing that the trailer was a good hiding place for an ambush. But sure enough, it was stacked floor to ceiling with boxes of food and supplies.

Lloyd walked up. "Reckon I'll start unloading."

"How 'bout lettin' us use your kitchen to settle up. It won't take but ten minutes," Tommy said.

"That'd be fine," Lloyd replied.

Everett and Kevin retrieved the AR-15, ammo, and silver from the truck then brought it inside to Tommy. Tommy selected two of the five tubes of the one-ounce silver American eagles. He removed the coins, inspecting each one.

"Seems like country folks like to make sure they're not being had either." Kevin chided Tommy playfully.

Tommy chuckled. "Trust but verify, my friend; trust but verify." Next he checked the AR-15, and examined a few boxes of the ammo. "Looks good. I sure hope we can do business again sometime."

Everett shook his hand. "I hope so, too."

Everett and Kevin pulled around to the back of the barn so they could unload boxes straight from the trailer, into the truck. The four men quickly worked out a system to get the boxes unloaded. Everett and Kevin had the pickup filled with boxes of canned soup, biscuit mix, canned vegetables and fruits, canned pasta, canned meats and several cases of MREs. The trailer had been destined for the Winchester census station where its cargo would be used to exchange for the souls of men and women, willing to take the Mark for a mouthful of food.

Everett and Kevin assisted Tommy and Lloyd in unloading the rest of the goods, as Tommy had to get the driver back before he was missed. It took just over two hours to completely unload the truck. Lloyd brought out a pitcher of tea when they were finished. It was cool from being in the brisk mountain air, but not cold like the Cokes at Tommy's, and it was sweet.

Tommy took the bandana off of his head and

wiped the sweat from his face. "You boy's know when you'll be back for your second load?"

"How is next week, about the same time? We should probably give it at least that long to cool off. I'm sure the GR will be lookin' for this stuff soon." Kevin looked at the boxes strewn about the barn.

"That's fine by me. As long as Lloyd's all right with it." Tommy stuck the bandana in his back pocket.

"Y'all come when you want," Lloyd said. "And I've got a tarp you can throw over your boxes. Just bring it back when y'all come for the rest. Put a layer of wood on top, and it'll look like a truck full of firewood."

"Nice to know a shine runner in times like these." Kevin winked at Lloyd.

"Always nice to know a shine runner. My grandpappy would throw a tarp over his haul and cover it with pig manure. Never lost a load."

Kevin rolled his eyes. "I bet."

Everett winced and looked over at Tommy who was laughing. "You worked up quite a sweat. I'm surprised you didn't have someone else handle the heavy lifting for you." Everett took a long drink, finishing his tea.

Tommy nodded. "Less people knows where my vittles are, the better I'll sleep. Besides, work is good for a man."

Lloyd helped them get the tarp over the boxes then they covered it with some firewood. "Y'all be safe. See ya soon."

Everett breathed a deep sigh of relief as he got in the truck, and started the engine. He waved as they pulled away. "That went well."

"Yeah. Now we just have to get it to the cave." Kevin seemed less willing to relax than Everett.

The next big hurdle was driving through Wardensville. They hadn't seen any Global Republic presence in the small town thus far, but the out-of-the-way community was not out of reach from the tentacles of the New World Oder. Everett maintained a steady pace as he approached the little town. He saw no activity on any of the cross streets as they drove through town, and Wardensville looked nearly abandoned. Everett turned onto Trout Run and accelerated.

"Did you see that?" Kevin sat forward in his seat and looked toward the sky.

Everett glanced up in the direction Kevin was gazing, but saw nothing. "No. What was it?"

"A massive fire ball."

"You mean like a shooting star? In the daylight?"

"Whoa! There goes another one!" Kevin pointed out the front windshield.

Everett saw that one. An enormous ball of fire shot across the sky, followed by a glowing tail that became a trail of smoke. Everett pulled to the side of the road. "You think it will burn out before it hits the ground?"

"I don't know. I've never seen anything like it." Kevin scoured the heavens with his eyes. "Look, back behind the mountain. Another comet! We better get going. The earth has just crossed paths with a massive asteroid field."

Everett followed Kevin's pointing finger and caught yet, another falling star, this one more distant and less brilliant, but easily viewed, even in the early afternoon light of the sun. He hit the accelerator and speed back onto the road.

As they entered the mountains, they had less of a view of the sky, but Kevin continued to watch for more shooting stars.

The truck suddenly shifted to the left pulling them into the lane of oncoming traffic. Everett quickly jerked the steering wheel to pull them back over the center line. "Did you feel that?"

"Yeah, I thought you fell asleep or something." Kevin's eyes were open wide.

"No, it felt like the power steering or something. It's like it grabbed the wheel and jolted us to the other lane."

Kevin looked in the passenger's side view mirror. "It's a bad time to be having mechanical problems."

Everett didn't even have to ask. He knew from the tone in Kevin's voice that they had company.

Kevin positioned the AK-47 next to his leg. "If we can't lose them, we have to engage. And the second they hit the lights, you can assume they've already called in the plates. Even if we didn't have a truckload of supplies stolen from a GR truck, we've got no Marks. Fight-or-flight. No in-betweens."

A sense of doom came over Everett as he looked into the rearview. A GR Humvee was behind them and closing in fast. Everett hit the gas to speed up. Maybe he could navigate the sharp curves and gain a little distance.

Kevin turned around to watch the Humvee behind them. "If you can't lose them by the time we get to the cave, turn off onto one of the side roads. The last thing we want to do is lead them in the direction of the cabin. If we have to, we'll stick the truck in a ditch, and run into the woods. I'll lead, as soon as I find a good spot with some cover, I'll drop down and wait to see if they pursue us on foot. If they do, we can snipe them off from cover. If they keep coming, we'll keep shooting. Remember, they're probably all British, Australian or South African, so we've got the home court advantage. If we can recover the truck, great. If not, we'll hike back. The good news is it's not in our name and has no link to the cabin."

"Sounds like a plan." Everett pulled the wheel hard to take the next curve. The tires squealed.

"They're picking up speed, also." Kevin kept Everett briefed on the position of the Hummer so he could focus on the tight curves of the pavement.

Everett pushed the pedal all the way down as he came out of the curve and onto a short stretch of straight, even road. He hit the brakes going into the next curve then gunned the gas again. Suddenly, the truck pulled to the right, pushing Everett onto the shoulder. "Woe! There goes the power steering again."

Kevin braced himself on the dashboard and the back of his seat. "I don't think it's the steering."

Everett accelerated nervously, not feeling comfortable to drive at such high speeds when the steering was not working properly. "Why? What do you think it is?"

Kevin shook his head. "I'm not sure, but the Hummer swerved at almost the same time we did.

Like they got hit by a wind gust, and the trees all shook, also."

Everett looked at the trees before him. "I don't think the wind is blowing." Suddenly the wheels shifted again, but more violently, shaking the truck so bad that some of the wood on top of the cargo went rolling out of the bed of the truck, nearly sending Everett off the road. He had no choice but to hit the brakes.

Kevin held on tightly to the back of his seat. "They just went off the road. A huge crack just opened up in the pavement. We're having an earthquake!"

"Are they still coming?" Everett asked.

"Yep, they're pulling back on the road. Go, go, go!"

Everett hit the gas again, but kept it slow to deal with the earth moving beneath the truck. As he came around the next curve, he saw a massive landslide moving down from the cliff above. His instinct was to slam the brakes, but he knew this was his one chance to lose the Humvee. He pushed the pedal to the floor and gritted his teeth. "Hang on!"

Kevin saw the earth giving way in front of them and turned away.

Small pieces of dirt and rock hit the windshield from the left as the truck collided with a wave of debris, which was racing down the hillside. Suddenly, Everett was driving in a complete haze, unable to see the road. He took his foot off the gas, but kept moving forward, hoping he wouldn't go over the cliff to his right.

Soon, the darkness faded and he could see the faint yellow lines which indicated the road. The pavement was still moving and large cracks were appearing, one after the other. Everett had to swerve into the other lane to avoid a vast chasm from where the road had given way and descended down the hill to his right.

"We lost them. You can slow down." Kevin continued to watch behind them.

"I want to get as far as we can. I have a feeling we won't make it all the way home."

"Okay, but take it slow. We can always walk, even if we have to leave the supplies behind. But if you're going too fast and go over the cliff, we're done for."

Everett took his foot off the gas and drove more cautiously as the earth continued to shake. As he came around the next curve, a large mass of trees, roots, rock, and mud blocked the road. The pavement disappeared under the mess as if the builders of the road had just given up at that very spot. It was as if there had never been any route through this particular stretch of the mountains. Everett drove to the edge of the solid mass of earth and stone, stopping just short of hitting it. "Do you think the comets could have triggered the quake?"

Kevin looked all around as if he were wondering where the next threat would appear from. "I don't know, but the sky is falling in, the earth is giving way beneath us, and we're being pursued by Satan's henchmen. I guess this is officially an apocalyptic nightmare. We need to get our packs and keep moving."

Everett nodded and began to open his door. Another tremor began to shake the earth once more, rocking the truck. Everett looked up to see more debris rushing down toward the vehicle. "Get out! Go!" He pushed Kevin out the open passenger's side door and followed him. Everett sprinted behind Kevin, down the hillside, trying to outrun a wave of falling rocks and dirt. Everett hit a sleek spot and lost his footing. He fell back on his butt and slid for another five feet, stopping himself by grabbing a sapling. The earth quit shaking and Everett looked behind him. The landslide had also ceased.

Kevin walked over to Everett and helped him up. "Are you hurt?"

Everett's adrenaline was still pumping. He was shaking like a leaf. He ran his hands along his legs and torso, finding no blood. "I don't think so."

"Okay, let's get moving." Kevin led the way back up the hill.

Everett's legs were still shaking from the utter terror he'd just experienced, but he fought to keep up with Kevin. When they reached the truck, it had been moved into the other lane by the impact of a four-foot high boulder which had smashed into the driver's side door. The windshield was shattered and the driver's side door had been pushed all the way into the steering column. Everett took a moment to survey the damage, knowing that he would be dead, had he not moved out of the way before the giant rock collided with the vehicle. He crawled through the passenger's side to retrieve his HK rifle and pack. He handed the AK to Kevin, along with his pack.

Kevin put his pack on and picked up his AK. "We're probably going to be getting some aftershocks, so be ready."

Everett put on his backpack and looked up at the sky just as another large fireball streamed overhead. "There goes another one. This isn't over with yet."

The two men began carefully climbing onto the hill of solidified mud, rock, and debris. It resembled a dam that a mammoth beaver might have built. The mountain of earth and rock that had slid onto the road was more than fifteen-feet high. As they approached the top, Everett could see that the landslide extended for roughly seventy yards. Anyone buried on the road below would never be found.

Kevin stayed low to the ground as he worked his way through the trees and roots sticking out of the mud. "How could such a colossal asteroid field get so close to earth without it being detected?"

Everett followed Kevin's path. "The GR knew. They just didn't bother to tell any of the rest of us. For all we know, the meteorites we've been seeing could be the remains of a larger comet. Perhaps they nuked a bigger asteroid that was on a collision course with earth. Whatever happened, you can bet they knew about it before hand. You saw the seismic isolators being put in the foundations of the new buildings in DC. Luz and his minions are reading Revelation like a playbook."

Kevin kept moving. "Yeah. It's hard to understand how they can put so much faith in the prophecies of the book and still think they have a chance at winning."

"I suppose Luz looks at it from the standpoint of seeing how many souls he can drag down with him."

"Yep. You're probably right." Kevin reached the end of the mud, rock, and tree roots and began to work his way down from the mound. "At any rate, all of this destruction is going to put a damper on Luz's plans."

Everett slung his rifle over his back so he could use both hands to hang onto roots and limbs sticking out of the mud as he descended the immense field of wreckage. "If we saw that many meteorites in the daylight, you can bet there were a lot more outside of the atmosphere. I guarantee Luz is missing a good number of his satellites. He'll be confined to terrestrial communications and surveillance until he can get replacements into orbit."

Once they reached the bottom of the mudslide they stopped to look for the road. Kevin took out his compass to check their general direction. He furrowed his brow as he looked toward the afternoon sun. "Something isn't right."

Everett looked down the hill in search of the place where they'd find the pavement. "What do you mean?"

"Look at my compass. If that's west, the sun should be way over there, much closer to due west. It's way off to the south, almost like you'd expect it to be for the winter solstice. Today is the spring equinox. That just isn't right."

Everett wasn't that well versed in celestial navigation, but trusted what Kevin was telling him.

"Could the earth has been shaken so bad that it moved the poles?"

Kevin looked at his compass again. "I guess that would explain it. Even if Luz has any satellites remaining, the GPS functionality won't be worth a dime."

Everett finally spotted an area where the trees were thinner. "I think that's the road down there. Let's check it out."

The two men quickly worked their way down the hill and found the place where the pavement began. They walked quickly in the direction of their destination.

"Do you have any idea how far we are from the cave?" Everett asked.

Kevin shook his head. "We've been on this road twice. I'm not that familiar with the landmarks."

"Not that the landmarks are still in the same place as they were an hour ago." Everett joked.

"Yeah. And I don't remember the roads being in this bad of a condition." Kevin snorted. "Figuring the time it took us to get to Lloyds' and the time we left, I'm guessing we've got about two or three miles to the cave. We should be able to make it in an hour or so. Of course, that's assuming we don't hit anymore major obstacles."

While the pavement was more than adequate for foot traffic, the massive buckles, fissures and up-ended segments would make navigation by vehicle extremely tricky. The two men had to walk around several gapping crevices where the surrounding asphalt looked unstable.

The men concentrated on moving as quickly and

safely as they could for the next half hour. Everett paused. "I smell smoke."

Kevin nodded. "Yep. Forest fire. I bet one of those meteors started it."

"Or there could be multiple fires, started by multiple comets." Everett resumed walking, now with more determination. "Either way, we better get back to the cabin and hope we can clear out a large enough area to keep the fire from burning it.

"If it's still there." Kevin had just verbalized a fear that Everett did not want to confront just yet. If the cabin was in danger, that meant Courtney was in danger. There was nothing he could do to help her at the current time and he did not want to think about what might have happened to her in the quake.

Their steady, even pace turned into a light sprint as they made their way toward the cave, and ultimately the cabin. After twenty minutes more, they reached the location where the trail head was that led to the cave. As they looked down toward the stream, they saw the green truck.

Kevin pointed. "The girls are here."

Everett raced down the hill to find Courtney sitting next to Sarah at the edge of the creek.

Courtney turned to see him and jumped up to run toward him, wrapping both arms around him as they collided. "You're alive!"

Sarah sprinted to meet Kevin and embraced him, also. "We were so worried. The meteors, the quake."

Everett kissed Courtney then looked at Sarah. "They may have saved our lives, actually."

"How's that?" Courtney inquired.

Everett told her of the GR Humvee that had been chasing them when the quake began and how the Hummer had most likely been buried in the landslide.

Kevin looked toward the truck. "We need to get back to the cabin. There's a forest fire burning and it could be coming this way."

The four of them rushed to the truck and began driving back in the direction of the cabin. Sarah drove the truck. The roads were in bad condition, and she couldn't go faster than five miles per hour as she had to continually drive from side to side to negotiate through the cracks and crevices. They drove past Elijah's house.

"I think we should stop and check on Elijah." Courtney's tone was insistent.

An ancient oak had fallen and was blocking Elijah's drive, so Sarah pulled up to the edge of the downed branches. Courtney jumped out of the truck and ran to the house. Everett got out and followed her, with Sarah and Kevin close behind him.

Courtney knocked at the door and Elijah answered. "Is everyone all right?"

Courtney turned to look at the others walking up the drive. "Yeah. We're all okay."

Elijah lifted his hands to heaven, "Glory to God Almighty who has protected us from the perils of this judgement."

"Yes, praise God." Kevin approached the porch. "We smelled smoke when we were coming back, so there may be a fire coming. We're going to go check the cabin and clear the trees back in case it's coming this way."

"What will you use?" Elijah asked.

"Axes and shovels. That's what we have to work with," Everett said.

"I've got a chainsaw." Elijah smiled.

Everett's eyes showed his joy. "Of course you do."

Elijah put his finger in the air. Wait one moment for me. I'll fetch it. We'll get your place cleared out, and then come up here and see what needs to be cleared."

Minutes later, the five of them were down the mountain, at the cabin. The structure was still standing, but Everett could see that the roofline was crooked. He walked up the stairs to the porch and was greeted by Danger.

"Cupcake! Come here." Sarah knelt down to hug and kiss the animal when he ran to her.

Everett opened the door to see that everything that had been on a shelf was now on the floor. Broken glass laid all over the cabin. He walked carefully through and looked up into the loft. Sox peeked cautiously over the edge, and down at Everett, as if he suspected that Everett could have somehow been the cause of all the commotion. "Glad to see that you're safe."

The cat turned and sauntered off to go lie back down on the bed, no doubt. Everett went back outside with the others. "It's a mess in there, but we'll get it cleaned up. Everybody is still alive and that's what counts."

The next few hours were spent clearing trees in the immediate vicinity of the house. Next, they cleared the trees and brush around Elijah's house until dark. When that was finished, everyone was completely exhausted, but inside, the homes still had to be straightened up somewhat before anyone could rest. The five of them worked to clean up the mess in Elijah's house first then the old prophet assisted them in clearing the rubble from Everett's cabin. Once finished, Everett washed up and went to sleep.

CHAPTER 13

And when he had opened the seventh seal, there was silence in heaven about the space of half an hour. And I saw the seven angels which stood before God; and to them were given seven trumpets. And another angel came and stood at the altar, having a golden censer; and there was given unto him much incense, that he should offer it with the prayers of all saints upon the golden altar which was before the throne. And the smoke of the incense, which came with the prayers of the saints, ascended up before God out of the angel's hand. And the angel took the censer, and filled it with fire of the altar, and cast it into the earth: and there were voices, and thunderings, and lightnings, and an earthquake. And the seven angels which had the seven trumpets prepared themselves to sound.

Revelation 8:1-6

The fires burned all through the mountains on the days following the great earthquake and the meteor shower, but by God's grace, they never threatened the side of the mountain where Everett's and Elijah's homes were. Nevertheless, the thick blanket of smoke and ash was inescapable. A rain storm which lasted from Friday night through Saturday morning finally quelled the fires and provided them some respite from the ash and smoke.

The only information the group was able to gather was from the occasional ham operator in the area. None of the Global Republic's affiliate stations were broadcasting.

The group had spent the week cleaning up the mess and making structural repairs to shore up the cabin, which had been severely shaken and left out of plumb, as well as unleveled.

For the most part, things were back in working order by the following Saturday. Everett and Kevin used a log, leaned at forty-five degrees, as a brace against one wall that seemed to have shifted more since the quake. The log was from one of the trees they'd cut the previous Saturday, when clearing the area around the cabin to prevent fire reaching their home. Once it was hammered into place with the sledge hammer, Everett would be finished with all he'd hoped to accomplish for the day.

Courtney came outside. "Don't forget we're supposed to be at Elijah's for Passover dinner in an hour."

"That's right. Thanks for reminding us." Everett leaned the sledge hammer up against the log.

Kevin pursed his lips. "I guess we won't have time to drive down towards Woodstock. I wanted to see if the road was clear. This is the first day the smoke has been clear enough to drive on these busted up roads."

"Yeah, me too. Let's get cleaned up really quick and take a drive down the mountain."

Both men rushed to get ready. When they told the girls of their plan, Courtney and Sarah insisted on riding along. The four of them got in the green truck. Kevin drove.

Everett sat in the passenger's seat and tried the radio, once more as he kept hoping to find a station that had come back on the air. The rumors traveling across the local hams ranged from DC being completely destroyed to everything west of the San Andreas Fault being five feet under water. As he scanned the AM frequencies, suddenly he heard a faint signal. He hit the button once more and picked up a station. "I think we've got something. It must have just came back on line. I checked all the AM frequencies this morning!"

". . . Puente Hills thrust fault completely leveled the city of Los Angeles when it was triggered by last week's global mega quake.

Tsunami waves which hit the LA coast were not

as high as the fifteen-foot wall of water which rushed the upper West Coast of North America, pushing up to five feet of water into the streets of Seattle and Vancouver, via the Straight of Juan de Fuca. Sea water also rushed up the Columbia and Willamette Rivers, devastating the city of Portland. The loss of life from the combined effect of the quake and tsunami in Santa Cruz, San Francisco, and Monterey is also thought to be near total.

"Search and rescue efforts have been suspended for the West Coast, as almost no bridges or overpasses survived the quake, and the complete lack of navigable roadways leave the Global Republic unable to respond to the crisis. Emergency management officials have decided to focus their efforts on the East Coast where there are still lives that can be saved.

New Atlantis is just now digging itself out from beneath the rubble and getting to a state of operations in which it can care for its own wounds. The most recent architectural additions to New Atlantis were built using the latest technology and faired the great quake quite well. Many other structures in the city, including the old US Capitol, The White House and the Washington Monument were completely destroyed.

"His High Prepotent Majesty Angelo Luz issued a statement to the press earlier this morning vowing to rebuild the Monument as a symbol of the world's ability to overcome such utter catastrophic destruction. He stood upon the fallen stones of the Washington Monument and read from the ancient Book of Isaiah, which reads, 'The bricks have fallen down, but we will rebuild with dressed stone; the fig trees have been felled, but we will replace them with cedars.'

"The New Madrid fault sent waves of destruction in all directions, causing massive loss of life from Memphis to Saint Louis.

"Thank you for listening to this emergency operation update. Our station will be signing off for now to conserve power for critical needs, but we will be broadcasting ten minute updates every hour from now, until we resume normal operations. We hope to be back to our regularly scheduled programming by this time next week."

Everett turned off the radio in time to look up and see a huge walnut tree laying across the road.

Kevin rolled to a stop. "I guess that's the end of our field trip for today."

Sarah leaned forward from the back seat. "The roads are so bad. It almost doesn't matter."

Kevin put the truck in reverse and began turning around on the severely damaged pavement. "So we're cut off on this side by this tree and from Trout Run by the land slide."

Courtney spoke from the back seat. "That's not necessarily a bad thing."

"Other than not being able to get our supplies, I agree," Everett said.

"That tree can be cleared in a day or two. We need to take a hike down the mountain next week to see how bad the rest of the road is." Kevin pulled back on to the jagged asphalt and slowly drove back towards Elijah's "Somehow, we have to figure out a way to get the rest of those supplies, and we need to do it before the GR is back up and running at full throttle."

The group arrived at Elijah's just as he was ready to serve the Passover Seder. They sat at the table together as Elijah explained each part of the meal, tying the meaning of everything to Messiah.

Afterwards, Everett thought about the different aspects of the meal, the Old Testament meaning and the New Testament application. A sense of deep peace and quiet came over his spirit and he felt the sudden urge to go outside, to be alone and quiet before God. Almost in a whisper, he said, "Please excuse me. I'll be right back." He walked outside into the night and looked up at the heavens. All was still and silent. He listened for the crickets which should have been chirping. There were none. He listened for the wind, but it was still. He listened for the frogs which should surely be making noise after so much rain the night before, but everything was hushed. Everett stood on Elijah's porch, motionless for the next half hour, listening to the soundless tranquility. He slowly looked up to see storm clouds gathering above. And then with a mighty and fierce crack of lightening, deafening thunder shattered the calm. Yet, Everett remained on the porch, determined to drink it in. The ground began shaking again as the biggest aftershock since the great quake shook the entire mountain. Everett took hold of the post which held Elijah's roof over the porch to steady himself. This was it, the Seventh Seal of which he'd read, and Elijah had explained. According to the prophecy of Revelation, next would be seven angels sounding seven trumpe. which would announce the coming of blood, and fire, and death, and destruction, and the bitterness of God's Wrath. Everett, Courtney, Kevin, Sarah, and Elijah had survived the Seven Seals, but would they be able to endure the next devastating wave of the Great Tribulation?

DON'T PANIC!

⌐ks like this will wake folks up to the ⌐ be prepared, or cause those of us who are ⌐lready prepared to take inventory of our preparations. New preppers can find the task of getting prepared for an economic collapse, EMP, or societal breakdown to be a source of great anxiety. It shouldn't be. By following an organized plan and setting a goal of getting a little more prepared each day, you can do it.

I always try to include a few prepper tips in my novels, but they're fiction and not a comprehensive plan to get prepared. Now that you're motivated to start prepping, the last thing I want to do is leave you frustrated, not knowing what to do next. So, I'd like to offer you a free PDF copy of *The Seven Step Survival Plan.*

For the new prepper, *The Seven Step Survival Plan* provides a blueprint that prioritizes the different aspects of preparedness and breaks them down into achievable goals. For seasoned preppers who often get overweight in one particular area of preparedness, *The Seven Step Survival Plan* provides basic guidelines to help keep their plan in balance, and ensures they're not missing any critical segments of a well-adjusted survival strategy.

To get your free PDF copy of
The Seven Step Survival Plan, email me,
prepperrecon@gmail.com
with **Seven Step Offer** in the subject line.

Thank you for reading
The Days of Elijah: Book One
Apocalypse

Reviews are the best way to help get the book noticed. If you liked the book, please take a moment to leave a five-star review on Amazon and Goodreads.

I love hearing from readers! So whether it's to say you enjoyed the book, to point out a typo that we missed, or asked to be notified when new books are released, drop me a line.
prepperrecon@gmail.com

Stay tuned to **PrepperRecon.com** for the latest news about my upcoming books, and great interviews on the **Prepper Recon Podcast**.

Keep watch for
The Days of Elijah: Book Two
Wormwood

If you liked *Apocalypse*, you'll love the prequel series,

The Days of Noah

In *The Days of Noah, Book One: Conspiracy*, You'll see the challenges and events that Everett and Courtney have endured to reach the point in the story that you've just read. You'll read what it was like for the Christians in Kevin and Sarah's group in their final days before the rapture and how the once-great United States of America lost its sovereignty. You'll have a better understanding of how the old political and monetary system were cleared away, like pieces on a chess board, to make way for the one-world kingdom of the Antichrist.

You'll also enjoy my first series,

The Economic Collapse Chronicles

Matt and Karen Bair thought they were prepared for anything, but can they survive a total collapse of the economic system? If they want to live through the crisis, they'll have to think fast and move quickly. In a world where all the rules have changed, and savagery is law, those who hesitate pay with their very lives. When funds are no longer available for government programs, widespread civil unrest erupts across the country. Matt and Karen are forced to move to a more remote location and their level of preparedness is revealed as being much less adequate than they believed prior to the crisis. Civil instability erupts into civil war and Americans are forced to choose a side. Don't miss this action-packed, post-apocalyptic tale about survival after the total collapse of America.

ABOUT THE AUTHOR

Mark Goodwin is a Christian author, creator of PrepperRecon.com, and host of the popular Prepper Recon Podcast which helps people prepare for the uncertain times ahead. His fiction series, *The Days of Noah*, spent several months at #1 on the Amazon best sellers list for Christian futuristic fiction. His first series, *The Economic Collapse Chronicles*, also hit the Amazon best sellers list in multiple categories. His latest book, *Behold Darkness and Sorrow*, also hit #1 best-seller for Christian futuristic fiction on Amazon.

Made in the USA
Columbia, SC
30 November 2018